MAP

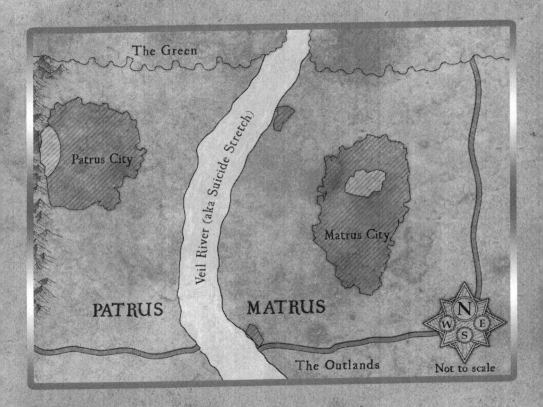

The Green

Patrus City

Matrus City

Veil River (aka Suicide Stretch)

PATRUS

MATRUS

The Outlands

N
W E
S

Not to scale

THE GENDER LIE

BELLA FORREST

CHAPTER 1

Violet

The steady beep of the equipment monitoring Viggo's vitals had become a soothing and constant reminder that he was still alive. I shifted in the chair that had become my second home and stared at his unconscious face, both here and miles away at the same time.

When I had first sat by his bed, the beeps of the machine had felt like a metronome, counting down the minutes until he died. Every missed beat or change in rhythm would cause my heart to leap into my throat—out of both fear for the worst and hope for the best. By now, I was numb to it. I knew that there would be no change, no miraculous recovery, until we got the laser that was needed to seal the tear in his heart.

The tear that he had put there while protecting me from the twin princesses of Matrus. He had used adrenaline patches to try to buy me time to escape and in doing so, his heart had given out. He would have died, if not for the intervention of a group whom I'd since learned called themselves the Liberators—run by Desmond Bertrand, former spy of Matrus.

When I first met Desmond, I didn't know whether to trust her or not. She seemed honest and allowed me to stay, promising to help me with Viggo and Tim if I would consider joining her side in a war against Matrus. But then again, her son had seemed honest, and he had tried to kill me.

Still, Desmond's offer was tempting. Matrus hadn't done me any favors in the last eight years, and after all I had been through, I was in no rush to return—especially since I was being blamed for Queen Rina and Mr. Jenks' deaths.

My eyes glazed over as I stared at Viggo's chest, and my thoughts wandered to my brother. So much had changed in him during the years he'd been used as a guinea pig with the other lost boys of Matrus, as my homeland had tried to turn them into a better breed of human. Enhanced speed, strength, endurance, intelligence—all tested here in this hidden facility within The Green.

When Tim fought with Marina, he had held his

own with her for several minutes because of his enhancement. It was why I had assumed he possessed the same enhancement as hers: Strength. But after looking at a file pilfered from Mr. Jenks' lab, I learned differently. It was Tim's reflexes that had been enhanced, making him able to react faster than a normal person.

All the enhancements came with a price, however. I had discovered that Tim's was tactile sensitivity—everything that touched him hurt him in some way. Even his clothes caused discomfort. He was also dealing with years of isolation and trauma due to the so-called stress tests that Mr. Jenks had designed to test the boys' limitations and weaknesses.

It was lucky for Mr. Jenks that Lee cut his throat. If he were still alive, I would've done a lot worse to him.

And to Queen Rina, considering she allowed her unborn children to be among the first experiments.

As my mind returned once again to our narrow survival of the twins' attack, I frowned, thinking of Ms. Dale. Desmond kept her locked in one of the cells that had been empty, and I hadn't seen her since that day. I had asked about her more than twice, but Desmond had warned me that Ms. Dale was their enemy. I had tried to argue on my old teacher's behalf, but my words fell on deaf ears, and I needed to be cautious when it came to Desmond. She had the power to keep me off the mission to procure Viggo's cure, so I had resigned myself to keeping my mouth shut and my ears open.

Although, given what I had learned about the Liberators, they all seemed… reasonable. They were people, just like Viggo and me, who had found out their government was lying to them. The majority of them were from Matrus, but there were a few here and there—mostly women—from Patrus.

All were disillusioned like me, but I had been a pawn in this game for far too long—which was why I didn't want to join Desmond's rebel faction. I didn't believe that there was any way to win a war with Matrus, let alone start one, so I had kept my mouth shut and fended off her requests to make me a full member. I'd told her that at the moment, I was only concerned about Viggo, and making him well.

But, if I was truly honest with myself, I was starting to like Desmond.

She was brusque, but fair. Her orders were rarely ever refused, but when they were, she opened her door to whomever had problems with them, and heard them out. Sometimes she even changed her mind when a good argument was presented. It didn't happen often, but I had seen it once with Owen—the young man who'd tried to kidnap me in The Green—and it impressed me.

Tearing myself away from my thoughts, I

refocused my eyes on Viggo. I had come here to tell him that I was leaving.

Reaching out a hand, I smoothed a lock of hair from his face. I still didn't feel ready to say goodbye—even if it was to depart on the mission to procure the object that could heal him.

As much as I was excited, I felt nervous for several reasons—the first and foremost of which was leaving Viggo and my brother behind for any amount of time. I was entrusting their well-being to others—something I wasn't remotely comfortable with. My imagination kept running amok, visualizing worst-case scenarios that could take place in my absence.

It took every ounce of self-control I possessed to push my worries aside and remind myself that what I was doing, I was doing for *Viggo*. I had waited too long for this mission, and I couldn't falter now. Not with his life on the line.

Desmond had located a warehouse in Patrus that had exactly the type of laser we were looking for, and if we did things right, Patrus wouldn't even know it was missing. So, I was going into Patrus, where I was wanted as a terrorist. I was just glad I wasn't going alone.

Desmond had made good on her promise. For two weeks, I had trained side by side with a small team of Liberators. Owen was serving as the *de facto* leader of our group. When he had grabbed me in The

Green, I had thought him some man-snake creature, but in reality, I had been reacting to the suit he wore. A suit that allowed him to move undetected. It was one of the most advanced forms of camouflage I had ever seen—and they had trained me to use one.

Owen was clearly Desmond's second-in-command, which was interesting, due to his Matrian status and his young age—he was barely older than me. It had taken me a while, but I'd come to realize that I actually liked Owen—he could be annoying at times, too jovial, but he had a good sense of leadership.

Besides Owen and myself, there were three others joining us.

Amber—who was a bit younger than me, with curly orange-red hair that she cut artfully by shaving the sides of her head while keeping a thick curly mop on top. She was outgoing and upbeat, but I had learned that she had originally escaped from Patrus, where her father had 'sold' her to a wealthy man to pay off his debts.

Then there was Solomon. When I had first met him, he had been incredibly intimidating—taller and broader than Viggo, roped with muscles that seemed ready to burst. Everything about him seemed dark, from the duskiness of his skin and the deep inky black of his hair and beard, to his intense black eyes. He gave off a dangerous vibe and I had kept my distance until I had heard him laugh—a rich, joyful sound—after

which I'd realized he was a kind and considerate individual. He had gone out of his way to bring Tim little
gifts like softer clothes that wouldn't irritate his skin,
and pilfered cookies his mother Meera (who was a
cook for the Liberators) had made. Solomon's own little brother was a failed test subject and a captive of the
facility.

Lastly, there was Quinn, whom I knew little
about except that he didn't have any family among the
Liberators, and was a little older than Tim. He kept
mostly to himself but seemed nice enough, if not a little excitable.

Having spent the last couple of weeks going
through training with the team, I felt reasonably confident that we could work together. That didn't stop
me from feeling nervous that I was leaving for an un-
determined length of time though. Anything could
happen while I was gone.

But Viggo's condition was steady and sure—just
like him—and I had to believe he would remain that
way. I couldn't accept anything less than success on
this mission, because the thought of losing him was
too painful to even contemplate. It amazed me how
far we had come, given our sordid history, and I wasn't
ready for it to end.

I wouldn't let it end.

With that thought, I stood and moved closer to
him, resting a hip on the bed near his elbow.

"As far as I see it, you've saved my life a total of four times," I said conversationally to him. I didn't know if he could hear me, but I didn't care. Talking to him made me feel better, and I liked believing that he did hear me. That somehow my voice was able to penetrate his dreamless coma, and remind him that there was someone waiting for him to come back. It was romantic drivel, but sometimes that was the best kind of drivel to hold onto.

"Once with the Porteque gang, twice with the centipedes (though I still think it counts as once) and once with the princesses. And I've saved your life three times. Once with the red flies and twice with the same princesses. Now, any good Matrian will tell you that being in debt to a Patrian is the worst fate imaginable, but truthfully, I don't mind. However, given that you essentially—and stupidly, I might add—put yourself into a coma for me, you've set the bar way too high. Well... challenge accepted. I'm going to break into a country that restricts female movements, break into a warehouse, get what you need, and bring it back for you. And then... I'm going to kiss you right before you wake up, just so that I can tell everyone you're my princess. Then, it'll be your turn to top that."

I smiled at my stupid speech, knowing that if Viggo was awake, he would offer some dry comment that would cut through it.

I was beyond anxious to have him back—I craved

the strength of his arms as he held me, and the surety of his heartbeat under my ear. More than that, I craved the way he just listened. He didn't always agree with me, but he did listen to me just as I listened to him. We were a great team, and he was a person I truly viewed as a partner.

I heard the door swing open behind me and turned toward it. Owen was standing there.

"Everyone's getting ready in the antechamber," he said softly, and I could tell he felt bad about intruding on my moment with Viggo.

I nodded and he swung the door closed behind him. I turned back to Viggo and studied his face, trying to commit every line and angle to memory. "I'll be back for you," I whispered. "Just please… don't give up. Stay here. Wait for me."

The machines chirped in response. Leaning over, I carefully positioned myself over him and pressed my lips against his.

Then, before I could talk myself out of it, I scooped up my pack and headed for the door.

CHAPTER 2

Violet

I turned left and moved toward the antechamber. This level was the only one above ground and featured an airlock for entrance and exit. It was the only way in or out of the facility, although a few of the engineers who worked with Desmond insisted there would have to be ventilation ducts that could serve as exits if the top level was ever compromised. I hadn't heard if they had found them, but so far it hadn't been a problem.

Owen was holding open the door for me and I could see Quinn, Amber, and Solomon already inside. I stepped through the door with a nod to Owen. He offered me a smile and a nod of his own.

Amber and Quinn were busy organizing all of the packs. I recognized most of the equipment that they were packing, my eyes running over and cataloging it. My own pack was mostly empty—I had left the false egg that was in my possession behind in my wardrobe and made Tim promise to keep a close eye on it—but I had grabbed the key to the real egg. I had found a chain buried in the back of a drawer in one of the rooms, and now it was hanging under my suit, pressed against my skin.

Quinn shot me an enthusiastic look and I sighed, steeling myself. This was a fundamental worry I had—Quinn and Amber had never been on a mission before, and I was nervous that their inexperience would get us into trouble. I couldn't afford for there to be any screw-ups in getting the laser.

The room was silent while everyone put their gear together. Amber handed me a few items—a handgun, some silver canisters, a face mask, and a few cans of food. I frowned, calculating how much food we were packing versus how many days it would take to walk out of The Green, and I felt certain it wasn't enough.

I shot a questioning gaze at Owen, but he returned a sly smile and shook his head. He knew that lack of information chafed at me, but I had to trust him enough not to make an issue out of it. He would tell me when he was ready. Besides, I was not going to jeopardize my position on the team by being argumentative. Not with Viggo's life on the line.

The four of them were in the process of strapping

something over their forearms that I had never seen before. It was like a bracelet, except it wrapped around the wrist and just under the elbow. Two thin pieces held the two bracelets together, and there was a flexible piece that ran over the meat of the thumb and then across the palm of the hand, reconnecting on the other side. It was like a wire cage for their forearms.

"What are those?" I asked, studying the strange contraption.

Amber and Owen exchanged looks.

"Remember that time I kidnapped you?" Owen asked.

I let out a surprised laugh, and nodded. "You mean the time you *tried*?"

That elicited a deep chuckle from Solomon and I met his grin with one of my own. I really did like Solomon. He had been one of the few people who had been kind to Tim, and tried treating him like a human being rather than a broken boy. It was hard, though— more often than not, Tim stayed in our room with Samuel, only ever venturing out at my insistence. The rest of the time he spent on the floor on his makeshift nest of pillows and blankets, curled up around the dog.

It was harrowing seeing Tim struggle like that. I'd had several conversations with Desmond about how to help him, but there was not a lot on Mr. Jenks' computer that even speculated how to rehabilitate the boys. If anything, the scientist had remarked on the side-effects with clinical detachment.

It made me furious to know that Mr. Jenks had dismissed the possibility of rehabilitation, or even developing some sort of medication to help them overcome their problems. Instead, he had focused on trying to replicate his results with minimal side-effects in future children, and creating a pill that would activate the genes temporarily in a regular human. He hadn't quite nailed the science, but after a long conversation with Desmond about it, I had asked her to destroy those pills, and she had agreed.

Yet another reason I liked her. The pills Mr. Jenks had been developing could have helped her people immensely—but the pills were unstable, and might damage whoever took them. I knew she had toyed with the idea of having her own scientists try to fix the problems with the pills—she had told me as much—but I'd reminded her that anything that came from Mr. Jenks' research had been paid for in the blood of our loved ones, and she had taken that to heart, thanking me for reminding her about what was important.

I turned my attention to Owen as he explained, "These things are what helped me swing you through the trees using the vines. They're grip enhancers."

"Oh… Do I get a pair?" I asked.

Owen shook his head, a flash of regret crossing his face. "They are more dangerous than the suit.

Quite commonly, you can get radial fractures in the bones of your arms if you're not careful. We normally start training on them at a lower setting, and it's not something we can move quickly through, like the suits. They take months to master. But don't worry… I can carry you again if need be."

He said this with a smile and a wink, but the thought of swinging through the vines again with his arm around my waist and the forest floor rushing up to meet us was too nauseating for me to register his good humor. I shuddered, shouldering my pack.

We slipped our masks over our faces and then stepped into the antechamber. Quinn closed the door behind us and twisted the handle, sealing us in. Amber pressed the button on the opposite door, and there came a soft hiss as the chamber began to filter in the toxic air from outside, equalizing the room.

After a few seconds, the light over the door flashed from red to green, and Solomon opened the door. Immediately, the sweltering heat from The Green filled the room, as did a little of the ever-present mist.

As we stepped outside into the toxic atmosphere, Solomon closed the door behind us. Owen consulted with his handheld before pointing out the direction. We began walking. Owen took point and Quinn the rear, and I was sandwiched between Amber and Solomon.

For the most part, we were quiet. It made

sense—the dangers of The Green required caution at all times. I would never forget my own time here, and I reflected on how this felt different. For one thing, I had been completely alone at the start of my journey through The Green, and for another, I had been completely unprepared for it given that I had crash-landed here.

Now I felt confident, like I knew what I was doing, and I trusted Owen—and by default, the others—enough to know that they'd watch my back, just like I would watch theirs.

We moved slowly through the foliage. A few times Owen had signaled for us stop by bringing up a fist. Immediately, weapons were drawn. Solomon pulled out a stick that was strapped along his thigh—he clicked a button, and the stick morphed into that of a broad axe, the massive head resembling a half-moon.

Quinn and Amber had similar weapons—Quinn's stick morphed into a spear that stood almost a foot taller than him, and Amber had a pair of short swords. Owen's was short and fit in his palms, forming over his fisted knuckles into punch blades with four blades instead of two. While I simply had a gun.

Periodically, Owen would make us go invisible to avoid detection from the wildlife. For the most part though, we just walked.

We traveled for hours, the sun marching along with us in the morning, and then past us in the evening. Not that we got much sunlight in The Green—the canopy was too thick to let any light through, save a few rays that managed to push past the dense thicket of leaves.

Toward the evening, Owen had us spread out, and we began searching in a straight line, looking for prospective camping sites. It was ultimately Owen who found the perfect place against a massive boulder covered in green and brown moss. We sprayed it down—luckily no centipedes emerged from beneath—and fixed a simple roof using some of the polymorphic blankets we had brought.

Amber set up a light, and we all sat and ate in silence.

It was Quinn who broke it first. "Violet?"

I turned my head at his questioning tone, my hand on my mask, preparing to remove it to take another bite of my protein gel. "Yeah?"

Quinn leaned forward. "What happened to you when you were out here?"

"What do you mean?" I asked.

Quinn looked over at Amber, who looked at Solomon. There was a long pause before Solomon began speaking. "We heard you survived out here on your own for several days, with no suit," he said, his dark eyes glittering with questions.

"But… people do that all the time, don't they?"

The group collectively shook their heads.

"No—because of our suits, we rarely encounter any-thing out here," said Amber, an almost wistful quality to her voice.

I frowned at her. "Then that's a good thing. Because it was not easy, and I almost died."

CHAPTER 3

Violet

Amber scooted forward a few inches, her face reflecting her excitement and anticipation behind the plastic faceplate of her mask. I looked around at everyone, who bore similar expressions.

Letting out a breath, I set my gel down, crossed my legs and began to explain. "I crashed into the forest thanks to a flying motorcycle, and when I landed, I wasn't wearing a mask—I was hanging in a tree. I managed to get to the motorcycle before it plummeted to the ground and I put my mask on. Then, I heard some red flies. I leapt into a hiding place before they could get me, but I got bitten by a black centipede. I didn't have medication, so I was trying to make my way to Matrus before I died, but I passed out. Viggo…

well… he found me, patched me up, and then arrested me for what happened in Patrus.

"Anyway, one thing led to another, Owen grabbed me—although I didn't know it was him at the time—we found Ms. Dale, ran from some more red flies, and then stumbled upon the facility. It was a hellish nightmare, and frankly, I really kind of hate this place."

I picked up my tin from where I had set it, determined to start eating again.

"Wow… that's intense," Quinn said, his voice holding a note of admiration. "You've really been through it, huh?"

The others' faces reflected Quinn's admiration, in a way that made me uncomfortable.

"No more than anyone else," I muttered.

"That's not true," Amber said, her voice burning with vehemence. "You've done more to hurt Matrus than we could ever dream of!"

I hunched my shoulders. "If you're talking about the twins… it's not as simple as it sounds. I… I wish…"

I honestly wish that we hadn't been forced to kill them, was what I wanted to say, but the words stuck in my throat. It had been in self-defense, but their deaths weighed heavily on my conscience regardless, even after one of the twins shot Viggo. She had done it to save her sister, and I had killed her to save him. It was a war of attrition, one that promised to never end.

Owen quickly came to my rescue. "Violet did

what she had to in order to survive, and if you had any idea what that was like, you wouldn't push her for details or praise her. She's just like us—she wants to take care of the people she cares about."

I shot Owen an appreciative glance and he winked.

"Believe me," I said, lowering my voice so that they would pay closer attention. "I would not wish what I have been through on my worst enemy."

"Not even the queen?" whispered Quinn, his eyes wide, and I was momentarily struck by how young he was—older than my brother, but not by much.

I shook my head. "Not even her," I said.

Amber watched me, her eyes flickering. "No offense, but I think that's really dumb."

"Why would you say that?" cut in Solomon.

Amber tossed a glance at him and then frowned. "The queen is the reason we're doing this. She took those boys from their mothers and family and subjected them to that awful place." She shuddered. "What she has done is no different than my father using me for his benefit."

"Well, to be fair, it was Queen Rina," Owen said, standing up. "Queen Elena might be a nicer person— we don't actually know."

Quinn scoffed and banged his empty tin down on the ground. "They're all the same," he said. "I mean… aren't they trying to frame Violet for something she didn't do?"

I leaned back, my eyebrows climbing to my fore-head. "There aren't many secrets in this group, huh?"

Amber rolled over on one side, propping her head up with one hand. "Not many, though we didn't know what happened while you were in The Green alone. I don't even think Desmond knows actually... and she knows everything."

I nodded. "Right, well, yes, blaming me doesn't speak too kindly of Queen Elena. Not to mention she left the boys in the facility, presumably to cover up what her mother was up to. Except..."

I trailed off, my mind working. The group sat patiently for a few seconds before Owen chimed in.

"Except what?" he asked, his blue eyes on me.

"Except... why would Queen Elena? They were close to achieving their goal, right? Even without Mr. Jenks, there was a chance someone could be hired to replicate his work, but they would need access to his original research and test subjects. Why did the queen just abandon the facility instead of destroying it, if her goal was a cover-up?"

The group exchanged a series of looks. "That's astute," Solomon commented after a pause. "And a good point—although I'm sure Desmond's considered it."

"Yeah, I'm sure she has," I muttered.

After another span of quiet, Owen stretched out. "All right, enough chitchat. We can continue the conversation tomorrow, but for now, we rest. Amber, you're up on guard duty, followed by Solomon, me, Quinn, and Violet, you're last."

The next morning dawned too soon in my mind. My muscles were sore from the previous day, but I used the two-hour morning shift to stretch them out. Everything was quiet and there was an eerie sense of calm in The Green, but nothing that stood out.

I woke Owen when it was time, and he helped me wake the others. We quickly ate, packed up camp, and started trudging along again. I had figured out yesterday that we were cutting a clear path toward Veil River, the toxic body of water that served as a natural boundary between Matrus and Patrus.

I wondered if Owen planned for us to cross there and head directly south afterward. It made sense, but the glaring exception was that there were no bridges, and the river was wide. It was also turbulent, so taking anything smaller than a barge was risky. If we capsized on the river, we might die within minutes of exposure.

I reminded myself again that I had to trust Owen—this was what it meant to work in a team. He knew what he was doing. After all, the Liberators operated from The Green, which meant they knew how to get in and out of it safely.

We walked for several hours before Owen stopped us abruptly. Immediately, a flurry of motion exploded from everyone as they began redistributing stuff from their packs and removing their weapons, placing them inside the bags. Curious, I stepped through the trees and gaped at the massive crack in the earth before us.

The two jagged pieces of earth were at least a hundred paces apart, and the crevice ran deep. The earth was red underneath—a violent, unnatural crimson that looked bloody and raw. The opposite facing wall jutted out at least twenty feet overhead.

Instinctively, I took a step back before I could look down to see how deeply it ran.

"We're not going to climb that, are we?" I asked, my heart leaping into my throat.

Owen chuckled and shook his head. "No," he said. "We're going to climb a tree, and then swing across."

A wave of dizziness hit me and I took another step back. "Oh God," I breathed.

Owen looked past my shoulder and I whirled—directly into Solomon's arms. He scooped me up and slung me over his shoulders almost casually, fitting me over his back like a human backpack. I gripped him tightly, my muscles tensed in preparation to leap off of him, when he started climbing.

I closed my eyes and tried to calm my breathing as a wave of panic slammed into me. I could hear the others grunting as they climbed, and a small whimper escaped my throat.

"It's okay, Violet," Solomon whispered, low enough so only I could hear. "It will be over in about forty-five seconds. Count for me."

I considered ignoring his request, but it seemed reasonable, all things considered. I started counting, focusing on the numbers.

At twenty, I clenched him tighter as the wind began to whistle past my ears. Amber shouted in joy and exhilaration, and in that moment, I envied her ability to enjoy heights.

I felt the impact as we hit the ground just as I reached thirty-seven seconds and opened my eyes to make sure we had landed.

I leapt off Solomon's back and moved a few more feet away, putting as much distance as I could between myself and the cliff face. We had made it to the other side effortlessly, but I was not exactly okay with how.

"I hate you," I said to Owen, who laughed.

The others laughed too, but it didn't feel like they were laughing at me. Quinn and Amber patted me on the shoulder, and Solomon shot me a grin. I crossed my arms and glared, but the truth was, it was nice having a team to work with. They made up for my shortcomings, namely the intense fear of heights I had developed recently, and I was truly enjoying being around them.

It had been so long since I had worked with a

group of individuals like this that it actually felt like I had friends. It was a nice feeling after being on the run and in prison for so long—yet I knew I had to keep my eyes on the goal.

Viggo was my only reason for being out here with them.

The group quickly reorganized their packs, pulling out their handheld weapons. I kept a look out, as I was the only one with a weapon available, until they were ready. Once they were, Owen took point again and led us deeper into the trees.

About an hour later, I became aware of the sound of the river. Perking up, I went on my tiptoes to see if I could catch a glimpse of it. I was excited to see what Owen had in store.

We broke through another copse of trees and suddenly, the river was there. We lined up next to it, and I stared at the massive body of water churning in front of us. The water was an unnaturally brilliant blue—a hue so deep and bright that it almost matched Owen's eyes. Like the earth of the cliff face that we had swung over, the shade looked artificial, and vibrantly different than further downriver by Matrus. There, it was a deep brown, almost muddy.

"It looks so different," I said.

"That's because it's ten times as potent here," Owen replied. "It becomes more diluted as it moves downstream."

"What really makes it so toxic here?" I asked.

"The Green," replied Amber, moving closer. "Whatever is in The Green gets flushed into the river and is carried downstream for miles and miles."

I nodded, absorbing the information. "So, what if one of us falls in?"

"Don't," replied Owen, pulling a lantern out of his bag. He clicked a button and a red light began to shine from it. He slid the lantern's hoop over a tree branch and then leaned against the connecting tree trunk, his arms crossed.

I watched him curiously. "What are you doing?" I asked.

"Ordering a taxi," he replied blithely.

Just then, a shout came from the water. I turned, my hand sliding to my gun. Owen placed his hand over mine and shook his head. "Don't shoot our ride, Violet."

I relaxed my hand and he let go. I narrowed my eyes, gazing out at the river. The mist over the water hung thick and glowed a slight blue, illuminated by the liquid flowing beneath it. I watched the mist as it roiled and writhed, when suddenly the bow of a ship slipped out of it.

The ship wasn't big—maybe thirty to forty feet long—and there was one lone man standing at the helm, his white hair sticking out from under a cap which was precariously perched on his head. Owen held up a hand in greeting, and the man raised one in return.

Quinn waved an arm and gave a small yell as the ship drifted closer, cutting a path through the churning water. The man on the boat was swinging something over his head, and I had just begun to realize it was a rope when he released it, angling it toward Quinn. Quinn caught it and quickly tied it to the tree next to him, wrapping it around the trunk. Amber was in the process of catching the other line, about twenty feet upstream from Quinn. She too, tied the rope to a tree.

The water behind the engine churned as the man on the boat revved the engine, bringing the vessel closer to the bank.

"Violet, why don't you come on board—I'll introduce you to Alejandro," Owen chirped.

Dazed at the coordination and planning—as well as a large boat appearing in The Green—I followed Owen down to the shore, eager to meet the man crazy enough to travel so far up Veil River.

CHAPTER 4

Violet

The boat churned downriver at a frightful pace, but nobody seemed concerned about the speed we were moving at, especially not Alejandro, the elderly man who owned and piloted the boat.

We had been cruising for several hours, and Owen had said that it would take many hours more to reach our extraction point. I had spent more than a few of those hours repacking my bag, but after a while, boredom set in, and I found myself wanting to talk to Alejandro.

Before we boarded the boat, Owen had pulled me aside and told me that Alejandro was not a part of the cause, so we had to be cautious about what we said to him. As far as Alejandro knew, the five of us were a research team, collecting specimens for study.

Now that we were on the boat, I found that I liked Alejandro. The rest of the group seemed perfectly content to ignore him, but I was fascinated by the old man. For one thing, he loved to talk—his voice constantly filled the air. Whether it was a narration of what he was doing or holding one-sided conversations with us, he was constantly chatting.

For another thing, there was a fierce intelligence burning behind his eyes. Maybe the others picked up on it as well, but I could tell that he knew we weren't what we said we were. However, he didn't say anything to the contrary, he just continued talking and watching, all while he navigated the boat through the bubbling waters.

I looked over to where the group was sitting, toward the bow of the ship, and realized Amber and Quinn were asleep. Owen and Solomon had their heads bent toward each other and were whispering. A part of me wanted to go over and interject myself in the conversation.

Owen's tight-lipped attitude toward the mission was still a bone of contention with me. I didn't like being left out of the loop when it came to missions, but then again, it wasn't a surprise. Lee had left a lot of details out of his plan to bomb the lab and retrieve the egg. However, he had told me the plan in general, with several glaring exceptions. I understood the need for operational security, but not at the expense of leaving everyone blind.

I also wondered how much Amber, Quinn, and Solomon knew compared to me. This was Amber and Quinn's first mission, but they had done far more training with Owen and Solomon than I had.

In all likelihood, this wasn't the first time Owen had infiltrated Patrus, and he probably used Alejandro to help move his team up and down the river all the time.

The boat dipped sharply, breaking my train of thought, and I grabbed the edge of the boat to steady myself. Quinn and Amber jerked awake and grabbed the bench they were sleeping on, while Solomon and Owen simultaneously gripped each other's forearms and turned their heads toward the stern of the boat.

"Yeeeeeeeeehaaaaaaaaaaaw!" bellowed Alejandro, a wild smile on his face. We reached the apex of the dip with a splash, and I ducked, covering my head with my arms. The move proved to be pointless—none of the toxic water that the boat kicked up made it over the sides. We leveled out and I sat up, picking a stray lock of hair off of the faceplate of my mask.

We all looked around, checking to make sure we were okay. Owen's gaze slid over mine and a small smile formed on his lips—I imagined how disheveled and panicked I must have looked, and relaxed my features. My only experience with boats was with the one that took me to Patrus. Had that been so recently? It had actually only been a little over a month ago, but it felt like a lifetime.

Alejandro sauntered up, his rolling gait confident as he moved. He was definitely a man of the river—every time I tried to stand up or walk, it was in the form of a controlled stumble. I couldn't anticipate where the deck would be as the boat was constantly being rocked by the turbulent waters below.

"We're through the worst of it," Alejandro announced. "Should be a peaceful trip to your drop-off point."

Owen nodded in acknowledgment and turned back to Solomon.

I frowned, and looked up at the old man. "Thank you," I said.

Alejandro tipped his head to me, the glare that he had been directing at Owen and his rudeness dissipating. "Think nothing of it, my girl," he said.

"No," I said, moving unsteadily on my feet. "It really is generous of you to risk your life and your boat for us. I understand that we're paying you to, but I can also imagine that some jobs aren't worth the risk. I, for one, appreciate the sacrifice."

Alejandro flushed behind the clear plastic face of his mask. He whipped off his hat and ran an embarrassed hand through his white hair. "You're much more sociable than your compatriots," he said after the red of his cheeks had faded.

I gave a small laugh. "Well, let's just say they take their work very seriously."

"And you?"

Ducking my head, I shrugged. "I'm serious… but being serious is no cause for being rude."

He guffawed and clapped me on the arm. It was my turn to blush—not from his laugh or even staggering under the force of his hand on me, but from the attention I was drawing from Owen and the others. I gave them a small shrug, and after a questioning gaze, they turned away.

I could tell Owen didn't approve of me talking to Alejandro, but I didn't really care. The man seemed sweet, if not a little eccentric, and since no one else seemed interested in talking to pass the time, I was going to make do where I could. Owen just needed to trust that I wouldn't do anything to jeopardize the mission.

Just like I needed to trust that he knew what he was doing, and that he wasn't doing anything to set me up.

It was unfair to Owen, but I couldn't help feel a little doubt. The last mission I'd been on with a partner had ended with me having to kill him, and I wasn't eager to relive that experience. I did trust Owen, but the doubt was always there in the back of my mind. I knew it wasn't rational, but drawing from history was never a bad thing. It kept me from blindly trusting people, and helped me keep an eye out for potential threats to me or the mission.

Alejandro moved back to the captain's station, and I followed him. I moved at a slower pace, my legs and arms stiff and ungainly against the roll of the deck. He shot a glance back at me, a knowing smile on his lips.

"You have to bend your knees, girl," he said. "You look like one of those wooden puppets on strings, but the river is alive, and your arms and legs need to be alive if you're going to master her."

I couldn't resist the urge to smile. "Have you mastered her yet?" I asked.

"Oh, no... no one can ever master a great beauty like this. She's far too wild and unpredictable. However, I'm one of the few operators who can navigate her. I like to think it's because she likes me." He winked at me and then began moving again.

"How long have you been working with her?" I asked. It felt a little silly, referring to the river as a woman, but a part of me admired Alejandro's reverence of the river. He had personalized it, and I recognized the importance of that act in his eyes. Every time he came up or down river, he risked his life. It was his way of coping with the dangers inherent in his job.

"A little over thirty years," he said, grabbing the wheel and turning it slightly. "I used to be a stevedore."

At my confused look, he chuckled. "We were dock rats—unloading and loading up cargo. Shipping goods to Matrus and unloading goods for Patrus. But I was obsessed with the boats, and Jenny—that's my wife—she told me to crew up." He paused and shot me a look. "She'd tell you that she did it for me, but honestly, I think I drove her a bit crazy being around all the time."

I laughed at his bluntness. "Really? I think that's surprising. You seem very upbeat."

The smile slid off his face like drops of water sliding down a window pane in the rain. "Nah… it's not because I'm so cheerful, it's because I tend to worry over her. She compares me to a mama dog hovering over its pups. I'm too protective."

It was a little strange hearing a Patrian man saying he was too protective over his wife. From what I had seen of Patrian marriages, men tended to expect the woman to jump through hoops and fulfill their every demand. Or at least, that was what the Matrus government would have us believe.

The truth was, I'd only had a handful of experiences with Patrian males. Viggo was perhaps one of the more equitable males I had met. There was my cousin Cad, but I hadn't spoken to him since he'd tried to help me smuggle my brother to safety. I wasn't even sure if he was married, but I could imagine that he would be kinder to his wife than the other males of

Patrus.

The laws of Patrus considered women no more than property, and the rules for women were in strict adherence to that. They couldn't even be in public without a male escort—if they were, they could be arrested, or even worse. I shuddered thinking about the Porteque men who had cornered me in the alley—my first encounter with those brutes. If it hadn't been for Viggo's interference, they would have dragged me off.

I shook my head to clear my thoughts and shifted my gaze back to Alejandro, who was looking at me knowingly. "Don't think about it, girl," he said, but with a kind edge to his voice.

"About what?" I asked, settling my hip against the rail I had grabbed onto to steady myself.

"Whatever darkness that was dragging you into the past."

I flushed, both embarrassed and curious at how he could read me so well.

"No need to get embarrassed," he continued, and I met his gaze. "You remind me of a man I know. Probably the closest thing I have to a son. He's arrogant and pig-headed at times, but if you can get past his prickly outer shell, he's got a heart as large as this river."

"Where is he?"

Alejandro's face fell. "I took him upriver some time ago. I haven't heard from him since."

I felt an echo of sadness in response to the older man's tragedy. "I'm so sorry. Do you think... do you think he's still alive?"

Frowning, Alejandro shook his head. "No," he said gruffly. "Nobody can live that long in The Green. But... have you seen any bodies out there, maybe? On your... expedition?"

"I'm sorry," I repeated, feeling stupid that I couldn't articulate anything better. "I wish I could help you."

"Ah, don't worry about it, lass. He's a resourceful man—if anyone could survive, it'd be him. Besides... you and your friends lasted for a bit... how long did you say you were up there?"

I caught a glimpse of the sidelong gaze he shot me and returned a bemused look. "All information regarding our expedition should be handled through Owen," I replied, and he laughed.

"You and my young man would've gotten along famously," he said, his eyes sparkling merrily. "He was also great at keeping a secret."

We shared a smile before I turned my gaze out over the river. The deep blue hue had faded the further downriver we went. The trees and sounds of The Green were also starting to fade, and I knew that in a few hours, we were going to be in even more danger than before. Yet in that moment, even with everything weighing heavily on me, I felt a strange contentment rolling over me.

It was the knowledge that I was finally doing something to help Viggo. Two weeks of waiting, trying to be patient when every day felt like the slow grinding of teeth. Now, in this moment, we were moving toward a goal where I could finally help him, and there was no turning back.

Owen called my name. Turning, I saw him holding a bag and waving an arm, beckoning me over. I noticed that he had taken his mask off, and I turned to Alejandro, who was in the process of taking his off as well. Grabbing the straps of my own mask, I removed it, taking a deep breath of fresh air and releasing it with a small sigh.

Then I moved toward Owen, hoping to finally glean more details of the mission ahead of us.

CHAPTER 5

Violet

As I stared at the bag in Owen's hand, resentment and understanding warred within me.

"Ugh, no," I said.

Owen gave the sigh of eternal patience, and I resisted the urge to childishly stomp my feet.

"Violet, even with the time that has passed, everyone will be looking for you. Maybe not as fervently as a few weeks ago, but your face will still be fresh in everyone's minds. The bombing of that facility killed dozens of people and wounded dozens more. Patrians want revenge."

His words were reasonable but I hated the feelings that the contents of the bag were inspiring. I knew it was irrational—I had done it before, so it shouldn't be such a big deal—but internally I was balking, trying to find another solution.

Ultimately though, there wasn't any, so I reached out and accepted the bag.

Owen patted me on the shoulder. "Alejandro said you could use the small room down at the end of the galley to change. Amber's already down there getting ready."

I turned reluctantly, heading for the small narrow stairs that led to the galley.

I moved through the slender hallway toward the door at the end. There was a small kitchenette just before the bedroom, with a small table and stovetop neatly set up. I pushed open the door and found Amber slipping a dress over her uniform.

I glowered at the dress while placing the bag on the bed and unzipping it. Sighing, I began pulling the folded items out and examining them. The suit was a simple gray—a little threadbare, but serviceable. A gray-blue button-down shirt and a black tie were next, followed by a fake beard and a small box of pills labeled *Deepvox*.

As I set them out one by one, I felt a pang of déjà vu. The last time I had been in Patrus, Lee had given me similar items to help with his mission. Dressing like a man had afforded me more liberties around Patrus, but it had also carried a great risk. Any woman caught impersonating a male would face punishment.

Not to mention it was downright uncomfortable. The opposite sex—especially the Patrian ones—were still a giant mystery to me. Acting like one was almost impossible, so most of the time I had tried to keep my head down and my mouth shut.

Amber was looking at me inquisitively while I started unfolding the clothes. "It's not your first time, is it?" I heard it as a question, but she said it as a sentence.

"Nope."

"I hate it," she said.

"Yeah," I agreed. It did make me feel better, knowing that Amber despised the costume as much as I did. I looked up at her. "Won't your hair make you stand out?" I asked.

Amber's fingers shot up to the sides of her head where the hair had been shaved down. She cast me a crooked smile, and pulled a glob of hair from the bag on her side of the bed. "Ta-da!" she announced, waving a blonde wig around like a white flag.

I chuckled as she plopped it on her head, winking at me dramatically. The hair, which needed to be brushed, chaotically fell around her face, making her look wild and deranged.

"Come here," I said, reaching over to grab the brush that was sitting by her bag. Dutifully, she sat down with her back to me.

Carefully, I began brushing the wig. It was tricky

to do, but I eventually made my way through the tangled mass. Amber sat patiently under my hands as I worked.

"There," I said, putting the brush down. She twisted around to give me a better look, and I nodded approvingly. The blonde helped to highlight the freckles across her cheekbones, and her normal aggressive appearance was gone, replaced with a pixie-like quality. "You look cute," I commented.

Her violet eyes tightened in annoyance, and I laughed. I moved back over to my costume and groaned. "My turn."

It took a while to get the padding sorted, but Amber helped me, and after about ten minutes, the curves of my hips and breasts had disappeared under foam and wool. Applying the beard took another few minutes. Owen had provided something a little simpler than I was used to—a goatee.

It framed my mouth well, however, and I felt more secure that it wouldn't fall off as easily if I smiled or laughed—not that I anticipated doing much of that.

I tied my hair up and dropped a cap over it. I looked a little effeminate in the face, but overall, the disguise seemed sound. I was glad I was wearing my invisibility suit underneath it—it helped to alleviate a lot of the heat wearing the entire outfit generated. However, it would be impossible to shed the disguise quickly if I needed to use the camouflage function, so

I made a mental note to keep a knife handy, just in case.

Amber gave me a nod of approval once I was done. "*Very* handsome," she declared with a mischievous look in her eyes, and I stuck out my tongue at her.

We moved back through the galley and up the stairs. Quinn gave a little wolf-whistle when Amber reappeared, but Solomon smacked him on the back of the head, making him flinch. The men had already changed—they were wearing suits similar to mine.

Owen threw us a thoughtful look, and then nodded his own approval. "It'll have to do," he said.

Alejandro walked up. "We're almost to the coordinates you gave me—are you sure you don't want to be dropped off closer to the city?"

Owen shook his head and offered Alejandro his hand. "No, this will be fine," he said. "We have arranged other transport into the city."

Alejandro looked dubious, but reached out and shook Owen's hand. "Be ready—I can only get within a few feet of the shore without risk of beaching her. You'll have to jump the remaining distance."

"Yes—we've been through this before," Owen reminded Alejandro.

"I know, but it's just worrisome to me—you've got two fine ladies with you." He shot me a gaze and I swallowed under his scrutiny. "I'd hate for something bad to happen to them, if you're discovered."

"Discovered for what?" asked Owen, his voice rising an octave in the appearance of innocence.

Alejandro arched a snow-white eyebrow, and just shook his head disapprovingly. "You young ones think you have it all figured out," he muttered. I wasn't sure if Owen heard or even cared, but I had to smile at his words.

I hoped this wouldn't be the last time I'd see Alejandro. There was a depth to him, and it felt like he was a kindred spirit.

Alejandro cocked his head and peered past Owen's shoulder. "All right," he announced, clapping his hands together. "Get your things, lads... and lady," he said, dipping his head toward Amber. He also shot a wink at me, and I hid my smile behind my hand. "Your drop point is about two minutes away, give or take."

He sauntered back up to the pilot's station, humming. I quickly got caught up with the rest of the group as we started inventorying our things and organizing the bags. I pulled my backpack on, tucking the mask into it.

Then we all lined up on the bow. There was a wooden plank extending from the tip. Owen stood at the front of it as Alejandro steered us toward the shore. There would be no mooring the ship to disembark—we would have to jump over the water below.

I felt my heartbeat accelerate at the thought—the water might be diluted here, but that didn't make it much less dangerous if one of us accidentally fell in.

Owen's posture was seemingly free of that fear. He stood tall, one hand resting on the rail behind him, while the shore loomed ever closer. Then his muscles tensed and he leapt. For a second, he seemed suspended in the air, frozen in that moment of flight until time caught up, and he landed on his feet on the other side.

One by one we followed, until only I remained. Solomon was waiting for me, so I took a deep breath and launched myself at him. For a harrowing moment, I thought I had miscalculated and that I would plummet into the murky waters below. But then Solomon grabbed me as my feet hit the soft earth, and he held me tight until I was stable again.

Owen had already climbed up the steep hill and had dropped to one knee, surveying the terrain above. We waited in silence for him to give us the all-clear. I glanced back at the boat, but it had already turned and was moving away from us, downriver at top speed. I waved at Alejandro, but his back was to me. I felt a little sad that I didn't get to say goodbye.

Just then, Owen let out a low whistle, and we were climbing. We crested the hill and looked around—the area was wide open, with barely any trees.

"Where's our ride?" I asked.

He gave me an apologetic smile. "About an hour

inland. We'd better get moving if we're going to meet them in time."

I grimaced, not looking forward to an hour long trek in my suit, and pulled my bag over my shoulder. I understood why Owen had made me change on the boat, but I resented the whole costume thing all over again.

Owen took point and the rest of us followed. Amber was holding up her skirt high as she pushed through the deep grass in the field, and I smiled.

Maybe my suit wasn't the worst thing to be wearing out here.

CHAPTER 6

Violet

The sun was uncomfortably warm on my head. We had been sitting for over an hour, waiting for our ride to show up. According to Owen, they were late but on their way. There wasn't much to do during the wait, so most of the group elected to take a nap. I refrained, mostly because I didn't want to worry about my disguise getting messed up from sleeping on the ground. Owen had also refused, saying that his contacts needed to see him first so that they didn't shoot everyone and ask questions later.

He said it in a joking tone, but I wasn't convinced. I was more than a little curious about the people Owen was using to shuttle us into Patrus.

I looked over to where he was sitting. He had his

back to me and was staring at his handheld. We had both decided to sit on the massive rock jutting out of the ground, while Quinn, Amber, and Solomon slept below in the shade.

"Owen," I called softly, so as not to disturb the others.

"Hmm?"

He didn't even turn his head to look at me, and I gave an irritated sigh. Picking up a small rock, I tossed it at him, hitting him on the shoulder. He froze as the rock clacked across the boulder, skittering to the grass below.

Turning, he arched a brow at me, and I gave him a fake smile and a little wave.

"*Yes?*"

I ignored his annoyed tone and asked, "Who are the people who are picking us up?"

Owen frowned, a line growing between his eyebrows. "It's not really important to the mission," he said, starting to turn away.

"Great! Then you should be able to tell me, right?"

He turned back, his blue eyes trained on me. "Why do you want to know?"

I crossed my arms. "Look, I understand the need for operational security and all that, but the lack of information is starting to get to me."

"I... I don't understand."

I gaped at him, but then closed my mouth when I

saw the seriousness in his face.

"Wow. Okay… well…" I paused, searching for the words that could make him understand my position. "The last mission I was on, key details were excluded, which sort of led to me being in this mess. I don't like walking into anything blind now, if I can avoid it. So… just give me this, okay?"

Owen considered my request as he leaned back on his hands and crossed his legs out in front of him. "All right," he said. "The people who are coming to get us belong to a different rebel faction based out of Patrus. They have ways to cross in and out of the border that we don't, so we employ them from time to time to help smuggle us in and out."

I frowned—another rebel faction based in Patrus? Why hadn't I heard of them? What did they stand for?

The last question worried me quite a bit, so I decided to ask, "Where do their loyalties lie?"

Owen's face looked resigned. "I'm not going to lie to you, Violet—they are Patrian through and through. Which is why I had you and Amber change before we even got off the boat. They are paranoid, enough to have set up lookouts to make sure we are what we claim we are."

"And that is?"

Owen's face flushed red—not in embarrassment, but in something else that I couldn't exactly place. "Matrian flesh dealers."

"WHAT?" I exclaimed, rising to my feet.

My shout was loud enough to wake the others, from the groans and whispers below.

"Everything okay up there?" Solomon called. I glanced over to see him backing away from the boulder, his hands over his eyes to shield his gaze from the sun.

Owen sighed heavily and hauled himself onto his feet to stand before me. "I guess it's a good thing we talked about this now," he spat, brushing dirt from his clothes. "Because if this is how you're going to react, you're going to break our cover."

"So what—Amber's our Matrian female, whom we abducted to auction off to a rich Patrian?" I asked.

Owen laughed, and I took a step back, stunned. How could he be so blasé about this?

"Violet, we aren't really going to sell Amber. You know that, right?"

"Of course I do, but—"

"And she's perfectly okay with it."

"Am not!" Amber declared from below.

Owen grunted. "Amber, what's the reason you're *not* okay with it?"

"Dresses are stupid," she said.

"But other than that?"

"Oh, yeah, if I didn't have to wear the dress, I would be perfectly fine with it. I don't care."

I rolled my eyes in annoyance. "Missing the point

here, guys," I said, addressing all of them.

Solomon pulled himself up the rock and came to stand next to us. "All right, what's the point?" he asked, his voice even and calm.

"If we have to pretend that Amber is a Matrian woman we kidnapped just to get a ride from these people, shouldn't we be asking if they are the kind of people we should be dealing with in the first place?"

Owen shook his head. "You're looking too deeply into it, Violet. They are providing a service. In order for us to complete our mission, we have to do it. There are no other options available."

"But—"

He cut me off, holding up a hand in warning. I felt my anger grow at being silenced so rudely, when suddenly I heard it—the distant sound of an engine. Solomon and Owen exchanged a look, and immediately sprang into action.

"Quinn, get Amber's hands tied up and get the remaining gear together. Solomon, go out in front of the boulder and have your weapon out, but not pointed at them. Violet... get off the rock and get down here to help us."

I raced to follow his orders. As much as I wanted to fight it out with him, now was not the time. I didn't want to risk jeopardizing the mission over an ideological squabble. My own reservations didn't matter at that moment, only Viggo did. Except that I was still unable to get the uncomfortable feeling in my stomach to go away.

I meant what I'd said to Owen—any people we had to put on an act for, especially one as demeaning as this, were people we should be steering clear of. It bothered me how matter-of-fact Owen and the others were about it, like it was just a walk in the park.

But I kept my mouth closed and began grabbing the gear. I could hear the vehicle getting closer while I worked to make sure everything was in order and accounted for. I was just pulling a bag onto my shoulders when brakes squealed.

The sound of the engine died, and Solomon gave a greeting. A deeper male voice responded, and suddenly I remembered I hadn't taken my Deepvox pills. Shooting a glance at Owen, I took off my pack and began rummaging around in it.

"What are you doing?" he hissed.

"I forgot to take the pills—if they talk to me, they're going to know."

Owen clenched his jaw and then nodded. "Just keep your mouth closed for as long as possible. They won't work instantly, and they're a little old, so I don't know how that affects their potency."

I grabbed the box of pills and dropped two in my hand. Pulling up my canteen, I swallowed them down and dumped everything back in the bag. Owen pushed by me with his own bag on his shoulders. I hurriedly replaced everything in my bag and pulled it on.

Running a hand over my face, I checked to make sure my goatee was still in place. It was hard to know without a mirror, so I looked over to where Quinn was passing me by with Amber in tow. I frowned at her bound hands and the rope that hung between them like a leash.

I knew I shouldn't feel so repulsed by it—after all, Viggo had tied me up like that once. Of course, at that time, he had been angry with me, and had a hard time believing that I was being honest with him. Still, I doubted I would be able to pretend to be the prisoner for something as disturbing as this.

Amber didn't complain though, just made a goofy face at me as she walked by. The face made me smile a little, and I pushed my complaints about the mission aside.

I was reacting too strongly—I needed to let it go.

I moved to follow, coming around the rock to take a good look at our escorts, and then froze. A man was standing before Solomon and Owen, talking with them. I didn't recognize him, but the tattoo under his eye told me more about who we were working with than talking to him ever could.

The black triangle tattoo was the mark of the Porteque gang. The gang that had been labeled terrorists, and were the ultimate form of misogyny.

My stomach turned as my mind took me back to that cell they had held me in. To the sounds and smells in that dank hole. I had been very lucky—Viggo had drummed up a response team quickly, and thanks to the tracking bug Lee had laced my water with, they had found me before things got too bad.

But I had still killed one of them, and that made me public enemy number one to these men. If they recognized me, there would be nothing we could do to stop them from taking me again. There were sixteen men standing behind the one talking to Owen and Solomon, each with a dangerous look in their eyes, and each holding weapons.

I swallowed hard and kept my head down, waiting.

After a while, the three men finished their discussion. I watched as Owen handed something off to their leader, who tipped his hat to him, a smile breaking out on his face.

Owen motioned for us to move toward the truck, and we did. A few of the men made leering sounds toward Amber, but were careful not to touch her.

Amber kept her head held high and ignored them. I followed behind at a more sedate pace, and paused when I was next to Owen.

"These men are in the Porteque gang," I whispered to him.

"I know, Violet. They're giving us passage to the

city."

"I understand that, but I was taken by them once. I killed one of their men. If they know it's me, then…"

I trailed off at Owen's glare. "Be polite and keep your head down," he ordered. "I promise… we'll get through this."

He moved away toward the truck and I followed, my eyes riveted on the truck as anxiety rose in me. I wasn't sure how I was going to do this, but if I wanted to make sure everyone with me made it out alive, I would have to.

CHAPTER 7

Violet

Surprisingly, the trip went smoothly. Owen had managed to pull Solomon and Quinn aside before they got on, and they made room for me and Amber between them. If the Porteque gang realized something was up, they didn't say anything.

I spent most of the ride pretending to sleep—which was difficult. The truck they had provided jostled over every bump and hole, throwing us up in the air multiple times. The seats were hard and made of metal, and after an hour of bouncing on them, it felt like I would never be able to walk again.

After three hours, the ride evened out. At my questioning glance, Solomon leaned over and whispered that we were now on a road, and that it would take another two hours to reach our destination. I exhaled, and then leaned back to try to pretend to rest again.

I actually managed to sleep until the truck came to a complete stop, jerking me awake. Stiff and sore, I stood and stretched, watching as the men leapt out of the back of the truck, pulling aside the heavy canvas flaps. I let everyone climb out first, and then slipped out behind them, dragging the bags to the tailgate.

Owen was massaging his lower back and looking around. We were parked behind a massive warehouse, walls enclosing the compound. I could smell the deep rich earth smell that seemed permanent in Patrus. We were close to one of the farms, but within the city, like they had promised.

Quinn passed Amber's rope over to Owen, who jerked her close. The Porteque men laughed at her cry of pain, and I turned away before anyone could notice the frown that his action caused. I knew it was an act, put on for the gang members' benefit, but it still didn't sit right with me.

Slinging the bag on my shoulder, I stood silently behind Owen while he and the Porteque leader shook hands.

"Thanks again, Peter," Owen said, a broad smile on his face.

"No problem, Sam," rasped Peter. He shot a glance at Amber, a calculating look in his eyes. "You sure you don't want to let me and the boys take her for a few days? She looks like she could definitely benefit from our education program."

The men behind him guffawed, and my hand clenched into a fist around the strap of my backpack.

Owen chuckled with him, but shook his head apologetically. "Sorry, Peter, but you know the drill. They don't pay for damaged goods—and they want to break in those Matrians themselves, y'know?"

I tried to keep my face neutral in the face of Owen's act, but it was hard. Maybe it was because I was so bad at acting, but Owen's ability to slip into a role this chauvinistic bothered me. A lot.

Peter was nodding in agreement. "I can imagine those Matrian women are quite a handful," he said. "Maybe I'll need to order one from you next time."

Owen laughed. "Peter, don't take this the wrong way, but I don't think you can afford it—these girls cost a lot, considering everything we have to do to get them."

Peter gave a laugh that made my skin crawl. "I hear you there, brother. Well, take care, and let us know when you need to smuggle another one in, all right?"

Owen nodded and extended a hand. "Of course."

Peter gave a whistle and the Porteque gang clambered back aboard the truck. We stood and watched as they started to drive away. Owen raised his hand in one final wave as they disappeared around the corner.

Almost immediately, he spat on the ground, as if he had a foul taste in his mouth, and dropped the rope leading to Amber.

"I hate working with them," he muttered, rubbing the back of his hand over his mouth in an attempt to clean it.

Solomon nodded in wordless agreement, his fingers already flying over the knots binding Amber's wrists together.

"I think you did a good job," Amber said, her voice quiet.

Owen shot her a look and then let out a breath. "Yeah, well, it doesn't make it feel any better," he said.

Amber wiggled out of her ropes and threw her arms around Owen's neck. "Don't worry about it, Owen. Let's just get to where we need to go so I can take this monkey suit off."

I watched the scene unfold, feeling relieved. Knowing that Owen hated doing what he did helped me feel a lot better. All the resentment that had been building up in me during our five-hour trip had receded, and I felt better knowing at the very least, the others felt as I did.

Owen shouldered his pack and turned toward me. "You okay?" he asked and I nodded.

"So, where to next?"

He studied my face for a few moments, then shot

me a mischievous smile. "You'll see."

I suppressed a groan and followed him. He led us away from the warehouse and over a few streets. The sky was starting to darken, the traffic on the roads becoming thinner. This area clearly wasn't a hub for nightlife—it appeared to be a series of factories for food processing and distribution.

Owen led us down an empty street and then stopped, consulting with the handheld. "All right—Solomon, get the cover."

I had a moment of confusion, until Solomon pulled a crowbar out of his bag and knelt in the middle of the street. Already, Quinn, Owen, and Amber were facing away from him, monitoring the streets around us.

I followed suit, but then I heard a loud metal clang, loud enough to make me jump. I whirled and found Solomon straining, shoving the manhole cover off the sewer pipe leading under the street.

"We're going down there?" I whispered, my mind recalling the dark, cramped space of the ventilation shaft from the facility where I had spent the better part of a day wiggling around, looking for a way out.

Owen looked at me over his shoulder and, seeing the hesitance in my face, smiled encouragingly. "Don't worry—we've been down there dozens of times. Not too many rats, and the smell isn't that terrible."

I swallowed and moved over to the edge of the

hole. The blackness was engulfing, the light from the moon and streetlamps barely able to penetrate. I pulled out my flashlight and then squatted down, clicking it on. There was a ladder leading down.

Placing the flashlight between my teeth, I stepped onto the ladder before I could have second thoughts.

I was down in a matter of seconds, my feet splashing as I landed in the middle of a puddle. I grimaced in disgust, and raised my hand over my mouth and nose. This place smelled awful.

"You lied to me," I said, skittering back a few paces as Owen splashed down from above. Through the flashlight, I caught his grin.

"Sorry."

"No, you're not," I accused, and he chuckled.

"You're right. I'm not. Also… you sound really funny right now," he said with a wink, referencing my deepened voice.

I rolled my eyes at him as Amber and Quinn dropped down next to us, and then Solomon, after some grunting and groaning as he worked the manhole cover back into place.

"Now what?" I asked.

Owen pulled something out of his bag and fitted it to his flashlight. It was a blue filter, which was weird, until he began pointing it at the wall.

"There," Amber said, tapping on Owen's shoulder and pointing to the left. He angled the flashlight

toward it and immediately, a green arrow was illuminated, pointing down the tunnel.

"We follow the arrows," Owen commented, in answer to my question.

Wordlessly, we all lined up in single file and followed Owen as he led the way.

The tunnels were dark and eerie, reminding me of
the ventilation shafts. At least these were much room-
ier, so it didn't feel quite as claustrophobic.

There was a network of tunnels under Patrus, used
to send waste into the river. We had a similar system
in Matrus, but supposedly ours was more efficient. I
had no idea if it was true, I just knew that being down
here was disgusting and I was more than looking forward to getting out.

"So, uh, how long will we be down here?" I asked.

"Who knows?" Quinn replied. "Apparently
Thomas likes to move every few missions, so it can
take a little while to find him."

"Who's Thomas?"

"Thomas is our eyes and ears inside Patrus," answered Solomon. "He's Patrian-born but hates the regime and what they stand for."

"That's interesting... why?" Everyone stilled and
turned toward me, and I froze, my eyes wide. "What,
too many questions?"

Owen's chuckle carried down the tunnel, and I felt
the tension of the moment drift away. "Violet, you are

terrible at spy craft," he stated.

"Why?"

"Because you ask way too many questions for your own good."

Everyone had a laugh at that, and I flushed. If anything, I thought asking questions was the trait of a good spy. But then again, if being a spy meant having to act and play the role of somebody else, then I was never going to be good at it.

We followed Owen for the better part of an hour, the green arrows winding us around until I had no idea where we could possibly be. After a few sharp turns, the sewer opened up into a junction point, with three feet of water ending at a concrete floor.

We were standing in a pipe draining water into the pool below. Several other pipes were doing the same thing. There was a door on the far wall of the room with a single light hanging over it, bathing the room in a soft yellow glow.

Owen pointed out the camera just behind the light and clicked his flashlight off. He jumped down into the water and pushed through it toward the concrete ledge. Climbing up on the ledge with a practiced grace, he motioned for us to follow.

Amber handed me her bag and jumped in after him, grimacing at the water. "It's cold," she said as I lowered her bag and my own to her. She held them up high as I splashed down next to her.

I hissed as the cold water seeped into my clothes. It came just past my knees, so it wasn't terrible. However, my mind was racing at all the possible diseases in the pool, and I just hoped I'd have access to a shower soon.

Owen extended a hand to Amber, helping her up, and then offered me one as well. I accepted it, and climbed up next to him. After we were all standing on the concrete island, Owen crossed over to the door.

He proceeded to knock twice, then once, then twice again, a pronounced pause between raps. Immediately the door swung open, revealing a man with a bushy brown beard and a balding head.

"Took you long enough," the man said, annoyance in his voice.

I studied him closely. He was shorter than Owen, and pudgy, wearing slacks that were slightly too big and a shirt that was slightly too small. Everything about him seemed disproportionate—from his small ears to his big mouth. Even his eyes were small, and they had a rat-like quality.

The man looked at me and skirted back a few feet. "Who is that? That's no man. Far too short, and lacking an Adam's apple! Why'd you bring a new girl here? You're supposed to tell me before you bring new people!"

Owen held up his hands. "Thomas, this is Violet. She's going to help us with this mission. Violet, this is

Thomas, and he owns all the cameras in Patrus."

Thomas squinted at me, studying me from top to bottom. I offered a little wave, and he gave a sharp huff, before whirling around and disappearing into the room behind him. Owen offered me a shrug before following.

Everyone filed in past me, leaving me standing there for several seconds with a stunned look on my face before following suit.

CHAPTER 8

Violet

The interior of the room where Thomas led us was much more luxurious than I had anticipated. The door opened into a short hall, which then opened up into a massive room. Large screens hung from three of the four walls, curving inward and around. Various images of people blinked in and out across the screens, presumably camera feeds that had been patched directly into the room.

In the center of it all was a long table containing three computers and a single chair. Against the walls was a mismatched assortment of chairs and sofas. There were doors to the left and right leading into two separate rooms—storage rooms, it seemed, gauging from what I could make out through the narrow vertical windows cut into the doors.

Thomas twisted around and gave an imperious tilt of his head. "This stuff is more important than you, so don't touch any of it," he announced.

I widened my eyes at Thomas' hostile tone and gaze, but Amber paid no notice. "Surely you don't mean me, Thomas," she crooned.

"Especially you," came Thomas' dry reply, and everyone burst out laughing. Amber clapped Thomas on the back before trapping him in a hug. He struggled for a few seconds, his face growing red, before eventually relenting to Amber's hug.

"It's good to finally meet you," Quinn said to Thomas after the hug was finished. He extended a hand, and Thomas wrinkled his nose at it before taking an index finger between two fingers, shaking it, and dropping it just as quickly.

"Quinn," he said, his tone stiff. I hid a smile by turning around, busying myself with taking off the bag I was carrying. Carefully, I peeled off my goatee and began sliding out of my jacket, shirt, and padding. I could hear the exchange of conversation behind me, little snippets of familiarity that reminded me of my outsider status.

"Still working the mines, huh, Mole?" came Solomon's deep baritone.

"I have asked you repeatedly not to call me that, Solomon," replied Thomas, his higher-pitched voice

66

containing a barely concealed impatient sound.

"Oh, come on, Thomas," Amber said, her voice filled with a teasing note. "All you do is work in this hole and you barely see anyone! We have to keep you socialized, or else you'll go off the deep end and destroy the city."

"Amber, that is a statistical improbability on all fronts—do you know how much Semtex it would take to destroy the entire city? No? Well, the answer is far more astronomical than you could guess."

I had just stepped out of my pants and padding as he said that, and I whirled around. "You... you haven't really made the calculation on how much explosive it would take to blow up the city... have you?"

Everyone froze and Thomas cocked his head at me, studying me behind the lenses of his spectacles. He pushed them up the bridge of his nose. "As a matter of fact, I have," he said, his voice flat and even.

I could feel everyone's gaze fall on me, waiting for my response. "But why?" I asked, not sure why anyone in their right mind would want to do that.

Thomas gave a small shrug. "Because I like math problems," he replied.

My jaw slackened as I took in the diminutive man in front of me. Everything about him—from his pudgy middle to his balding head—seemed so non-threatening that it was hard for me to wrap my head around his answer.

I transferred my gaze to Owen, who chuckled. "Thomas is good at what he does, Violet. He's a strategist."

Thomas nodded several times, reminding me of an over-eager child searching for his parents' praise.

"I... see..." I replied, uncertain of what else I could say.

Thomas and I eyed each other warily until Owen clapped his hands together. "Thomas, could you please bring us up to speed on the information you've gathered about the facility?"

Thomas moved to his workstation while the rest of us huddled close. He started clicking a few keys on the keyboard when he froze. "Do you mind?" he asked, and we all backed off. Solomon and Quinn busied themselves with dragging a few chairs over from near the walls, while Amber began to follow my lead and strip out of her costume.

Only Owen and I remained behind Thomas, watching the smaller man work. He was humming something under his breath, but I couldn't make out the tune, until I caught a word—"programming"— and I realized he was singing instructions to himself.

The mannerism was so strange that I had to shoot a glance at Owen to see if he heard it too. His blue eyes found mine and crinkled in a smile that made me want to throttle him for a moment. Him and his damned secrets—there was no reason for him not to tell me about Thomas.

In fact, I was even more irritated with Owen for putting us in a room with a clearly deranged lunatic. Who knew what sorts of things were going through his head? Was he calculating how to kill the five of us if the mission went bad, or had he already done that? Would he sell me out to the government? I wasn't naïve enough to think that the Patrian government had not put a hefty bounty on my head.

Thomas lifted his hands up in silent victory, breaking me out of my suspicious thoughts. He clicked a few buttons, and then the screen directly in front of us—which took up almost the entire wall—lit up to show an empty road.

We all fell silent as we searched the image, trying to see what Thomas saw.

It was Owen who spoke first. "All right, I'll bite, what is this?" he asked.

Thomas beamed up at him, his face squishing together like a toad about to fall asleep. "It's the only camera feed I could find remotely near to the location you and Desmond provided," he said, an edge of excitement to his voice.

Owen frowned, his eyebrows coming together. "Thomas… this video shows us absolutely nothing."

Thomas nodded. "They run their cameras on a closed system," he said, standing up. I watched as he waddled over to some file cabinets that were tucked

away in a corner. He pulled open a drawer and re-
trieved a thick folder. "You and Desmond are definitely onto something—it took a lot to get these
blueprints."

He rolled out the bundle of papers on the table.
"They don't even exist in digital media—if they had, I
would've found them. As it stands, I had to liquidate
the supplier just to be sure word about this didn't get
out."

Owen's gaze found mine and I frowned at him,
crossing my arms over my chest. "Thomas… you
know you're not supposed to liquidate the assets,"
Owen said.

I rolled my eyes at him. If he thought I was so
dumb as to not know what an "asset" was or what
it meant to "liquidate" one, he had another thing
coming.

Thomas raised a dismissive hand, his entire focus
on the blueprints in front of him. "He wasn't an asset,"
he said. "Not one of yours, anyway. The Porteque gang
are the only ones who will miss him, and as far as they
are concerned, he just disappeared." Thomas looked
at me, his lenses reflecting the white coming off the
screen. "I know how to cover my tracks," he finished.

The words sounded threatening, and I didn't like
them at all. I took a step forward, but Solomon placed
a heavy hand on my shoulder. I looked up at him, and
he shook his head, mouthing the word *don't* at me.

I felt my mouth flatten into a thin line as a wave of irritation rolled through me. I backed off though, distancing myself a few steps. Thomas was dangerous— he had just confirmed it—and for some reason he had decided to focus on me. I wasn't sure why he had, but if he did try anything, I was going to be ready for it.

Thomas had already continued speaking, in spite of my disturbance, and it took my brain a moment to catch up with him in the conversation. "The building is an original, which is why it's perfect! Lots of things were built and then torn down in the early days, so this place is practically a relic. The security around it will be antiquated at best. I also managed to get eyes on the facility, and there's only a handful of guards!"

"Inside?" Owen asked.

"No—all of my intelligence says that they are outside. I got a hold of the shipping invoices from the past year, and it helped me narrow things down considerably based on who signed for them. There are several buildings on the property—five, to be precise: two warehouses and three office-like structures. Now, I've managed to narrow the location of the surgical laser to one of these two buildings here. Most of the shipping manifests indicate that medical supplies are being kept in a specific office in this building, while in the warehouse, they're being housed between aisles A and D. It was the best I could do."

"How do you know all this?" I asked, cutting in.

Thomas faltered, his mouth working up and down. "I… I have a thing that… that I use…"

He floundered, looking to Owen for support. Owen patted him on the shoulder and I found myself frowning again at the tender support Owen was giving him. "It's okay, Thomas. Violet should know better than to ask a magician to reveal his tricks."

I gaped at the admonishment so casually leveled at me, and for a moment, I felt my temper boiling up. I wasn't trying to cause problems; I was just curious as to how he got his information. Until I reminded myself that it ultimately didn't matter—as long as I could get what I needed to help Viggo.

I smiled at Thomas. "Owen's right. I'm very sorry, Thomas. This is excellent work."

Thomas eyed me dubiously for a few seconds, and then nodded with a huff, turning back to Owen.

I didn't know what the deal was, but it was clear that Owen was indulging Thomas, and I intended to ask him about it later. Owen and Thomas were already bent over going over the plans, so I had little choice save interrupting them and risking antagonizing Thomas further, or being patient and seeing what the plan was.

I decided on the latter, and busied myself like the others with cleaning the clothes that we had brought in and then taking a shower.

Hours later, after examining every angle, we had come up with a rudimentary plan. More than that, though, I began to be more understanding of Thomas' weird mannerisms. A part of that, I admitted, was because Owen was right—he had a keen strategic mind that worked far better than the five other minds in the room. He had a knack for seeing the angle, and his ability to process numbers in his head was fantastic—he'd pitched and thrown away dozens of ideas, all based on some hidden formula for success that was buried in the recesses of his brain.

The other reason was because I began to notice how he looked at Owen from the corner of his eye. There was something hidden behind his gaze, an affection that I recognized on an instinctual level: Thomas was deferring to Owen for everything. He only listened attentively to him, focusing solely on Owen and *his* ideas.

Suddenly, a lot of his mannerisms clicked in my mind. He was a beta. Betas were males who were less aggressive, and tended to defer to whomever they felt their alpha was. Only betas were allowed in Matrus, alphas being considered too dangerous. But in Patrus, being a beta was not a good thing. They were bullied and beaten by alphas. Some elected to undergo a re-education program, but many of the subjects committed suicide during the process, unable to cope with their own existence.

I wasn't sure whether Thomas had undergone the re-education program, but it was clear that he had suffered a lot at the hands of the alphas, given his jumpy nature and childlike malevolence. It made me feel sorry for the smaller man, or at the very least, sympathetic. No wonder he had joined up with the Liberators— he had a grudge the size of both countries toward Patrus.

Looking around the table, I realized that we all did. Maybe not directly, but if I looked at it through the lens of a Liberator, then both countries had done one thing or another to harm their people. And, if I was honest, I had a grudge against them too—not just for myself, but for every male and female they had wronged over the years with their tyrannical dictates and legislations.

CHAPTER 9

Violet

Even though I knew that waiting was the longest part of any mission from my experience with Lee, this wait was really getting to me. I waited three whole days for Owen to announce that we were ready and if he hadn't told us the time had come for action on that third day, I felt I would have gone off the hinges on the fourth.

I understood, in part, the delay. There was specialized equipment that needed to be ordered from trusted sources. Then that equipment had to be moved, which took time and planning. If any of it was discovered on a routine spot inspection by the wardens, then it would be seized and the people we had hired to help us would be tracked down, questioned, and potentially executed.

I also understood Owen's insistence that I remain underground at all times. I hated it, but I understood it. Each minute topside represented a risk of me getting discovered or caught. One slip-up and I would jeopardize everything that we were hoping to accomplish on the mission.

Still, none of that helped me to deal with the claustrophobic feelings of being trapped down in the small space of Thomas' lair. I tried to remind myself that I had just lived for over two weeks underground in The Green's facility, but it didn't help. For one thing, that facility was much larger. I wasn't constantly having to step around someone or over something to get from point A to point B.

Calling Thomas' home a hole in the wall would be a fair comparison. The two rooms that were off to the side of the main one were cramped, with even tinier bathrooms to bathe in. Amber and I got more space in the second room, seeing as only the two of us shared it. Owen, Quinn, Solomon, and occasionally Thomas shared the room on the other side, and it was an equal size.

There were no beds to sleep on, so we made nests on the floor—similar to what Tim had done in my room in the facility—and curled up on the unforgiving concrete. It was cold, hard, and unyielding, and I hadn't slept well since we arrived.

Every morning after we woke, Owen would hand us our assignments. While everyone else received assignments that would send them topside—like going to see the weapons supplier or finding someone who could secure night vision goggles—I was always given the same duty: Stay with Thomas and make sure he had everything he needed.

Even though I had come to understand Thomas, that didn't mean I necessarily liked him. Pitied, yes—but the man was hard to read, and even harder to get along with. After a few tries at being social, I had given up and busied myself studying the plans or cleaning my weapon.

I tried to work out, but Thomas complained about me doing sit-ups and push-ups in the main room, then in any of the side rooms. He said the repetitive motion made him nauseous.

I didn't argue with him—there was ultimately no point. It was his place. I considered, briefly, moving my daily exercise outside, but the smell coming from the sewer alone was enough to dissuade me.

So, when Owen breezed in one day after meeting with his transportation guy, saying that the last piece of what we needed had fallen into his hands, I could've kissed him—that was how eager I was to get out of this hole and finally get what Viggo needed.

We waited an hour for Quinn and Solomon to return from their assignment for the day—securing the final shipment of ammunition we needed for the more high-powered rifles that Owen had secured—and sat down to discuss the operation once again.

It was fairly simple, although separating into two teams to secure one objective was a bit of a gamble. I had brought up the point with Owen a few days ago, and he had agreed, but there wasn't any better solution—I knew because we had talked all the options out.

The plan was for Owen, Quinn, and Amber to go into the warehouse to search for Viggo's laser, while Solomon and I were supposed to be inside the office building doing the same. Because we weren't sure which place it was located, lots were drawn to see who would go where. It was frustrating, because I wanted to be the one who found the laser, but there was no telling where it was. Ultimately, whoever found it would notify the others, and we would move to stage two.

Solomon and I were supposed to sneak out the side door of the office, avoid the guards, and come around to open the back door of the warehouse, meeting up with the other three. We would return together to the rendezvous location at the top of the hill.

All of that sounded simple, but we all knew that nothing ever went according to plan. However, it was impossible to plan for every contingency, so if things went bad, good communication was the only way to keep us all alive and have any hope of achieving our directive.

Owen passed out an ear bud and a black piece of fabric to all of us. He explained to me that it was a subvocalizer, a piece of tech that would allow us to talk to each other without articulating the words out loud. Securing these would have been very difficult, and very expensive. The electrical parts had been tucked into the black fabric, which was made from the same material our suits were—this meant the subvocalizer would vanish along with us after we activated the suits.

I put the bud in my ear and the piece of fabric around my throat. Immediately, a warm tingle spread out from where the two metal contacts pressed against my skin. I tried to speak—but my vocal cords were frozen and locked in place.

I looked around the table toward Quinn and the others. Amber smirked at me and placed her own ear bud in, and pressed the fabric against her throat.

It's part of the function, she subvocalized to me. I could hear her voice as loud as if she were speaking right next to me.

Feels weird, but kind of cool, I replied, and she grinned at me as she lowered her hand. I undid the bit of fabric and placed it gently on the table.

"All right—we've got an hour before sunset," Owen said. "Getting to the facility will take three hours by truck, so we need to get all the gear packed up and in the van."

I held up my hand and Owen paused. Leaning forward on the chair, I threaded my fingers together. "What exactly is the plan if we encounter resistance inside?"

"There won't be anyone inside," chirped Thomas, condescension thick in his voice.

"Right, but if this is a warehouse they want kept from the public eye…"

"They use it for storage," Thomas exploded, his face turning a violent shade of red. "They don't care what's inside, only that the outside is secure. If you can achieve complete obfuscation when you enter, they will have no cause to be inside! Your suits will help you with that, and after that, all you have to do is get to the rendezvous spot!"

I sighed. "Right. Just out of curiosity, what are the odds for success, Thomas?"

His expression calmed and he wet his lower lip. "Factoring in for a margin of error… I'd say about eighty-six percent."

I turned to Owen who shrugged. "We've had worse odds and beat them," he said, and I leaned back in my chair, trying to find an argument with eighty-six percent.

"Still… if there are people inside, you promise we won't kill them?" I asked, knowing Viggo would never be comfortable with us killing people in order to save him. I was also in that camp, so I wanted to be sure.

Owen blew out a deep breath and nodded. "Everyone knows that we shoot to wound, not kill. Let's just hope we don't have to pull the trigger."

I nodded, feeling relieved.

We worked in silence after the meeting was done. I inventoried the weapons, and stuck stickers on the stock to color-code them for each person. We had taken a little trip into the sewers a day earlier to set the sights on them. I wasn't very knowledgeable about guns, so Solomon had to explain to me why I should never pick up a random rifle to shoot.

Most people who were trained with the stronger weapons, like the rifles we were using, were taught to adjust their sights on the back of their gun to their own personal preferences. It took a little while for me to figure out what my settings were, but once I got the hang of it, Solomon explained that any other gun would feel strange to look down.

Hence the reason for the stickers—we didn't want to mix up weapons when we were distributing them. I also dutifully marked off every piece of equipment we were assigned. It felt a little bit like micro-managing, but I saw the need for it. With each piece of equipment marked off and assigned to an individual, we would know immediately if something was missing, and could adapt accordingly.

As I finished, Owen, with Amber in tow, snagged me and led me back to Amber's and my tiny room.

"You'll need to don the costumes now—Quinn, Solomon, and I will load up the gear. You've got twenty minutes."

He spun on his heel and exited the room, pulling the door closed. Amber and I looked at each other and then scrambled around the room, frantically grabbing what we needed to complete our costumes. Twenty minutes wasn't much, especially since Amber would be going in dressed like a man this time.

We were in the middle of wiggling into our body suits when Thomas strolled in. Amber shrieked and moved to cover herself, causing me to laugh. We were both still in the special Liberator uniforms—there was no need for her to react like that.

She realized that at the same time, and flushed a deep red that was almost as bright as her hair.

Thomas—for his part—wasn't even paying attention to us. His face was angled downward toward a file he was holding.

"Owen wanted me to tell you to bring your gear for The Green. If all goes according to plan, you won't be coming back here."

"Okay," I said. "Thanks, Thomas."

He lifted his hand in a half-forgotten wave as he left. I hobbled over to the door and shut it behind him.

"He really is a weird little guy," Amber said, as she

shimmied into the suit.

I had opted for a pulling technique on my own, my arms straining as I tried to force myself into the suit as quickly as possible. "I feel bad for him," I grunted.

"Really? Why?"

"Because... well... c'mon. Y'know, right?"

Amber blinked at me, her eyes wide and empty. "What are you talking about?"

I started sliding my arms into the padded sleeves. "You mean you had no idea he was a beta?" I asked, unable to keep the thread of amazement out of my voice.

Amber stared at me, her face reflecting her inner confusion. I resisted the urge to laugh in her face—it would be rude, and probably make her feel like I was Matronizing her. After a moment, her face turned contemplative, and her eyes lit up as realization set in.

"Holy cow!" she shouted, her voice a smidge too loud in my ears.

"Calm down," I said, shushing her. I had managed to get the padding on, as well as the slacks. I was buttoning up my shirt when she pushed my hands aside and fastened them for me. "He's just a person, like anyone else. Besides... who knows what he's been through."

Amber frowned as her nimble fingers did up the buttons. "Yeah..." she breathed, her voice small. "No wonder he hates people."

I didn't respond to that, because I didn't know how. A part of me didn't think Thomas hated people. If anything, I thought he craved more time around people. Just people who didn't hurt him. I didn't have any evidence to support it, just that look in his eye when he looked at Owen. A deep yearning to connect with someone—anyone—if only for a moment.

Owen rapped on the door, reminding us of the time, and we rushed to finish getting ready, the conversation forgotten for the moment.

CHAPTER 10

Violet

The van rumbled to a halt and I leapt into action, handing out equipment. Owen squeezed between the two seats up front and squatted in the middle of the van floor. I handed him his gun, which he systematically checked. The five of us began reviewing our gear in absolute silence.

The excitement I had been feeling before we left slowly drained in the long van ride, leaving a nervous tension that seemed to wrap around my spine and spread into my shoulders and neck. There was so much riding on this mission, it was impossible to not feel nervous. Dozens of scenarios ran through my head of every possible way things could go wrong, and it took every ounce of my willpower to set them aside and keep my focus on the task ahead.

My mind produced an image of Viggo's face and I drew a deep breath, using the lines of his smile and the peculiar color of his green eyes to anchor me. I would look at those eyes again. He would smile at me again. I would feel his breath on my face as he leaned close to kiss me.

I slapped the magazine into the gun and opened my eyes, feeling steady and sure.

Nothing was going to keep me from saving him.

Everyone looked at me expectantly, and I nodded. *I'm ready*, I subvocalized.

Good, came Owen's reply. Solomon slid open the side door and one by one we exited the van. We had parked next to a hill that overlooked the target—we were planning on approaching a kilometer to the southwest, and then fall back to the van in groups of two and three.

I'm going to be killing the power in five minutes, came Thomas' voice. *Get into position.*

Owen raised his hand to motion us forward, and we followed him. He was in front, flanked by Solomon and Quinn, and followed by Amber and me. We had shed our costumes shortly after leaving the busy streets of the city. It was inconvenient, the constant changing in and out of disguises, but once again, I understood the reasons—being spotted in the short trip between the exit of the sewers and getting into the van was still too risky. However, shedding all of that stuff in a moving van was no picnic either.

We crested the hill and gazed down on the factory. It was bathed in darkness. There were single lamps over the doors and under a few windows to the structure, cutting the darkness with little yellow cones. I could make out a few shadowed shapes of wardens roaming the perimeter. None were in the immediate area we had chosen for insertion.

We're in position, subvocalized Owen as he dropped to one knee, his gun against his shoulder. *I count... six guards walking the perimeter. We will have a window for another ninety seconds.*

Solomon knelt in the damp grass next to him. I stared at the office building that contained my target. It was a single story, with large windows running the length of the building. According to the blueprints, the windows were completely sealed, which meant we couldn't open them without making a lot of noise. There were two doors—one in the front and one at the rear. Our goal was the front entrance.

Ten seconds until I blow the power, Thomas responded.

Solomon looked at me. *Nervous?* he asked. I gazed around, thinking he had asked the entire group the question, until I realized he had directed it only to me. The subvocalizers had that ability.

I smiled self-consciously and raised my hand to

my collar, clicking the button that allowed me to speak solely to Solomon. *Of course,* I replied.

Really? His face reflected his surprise. *That's weird... this isn't your first time on a mission, is it?*

It wasn't—and he knew it. I had hoped that this kind of work was behind me, but it was clear it wasn't. *It's not, but it doesn't matter—I'm always nervous before stuff like this. It helps to keep us alive.*

Just then, the entire field of buildings before us went dark, preventing Solomon from answering. I clicked back over to the main channel.

Go, now, Thomas commanded. *Ninety seconds before the back-up generators restore power.*

Owen was already in motion with Quinn and Amber following close behind. Solomon tapped me on the shoulder, and I pulled down the night vision goggles. Immediately, the world changed to a bright green. Solomon did the same, and we began to move in long loping strides down the hill. We both kept low—just in case the moon came out and gave our position away—and moved quickly.

A glaring light caught my attention when we were halfway down. I reached out and grabbed Solomon, pulling him back as gently as I could without making him fall on the slick grass. He slid to a stop and dropped to one knee in front of me.

Guard to my right, I announced on the subvocalizer as I squatted down next to Solomon. *Approximately one hundred feet away, two o'clock.*

Everyone hold positions—Solomon, be ready to take him out, came Owen's reply.

I felt my jaw clench—I had told Owen that we absolutely needed to avoid killing people—and looked at Solomon. His gaze was trained on the warden and where he was walking. He had shouldered his rifle, and his finger was on the trigger. I could see that he'd already taken the safety off.

Slowly, I moved forward and placed my hand on the stock of the rifle. Solomon looked at me, and I shook my head, trying to indicate that we weren't killing this man. His jaw clenched and he shot me a warning look, but I shook my head again and kept my hand firmly on the stock, pushing it down. After a moment, he lowered it a fraction of an inch, and I turned my gaze back to the warden.

The warden held his light out directly in front of him, lighting up his path. He didn't swing it around, just kept it straight forward. I counted the seconds until the power came back on, my forehead sweating. I held my breath as he passed about fifty feet from where we were crouched in the darkness. He didn't even look our way.

Once he had passed, I counted ten more seconds, and then nodded to Solomon. We couldn't afford to wait any longer.

He's moved, I said as I started to head toward the

door. I kept one eye on the warden, and made sure to make as little noise as possible, but he never even looked back. It was sloppy, but if it kept him and us from being in a firefight, then I was all for it.

Even with the delay, it took us sixty seconds to get from the top of the hill to the door. Once there, I pressed my back against the wall, letting out a slow, controlled breath. The gun felt heavy in my arms, but I kept it tucked to my shoulder while I scanned the area and Solomon jammed the automatic lock pick into the lock.

The machine whirred softly in the silence, making me flinch. I knew the sound wouldn't carry that far, but any sound, as far as I was concerned, was too much. The whirring stopped almost as suddenly as it had started, and Solomon gripped the small black box and twisted. The door clicked open. He moved inside, tapping me on the shoulder. I took another last glance around before entering and closing the door behind me, then yanked off my night vision goggles.

The lights flicked back on just as I pulled the door closed and I breathed a sigh of relief. Turning around, I stared down the hall and froze.

At the end of the room was a warden, and he was staring right at us.

I hesitated as he reached for his gun, his young face reflecting his panic. From the corner of my eye, I saw Solomon raise his gun to his shoulder, leveling out. I didn't even have the opportunity to hiss, "No!" before Solomon pulled the trigger. The gunshot made a small sound, like pressurized gas escaping in a brief puff.

Red bloomed on the warden's chest where Solomon's bullet had caught him. The impact of the bullet sent him spinning like a top before tumbling to the floor with a sickening thud. Fury flared in me—I had not wanted anyone killed on this mission. Viggo would be sickened if he knew.

But I had to put it aside—anger didn't change the fact that the man was dead, his blood already spreading out onto the white linoleum floor. Regret wouldn't bring back the light in his eyes. Nothing would now.

We encountered guards inside, I subvocalized to Owen.

There was a pause, and then Owen replied. *Yeah, we found a few ourselves. Thomas' information appears to be wrong.*

I was not wrong—there were no signs that they had guards posted inside! Thomas shot back over the line.

I sighed. *It doesn't matter. Owen, are we aborting?*

There was a long pause before Owen spoke. *No. We're here—let's just keep on track, and improvise when it's called for. We'll keep with the original rendezvous point—meet back at the van in ten minutes. Don't be late.*

Solomon and I exchanged looks, and I raised my

hand to my collar, clicking the link over to Solomon's channel. *Keep moving,* I said and he hesitated. *What is it?* I asked, nudging him.

There weren't supposed to be guards in the building, he said, shifting his weight.

So? Owen gave us the green light. Let's go.

Still, he didn't move, and my patience was wearing thin. He risked a glance over his shoulder at me. *Protocol is that we bug out. We aren't supposed to die over this.*

And then I saw it—for all of Solomon's quiet confidence, he was afraid. I was too, but I had a clear image of what was at stake. I couldn't wait around for him to decide, and I didn't have time to waste in convincing him.

You do what you like, I told him, turning my gaze from him to the hall that stretched out before us. *I'm getting Viggo's cure.*

I started to move past him, but he held out an arm, stopping me. There was a long pause before he subvocalized, *I'm with you then.* He shifted and began moving down the hall. I followed, placing my feet as quietly on the floor as possible and trying to keep my feelings of relief at bay. I meant what I had told him—I was going to get Viggo's cure.

Even though we were using silencers, the wardens would figure out what was going on in a few minutes, especially if they found the guard. We paused long enough to shove the guard's body under a desk. I grabbed his jacket from the chair and used it to wipe up the trail of blood as best I could. I felt a sharp tug of regret and took a moment to close the man's eyelids, his blank expression seeming almost accusatory in my eyes.

I took a deep breath and met Solomon's steady gaze, turning my mind back to the mission.

Which room did Thomas say it was in? he asked me.

I knew exactly where it was, but I pulled my arm up and gazed at the handheld that I had secured to it.

Straight down the hall, right turn down the next hall, third door on the left, I reminded him.

He nodded and pressed forward in a crouching walk, keeping his body low to the ground. I followed, my gun pulled up. I gave one last look at the man under the desk as I did so, hoping that I wouldn't have to pull the trigger, and that his death would be the first and last on this mission.

CHAPTER 11

Violet

We had made it halfway down the hall when the sound of approaching footsteps forced us to halt. I leaned forward and tried the door directly in front of us, but the doorknob refused to turn.

What now? I asked Solomon.

I saw his reply as he quickly backtracked, his boots barely making a sound. I followed closely, and then watched as he shoved his gun and bag under the desk before activating his suit, disappearing in front of my eyes. I hurried to do the same, the footsteps approaching much more quickly than I was comfortable with.

It had taken a while to get used to the suit. Owen had explained that it acted as an electrical conduit when a user activated it by tensing muscles. Once they did, it allowed the wearer to go invisible. He had explained that it would also camouflage any organic matter it came into contact with, which was why we didn't have to wear face masks or gloves, but it wouldn't work on inorganic items that weren't under the suit. Which was why we weren't wearing bulletproof vests: It wouldn't work on them, and they were too bulky to go underneath. According to Owen, the scientists were working on a way of inserting plates in the suit, but the material used to craft it was rare and difficult to get, so it was slow going. It wasn't perfect—flashlights and thermal scanners would register a user regardless; however, it did allow people to turn invisible—provided they weren't holding something. If they were, it would look like the object was floating in midair.

At first, activating the suit had hurt—it created a sharp pins-and-needles sensation across the entirety of my skin. However, once I had gotten used to it, Owen and I had run through drills, from anything as simple as eating a bowl of food to more complicated drills that involved running, opening a door... basically anything where movement was required. I'd learnt rudimentary control over the suit, although interacting with objects was difficult when I tried to pair it with moving.

Almost immediately I felt the corresponding

tingle as the suit engaged. The electric thrill that coursed under my skin to all of my extremities might have become less painful with practice, but it was still weird. It felt like after my foot had gone to sleep, trying to force blood back into the area. It was a constant barrage of prickling, all over my body.

I focused on my breathing and kept my eyes on the hall in front of me. I wanted to avoid moving—my control over the suit was still tenuous.

The sound of the boots on the floor became a cacophony of rolling thunder down the narrow hall. I pressed up against the wall—a small movement that almost broke my concentration—just as one man walked in, holding a flashlight. I refrained from wincing and held my breath, watching the beam of his light as he swung it around the room.

The beam swept toward me, and I prepared myself to leap at him as soon as it interacted with the suit, hoping that the sudden appearance of me in the darkness would surprise him enough that I could get an advantage over him. Hopefully, Solomon would get involved as well—we had sparred a few times and he was a solid brawler.

It made me wish we had opted to enter these buildings while cloaked, but we had discussed using it as a backup plan. There were two main reasons for that: the first was that the suits were the Liberators' most carefully guarded secret. They were only issued full-time to Desmond, Owen, Solomon, and a few others—the rest were handed out before missions, and Owen had explained to me that if one of us were killed on a mission, we were expected to cut the suits off of them. Or burn the bodies if there wasn't enough time. Personally, I liked the second option better—there was something fundamentally wrong about stripping a dead body.

Using them, especially on camera, was only allowed in desperate situations, and if there did happen to be cameras, we had to go out of our way to destroy any and all footage.

The second reason was simply one of functionality. It didn't matter how strong I was, my muscles had limits. Eventually, they would relax, and I would reappear. There was a contest among the Liberators, who could stay cloaked the longest when standing, moving, or even fighting. Owen held all three records. He could maintain the cloak while standing still for over an hour, while walking for half of that, and for five whole minutes while fighting or interacting with objects.

The beam had slowed to a stop, and I slowly released the breath I had been holding until I realized it was pointed at the unmoving foot of the guard we had killed. I tensed my already tense muscles as the guard slowly made his way over to body, his hand on the butt of his pistol.

"McGee," he whispered, his eyes darting about.

McGee, of course, did not answer. After a second, the man moved his hand off his gun, switched the flashlight to his other hand, and pulled out his radio.

"Sir, Gustoff here," he said, taking a slow, measured step back.

"Go ahead," replied a tiny muted voice through the speaker.

"Sir, we have a code red—I just found McGee's body. He's been shot."

There was a long pause. "Are there any signs of the perpetrators?"

"Negative, sir. I must have passed them on my sweep. Or they've fled."

"Retrace your steps slowly. I'm sending Murtaugh and Lowens to sweep up from our end and see if we can't trap them between us. Be careful though, and don't shoot at one of ours."

"Roger," Gustoff said, before hooking his radio to his belt. He carefully switched hands again and slowly pulled out his pistol, turning around to head down the hall.

I was moving before he had even gone a step, quickly closing the gap between us. I was quite proud—I made it halfway there before I lost control of the suit. As I strode past the desk, I snagged a heavy-looking paper weight. The guard tensed, his body starting to turn toward me, when I lifted my arm and slammed the weight down hard on his skull.

He dropped like a bag of potatoes, his gun clacking loudly on the ground. I looked around and quickly grabbed him under the armpits. Solomon appeared next to me.

You all right? he asked, moving to the guard's feet. I nodded and we quickly moved him out of the way.

We need to move quickly—you heard the transmission.

Solomon hesitated. *Violet, more guards are coming. They know something's going on. We should scrub the mission.*

I checked the channel and breathed a sigh of relief that he hadn't transmitted that to Owen, only to me. *We are not leaving,* I said, staring him down. *I didn't come all this way to give up. Either follow me or don't, but we need to move. Now!*

Solomon's jaw tightened, but he quickly reached down and grabbed his bag. We pulled our gear back on and began moving down the corridor again.

It didn't seem to occur to Solomon that we should notify Owen, but as we moved down the hall, I clicked over to Owen's channel.

Owen.

There was a pause. *Vi? Why—*

Never mind that, I interrupted, my eyes on the hall. *Listen, another guard found the dead guard and alerted others by radio. I took him down but it's too late.*

I paused a moment, and then continued. *You also need to know that Solomon and I are pressing forward, even though we know it's against protocol.*

There was an even longer pause and then a click. *Vi, I can safely say I am not happy with this, and knowing Solomon, he's less than pleased as well. But if he's still with you, then we'll proceed. If he gets hurt…*

Understood, I replied, and then clicked back over to Solomon's channel as we continued to move down the halls.

Pausing at each door to make sure it was locked or that there wasn't anyone hiding inside was a slow process which made me feel the passage of time acutely. It felt like hours by the time we reached the correct door, but in reality, it was only a matter of minutes. Luckily, it seemed that the group from the back was taking their time—I still hadn't heard the faintest whisper of movement from up ahead.

I stood over Solomon, my rifle trained down the hallway, while he used the automatic lock pick to open the door. He gave it a twist once it stopped whirring, and the door swung open. He slid inside and I backed in behind him, keeping my rifle on the hall until I had closed the door.

I let the weapon drop as soon as the door was closed. We were lucky—many of the offices in the building had massive glass windows that allowed people to look into the rooms. This room, however, was completely enclosed. There wasn't even a window on the door. If we were lucky, they would never know we were inside.

My elation over the room was quickly dampened when I turned around and saw the staggering amount of boxes. Searching every single one would take forever.

Solomon was already sliding his knife through the tape securing the cardboard cartons. I frowned, and examined one of the boxes. They were devoid of writing except for a series of handwritten numbers on the top. Looking around the room, I saw a clipboard dangling from a nail and fetched it.

It was a list of numbers, followed by a description of each item contained within.

Solomon—look at the numbers. There are only a few boxes that have medical supplies listed within the contents.

He stopped and looked at me. *Okay. There are a lot of boxes, Violet—can you narrow it down any more?*

I scanned the numbers. Most of the first five digits were the same—it was the final four that were different. *Look for boxes ending in 4546, 5332, or 8991.*

He started sifting through the boxes, and I did the same, humming the numbers in my head to remember them. I found the first box under three other boxes in the second stack.

I got 5332, I conveyed to Solomon. I set it aside

and pulled out my knife, cutting through the tape and cardboard. I shuffled around the contents of the box, looking for something, anything, that vaguely resembled the picture that Thomas had supplied of the laser. The box was filled mostly with vials of medicine and boxes of syringes.

I placed it aside just as I heard Solomon's knife cutting through another box.

Which is that? I subvocalized, turning back to the stacks.

8991, he replied, ripping the box open. I continued to scan the other boxes, looking for box number 4546 in the midst of the chaos. After a moment, Solomon's voice came through my ear bud. *Not here.*

I could feel the tension coiling around us. Every second we were in the room was a second too long. I eased myself through two stacks of boxes, being careful not to press against them more than necessary. They were precariously stacked, and swayed under my passage.

Solomon turned to see what I was up to, his expression incredulous. I winced as I finally got through, expelling the breath I had sucked in to make myself thinner.

There were more boxes piled up in front of me, and I scanned them quickly. I found the last box, number 4546, under several boxes. As quietly as I could, I moved the other boxes aside, and pulled out my knife again.

I cut through the tape and felt disgusted as I gazed at the clear plastic tubing for IVs.

It's not here! I subvocalized, my frustration evident even though the vocalizer.

Then Owen will get it. Pass me your bag. And your gun too. Quickly, Vi! I can hear them coming.

I paused, and then heard what he heard—the distinct sound of boots on the linoleum in the hall. I pushed the bag through the small gap between the boxes. Solomon grabbed it, and then reached for the gun.

The footsteps were growing closer and I hesitated—if I pushed through the gap before they opened the door, there was a chance that they would see the boxes still moving when they opened it.

Go invisible, I ordered, as I sat down my gun and engaged my suit.

Solomon quickly placed both of our bags on the floor, as well as his gun, and faded from view. I risked a small amount of movement as I stepped a little bit further behind the stack, the pins and needles tingling through my extremities.

The door handle was starting to turn, and I saw a crack appear in the door as it swung open, emitting a light too bright to be anything but a flashlight. I held my breath, hoping that Solomon had thought to move behind a stack of boxes.

I ducked my head behind a box, my heart thudding loudly against my ribcage. I gently eased my back against the box and watched the circular light as it panned slowly toward me. A sudden ripple started as the light neared the center of the room, allowing me to see Solomon's eyes filled with horror.

CHAPTER 12

Violet

A loud burst of static made Solomon, me, and the light emitted by the flashlight jump to the left. I heard a loud curse, and the sound of a hand slapping against fabric. The light danced against the wall, just to the left of Solomon's position.

Get down slowly, I ordered, unable to make him out.

I didn't know if he followed my order, because another burst of static sounded, followed by, "I've got three hostiles in Warehouse B. They seem to be –"

There was a loud sound, and then a panicked series of transmissions.

"Shots fired! Man down! We need backup."

Through the walls, I could hear the sound of

rapidly retreating footsteps, followed by the soft popping of gunfire. I leaned out and saw that the door was wide open and the guards were gone. I relaxed my tensed muscles, and I saw Solomon doing the same.

There was another burst of gunfire, and I quickly switched over to the main channel. *Owen, what's going on?*

There was a momentary pause, and then—*Quinn was pulling a box and the stack shifted, alerting a guard. We're handling it.*

Owen, more are coming to you.

Yes, Violet, I am aware. We only have a few more boxes to search.

I paused, my mind working. *Is there anything in there we could use as a distraction? To buy you more time?*

It was Quinn who responded. *Actually, funny that you should bring that up, Violet—there's an entire crate of explosives in here...*

No, I countermanded, my mind racing. *However... any way you could rig a small charge?*

There was a pause, before Owen responded. *I see what you're getting at. Quinn's on it. Our timeline is all messed up though. Thoughts?*

I looked at my watch. We had agreed on ten minutes because that was how long it would take for roadblocks to come up after our burglary. *Not from me, but I'm guessing Thomas has an idea. Thomas?*

Well... as a matter of fact... I think I can buy you guys... five more minutes?

I crunched some numbers in my head. *That gives us eight. How much time does Quinn need?*

Quinn is already ready, said Quinn, in that smug way that made me roll my eyes.

I checked the diagram of my map, thinking. The building we were in was small, but ran rampant with hallways. It would take us about two minutes to clear the building. *You said reinforcements were coming?*

Yes, Owen replied. *They should be there any minute. Most of them will probably divert to us, but I'm betting a few will stay in that building with you.*

I studied the map. *They'll come in through the front, so we'll continue our plan to head out the back and over to you. We'll be about two minutes. Once I give you the all clear, blow the charge.*

Sounds good—we'll detonate as soon as—

Suddenly, a high-pitched screeching filled the ear piece, loud enough for me to pull it out of my ear. Solomon did the same.

"What's that?" I whispered, still flinching from the sound, my finger massaging my ear.

Solomon shoved his ear bud into his pocket. "They're jamming us. We need to get moving now."

He handed me my belongings and moved toward the door. I quickly slung on the backpack and rifle over my shoulders. I came up behind him and tapped his shoulder. He slowly opened the door, revealing the empty hallway before us.

I tapped him again, and we moved deeper into the building.

I grabbed Solomon by the arm, pulling him down just in time to be missed by the guard who had been prowling through the stacks. We had made it to the open storage space at the rear of the building, but the place was crawling with guards. We had been delayed four times in the last three minutes just avoiding them.

I was sweating, the fear of the mission causing a massive spike in my adrenaline. If we didn't find a way out of this room soon, we were going to be forced to shoot our way out, and I still wanted to avoid that if possible.

As the guard moved on, I wiped my forehead with the back of my hand.

Where do we go, Violet? Solomon subvocalized.

I looked over at Solomon, who was also sweating, and pulled up my handheld. I dimmed the screen as much as I could and cupped my hand around it to hide as much of the glare as possible.

There were only two ways out of this area— the way we came in, and the door at the back of the building. I was scrolling through the other blueprint images, trying to find anything that would help us, when Solomon nudged me.

Looking over to where he was pointing, I saw a gray vent at the base of the wall, about ten feet away. Immediately, images of the vents in The Green's facility flashed through my head. I looked over at him, giving him an emphatic *no* in the form of a headshake.

I turned back to the handheld, my frustration growing with every swipe of my finger.

I paused, and swiped back a few images. There was something labeled "ldr" along the far wall behind us. At first, I had thought it was the letters "IDR", but then it clicked. It was a ladder, leading up to the roof.

I tapped Solomon on the shoulder and made the hand signals for "follow me". He nodded, adjusting his grip on the rifle. Taking a deep breath, I straightened up enough to peek out from over the top of the crate. The immediate area was clear.

Moving cautiously, I squat-walked down rows of shelves containing boxes. At the end of the first row, I peered around the corner. There was nobody down the next row, and I could see the ladder just ahead of us. I turned back to Solomon and nodded before spinning around the corner, my gun held up.

I moved quickly, thoroughly checking each row we passed before advancing to the next. I felt the press of time and looked at my watch just as we got to the ladder. It had been four minutes since the last conversation with Owen. I had no idea what was going on with him, but hopefully he took the initiative and would blow the distraction charge soon.

Assuming he wasn't dead by now.

I pushed that thought away quickly and placed my back against a shelf full of boxes. I nodded to Solomon. He secured his weapon with a quick tug to the strap, tightening it to his back, and then sucked in his breath. Immediately, he faded from view, leaving his gun and bag floating in midair. I cringed, but it was the best we could do at the moment. Hopefully, no one would notice.

I counted to ten, trying to give him enough time to get up the ladder before I started my ascent. I envied his control over the suit, and dreaded having to use my own.

After enough time had passed, I slung the rifle over my back. I moved to the ladder quickly, and was just in the process of contracting my muscles when a warden came around the corner, his flashlight cutting over me.

A small sound of alarm escaped my lips, and I whipped around, grabbing the rungs of the ladder and climbing as the man let out a gasp.

I continued to clench my muscles, and was several rungs up when the first gunshot exploded about three feet to the left of me, concrete exploding and spraying me with dust and shrapnel. I narrowed my eyes and continued to climb, when another shot sounded, also going wide.

I felt a stinging in my side as a line of fire exploded by my ribs, a third gunshot going off. I looked up at the twenty feet of ladder I still had to climb before I reached the top. A chill rushed down my spine as I realized the man's next bullet wasn't going to miss.

Grabbing the left side of the ladder, I swung myself to one side and brought up my gun just as he fired. The bullet impacted a space between the rungs where my chest had been. I reached around and grabbed my rifle, bringing it up—one handed—and hip fired, catching the man in the shoulder.

He fell to the ground with a scream, clutching his arm, and I dropped the rifle, letting it dangle from the strap as I scrambled the rest of the way up the ladder. By the time I was at the top, Solomon had reappeared and was holding the door open for me, waving at me to hurry up.

The sound of more guards arriving sent waves of anxiety through me. I reached up a hand to Solomon, and his hand encircled my wrist, hauling me up. I kicked at the door as I slid through it, slamming it shut with my foot.

"Much better than ventilation ducts," I gasped, sucking the cool night air in through my lungs.

Solomon grunted in agreement as he placed his hands on my side. There was a small tear in the fabric, and I was bleeding, but fortunately, the wound was shallow. I pushed his hands away. "I'm fine," I said, as I got up.

I had been hurt worse during martial arts training. I was pulling my gun over my shoulder when a spattering of rifle fire filled the air. After exchanging looks, Solomon and I raced over to the side of the building it had come from. The scene before us was that of a nightmare—dozens of wardens filled the yard. Their attention was on the warehouse on the other side of our building, but there were too many for us to risk a mad dash to where we had left the van.

I checked my watch—only three minutes for us to get to the van and get out. I looked at Solomon, who returned my gaze, his face ashen.

We didn't have to say it—it was readily apparent that we were in deep trouble. I knelt and started going through the items in my bag. Solomon dropped down beside me, his expression inquisitive.

"Here," I whispered, thrusting a bundle of rope into his hands. "We're going to tie the rope to that vent there, and then, when I give you the signal, you're going to rappel down. I'll buy you some time."

He studied me for a long moment, and then shook his head. "No, I'll buy *you* the time. You have people to get back to."

I growled in irritation. "So do you. Besides, they'll want me more than they'll want you," I said, meeting his gaze with a hard one of my own.

"What are you going to do? Stand on the edge and announce 'Hello, my name is Violet Bates, come and get me'?"

I frowned at the dismissive quality of his voice. "It'll get their attention," I argued.

"You'll get as far as, 'My name is—' and catch a bullet."

"I can't have your death on my hands," I hissed at him, standing up.

"Well, that isn't your choice to make, Violet. We're a team. We need to—"

Whatever Solomon intended to say was lost in the explosion. The force of it shook the building, and instinctively we fell to the floor, curling our bodies into fetal positions to absorb the impact tremors. We stared at each other, waiting until the roar had slightly diminished.

I heard frightened shouts from the wardens below, and I stood up, running over to where a bright glow could be seen. Smoke plumed, filling the air with the smell of fire. Below me, the wardens were running around, panicked.

I scanned the area of the warehouse and spotted two lone figures loping away from the scene toward the van. There was a flash of gold as one of them paused, looking back, and I realized it was Owen.

But where was the laser? I looked at his hands but

saw nothing. Was it possible that they had decided to abandon the mission?

Solomon came up beside me. "There's a path that's clear to the south. If we hurry, we can make it back to the van in time."

I whirled and gave him an incredulous look, unable to process what he was saying. "Owen doesn't have the objective," I said.

He looked over my shoulder and his face tightened. "He's also missing a man—I don't know if it's Amber or Quinn, but if he had to abandon them in the warehouse, then the mission is over."

A fresh wave of panic bubbled up to the surface. "No! We can't just leave it there! We need it—Viggo needs it!" I grabbed his forearm, my fingers digging in tightly. "The wardens, they're distracted—we can just—"

Solomon yanked his hand out of mine. "No, Violet. We can't go get it now. The wardens are everywhere, and even more will be coming."

I shook my head, refusing to see reason in his words. I backed away slowly, pulling my gun around my body and putting it between us like a shield. "No," I said. "There's still time! We can do this."

He took a step forward, his hands raised. "Violet… please… see reason. We need to go, now."

Tears were beginning to form in my eyes. My vision blurred and I blinked, trying to keep the panic growing inside me at bay. I thought of Viggo's face, and it grounded me. I knew what he would do: He would go in after it anyway. I had to do the same. For him.

"You... you go back to Owen. You tell him to wait. Buy me time. I'll go get the laser and I'll find a way to get it to you."

Solomon took another step closer and I backed away from him. "Please, Solomon," I said, my voice breaking.

He paused and looked at me. Really looked at me. I couldn't imagine how I looked in his eyes—probably like some insane woman about to commit suicide. I didn't care—he just needed to know that I was serious about what I was saying.

"All right," he said reluctantly, and my knees buckled in relief. "If you're going to go, I think there might be a clearer path at the rear of the building. I'll rappel down with you, give you some cover, and then I'll get to Owen and tell him to wait, okay?"

I nodded emphatically. "Yes. Thank you, Solomon."

He gave me a tight nod and moved toward the rear of the building. I followed him, bending down to scoop up the rope from where Solomon had dropped it during the explosion. He was already by the ventilation shaft, digging through his pack.

"Here, use mine," I said, kneeling down next to

the vent to start wrapping my rope around it. I was just in the middle of tying the knot when I felt a sharp sting in my neck. Slapping my hand to the flesh there, I whirled around and saw Solomon standing behind me, a needle in his hand.

I had enough time to utter, "What the—" before blackness rushed in. I was barely aware of Solomon catching me as I fell into complete, unyielding darkness.

CHAPTER 13

Violet

I woke up with a jerk and gazed around. It took me a moment to remember what had happened, but then it all came rushing back—the explosion, Solomon, the syringe. The ghost of the sting on my neck made me lift my hand and rub the skin there, but I couldn't feel any evidence that it had happened.

Yet I was certain it had. I had woken up in a nest of blankets piled on the floor, and I recognized the room as the one Amber and I had shared in Thomas' lair. I braced my hand against the wall as a wave of dizziness swept over me, causing my stomach to roil in protest. I panted at the exertion, but refused to acknowledge my body's need to lie down.

Instead, I fought against it, forcing myself to stand

on shaky knees. I felt simultaneously feverish and freezing. It was likely a side-effect of whatever drug Solomon had injected into me. I checked the time and realized I had been out several hours. It was early in the morning now. I wrapped a blanket around my shoulders—the one thing I would allow myself—and stumbled to the door. I needed to know what happened after Solomon knocked me out.

I swung open the door with more force than necessary, and felt the graze wound on my side pull a bit. Lifting up my shirt, I saw a white bandage with a thin red line coming across it.

Entering the room, one of the sofas had been dragged to the middle of it, and Amber lay on it, moaning, one hand clutching her side.

"It hurts," she sobbed. "Make it stop—please!" The urgency coupled with the panic in her voice made me forget my own indignation for a moment.

I rushed over to her, dropping to my knees. Her violet eyes were large and luminous with fear as she looked at me.

"Violet… please… help me," she begged, reaching for me. I grabbed her hand and she gripped mine tightly. Shushing her, I noticed the bandage stained with blood low on her abdomen. She also had a patch on either side of her neck—I recognized them as blood patches.

"You were shot?" I asked in a hushed tone.

She made a little whimper and nodded, tears dripping from her eyes. I placed my hand on her forehead and she shuddered. "It's going to be okay, Amber. I'm going to find out what's going on and come right back, okay?"

I turned toward where Owen, Quinn, and Thomas were all standing around the table. Owen looked over at me, his face a mixture of sadness and anger. Thomas stood with his arms crossed, his head tilted defiantly as he gazed at the other two men. Quinn looked the most frustrated—his hair was disheveled and under his eyes were twin pockets of shadow, indicating he hadn't gotten much sleep.

I moved away from Amber and toward the men. They were having a heated debate in hushed whispers as I approached, which died as I inserted myself into their circle. I glared at each of them and crossed my arms.

"What are we doing about Amber?" I asked.

"We should be taking her to the hospital," exploded Quinn.

Frowning, I shook my head. "I'm sure that both Owen and Thomas have shot that idea down, with good reason, Quinn—you know taking a woman with a gunshot wound to the hospital is only going to land us all in jail. Does anyone have any medical training? Enough to assess whether, if we load her up with painkillers and prepare her to move, she'll stay stable on the way?"

All three avoided eye contact with me and I refrained from tapping a foot impatiently. It was Thomas who broke the silence.

"Solomon could have. But he can't now."

"Why not? Where is he? I kind of have a bone to pick with him after we get this situation handled!" Again, there was an awkward shuffling, and I exhaled a short breath in exasperation. "Just tell me."

"We have bigger problems than worrying about Solomon right now, Violet," Owen announced, finally meeting my gaze. I ignored his patronizing tone and angled myself toward him.

"Like?"

"Like why our intel was bad, and whether we have a mole somewhere."

I looked sharply at Thomas, who met my gaze. "As I was explaining to Owen," he said, "I don't think it was bad intelligence or a mole. It was probably just bad luck."

"You believe in luck?" I asked.

Thomas coughed and pulled at the collar of his shirt, looking wary. "Not as a rule, no. But Violet, it's the only thing that makes sense."

"How do you figure?"

"I checked every angle! I did weeks of research on my own and out in the field—something I despise, by the way—to make sure that the intelligence I received was accurate. Something must have changed since then, something that made the Patrians change their system."

"Owen, do you think Thomas could have betrayed us?" I asked.

Owen rubbed a hand through his hair and looked at Thomas for a long moment. Thomas, for his part, quailed under Owen's scrutiny.

"The Liberators, maybe—but me? No. Thomas wouldn't do that."

Thomas flushed bright red.

Seeing the awkward situation I had put him in, I felt bad and glossed over it as quickly as I could. "Well, then, it seems likely that it was bad luck." Owen moved to object, but I held up a hand and stopped him. "We don't have time to argue the point, Owen. Amber is in a rough place right now—we need to stop arguing and do something about it."

Owen froze, his mouth open, and I used his shock to my advantage. "What's the quickest way to get her back to The Green?"

"By boat, but—"

"Great. Thomas, can you get in touch with Alejandro and let him know that we need an emergency ride back to The Green?"

"Violet, you can't just—"

"Tell him we'll double his fee, provided he doesn't ask questions and allows us the use of his private bedroom."

"Violet! You don't even understand. We never, ever go back by the same means we enter a place. It's the quickest way to get caught!"

I stared at Owen. "These are unusual circumstances. I'm pretty sure Desmond and everyone else will understand. Now, will someone please answer my questions about Solomon? Also, please explain to me why he was carrying that syringe in the first place, and why he felt the need to use it on me!"

Thomas shot a look at Owen, who gave him a quick nod. Thomas moved over to the side and pulled out his handheld, presumably to contact Alejandro. I turned back to Owen and gave him a glare.

Owen shifted his weight on his feet for a moment, scratching the back of his neck. "Well... we felt that maybe you might wind up being a problem, if we weren't able to achieve the objective."

"Who's we?" I asked, bristling in righteous indignation.

"Solomon and me. We knew... we knew how much was at stake for you, so we came up with a back-up plan, in case things went sideways."

"I see," I murmured after a pause. There was a bitter taste in my mouth that I couldn't quite swallow. A part of me could see what he meant—after all, I had unilaterally decided to try to complete the mission alone. It had been a reckless and shortsighted move on my part. "That still doesn't tell me where Solomon is. Or where Quinn was when you and Amber were running from the scene."

I turned my gaze to Quinn, who flinched. "I was running the other way," he said.

I frowned in confusion. "The other way?"

Quinn nodded, and swallowed. "Yeah. Owen said it would be better if we split up, and he and Amber ran as a distraction to buy me time. We waited for you as long as we could after the coms went out, and then detonated the explosive. While they went left… I went right."

I frowned, confused as to why he would risk running a distraction with two people instead of one, and then my breath hitched. "So… were you able to get the laser after all?"

Quinn nodded and reached over to slide a long metallic case toward me. Wordlessly, I picked it up and opened it, staring at the silver laser inside. Inhaling deeply, I set it down, leaning heavily on the table with both hands.

It had been a diversion the entire time, and I had fallen for it too. The worst part was I hadn't had faith in Owen and the others, and that had led Solomon to whatever fate they were now trying to keep from me. I closed my eyes and fought to keep the panic at bay.

"Where is he?" I demanded, looking up at them. "Is he…" I trailed off, unable to force my lips to make the appropriate sounds.

Owen shook his head emphatically, and moved closer. "He's not dead, but… you're not going to like it."

"Show me," I demanded.

Owen fidgeted and looked at Quinn, who shrugged. Even Thomas looked uncomfortable—his fingers frozen over the handheld, his eyes were glued to the floor, unwilling to make eye contact.

I licked my lips and took a step forward, until I was within inches of Owen. He dragged his eyes up to mine, and I met his gaze sternly, letting him see my determination.

I couldn't explain it in words, but if Solomon had been severely injured—more so than Amber—then I needed to see it. I needed to see what I was responsible for due to my desperate need to save the person I loved. It was important, sacred, that I did, so I could burn into my mind that I had failed my team by not believing in them. So that I could see, directly, the consequences of my actions.

"Show me," I whispered, clenching my fists.

Owen stared deep into my eyes for a few seconds, then conceded. "All right," he murmured.

He turned and began leading me to the front door. Puzzled, I followed, ignoring the solemn gazes of Thomas and Quinn as we entered the hallway leading out of Thomas' lair.

CHAPTER 14

Violet

I could feel the tension squirming within me like a python. I followed Owen down the hall and through the door leading to the sewage system. We stepped down to the concrete platform, small puddles of water splashing as our boots passed through them. Instead of leaping into the murky water in front of us, Owen guided me left, heading into a different tunnel.

The concrete platform we were on narrowed, until it was approximately the width of our feet. Alongside us, a river of the same filthy water flowed into the darkness. Owen was using his handheld as a flashlight, the dim screen illuminating our path through the darkness. The tunnel shot off to the left, but then curved back to the right, leading to another junction, similar to the one we'd left behind.

Owen shimmied along the ledge as we neared, and then made a quick leap to the platform in the middle of the room. Hesitating, I made my way along the ledge to the point he had and then pushed myself from the wall.

I cleared the narrow gap easily, landing solidly on my feet next to him. Ahead of us was another door, similar to the door of Thomas' lair.

"I don't get it… were these rooms pre-existing?" I asked.

Owen paused his ascent up the stairs and shot me an incredulous look. "What, do you think that we built them?"

I shrugged, uncertain of how to respond, because, while I hadn't given it a great amount of thought, my thoughts had been along those lines.

Owen shook his head. "No, sorry, Violet. We're good, but not that good. These tunnels and rooms existed before us. It's part of the original design of the sewer system."

I wrinkled my nose. "Why would anyone build rooms in a sewer system?"

Owen gave his own little shrug. "Does it matter? They were abandoned long ago, and almost no one knows they're down here. It was Thomas who discovered them—by accident. The only records of them exist in physical form, and Thomas made sure to destroy them before he disappeared himself."

I frowned, but accepted the information. A lot of building, demolition, and rebuilding had happened in the early years after our predecessors had discovered the area. It wasn't too far-fetched to believe that the purpose of the rooms in the tunnel had been lost over time.

Owen's shoulders shifted lower as he turned and reached for the door. I wet my lips nervously, the moment of levity forgotten.

Solomon was somewhere within this room. My heartbeat increased slightly as my stomach contracted. Now that I was here at the threshold, I wasn't as certain as I had been minutes before. It was going to be bad, that much was sure.

I steeled myself as Owen pushed open the door and followed him as he moved into the oppressive darkness of the hall.

Unlike Thomas' place, this room was not well-lit. If it hadn't been for Owen's handheld producing light, I would have probably freaked out. I was not comfortable with dark and cramped places anymore. As it was, the shadows being cast by his handheld were giving me the creeps.

Luckily, we were through within seconds, and the lighting in the center chamber massively improved compared to the darkness of the hall. Just like in Thomas' lair, there were doors on either side of the room. The left room was dark, but the right room was lit.

Owen paused in the center of the room, eyeing me warily. "For the last time, Violet... maybe you shouldn't see this."

I tilted my chin up at him. I needed to see it. He sighed and moved over to the door, leaning against the wall next to it. He crossed his arms, not meeting my gaze.

I squared my shoulders and marched over to the door.

"Whatever you do, don't open it," Owen said softly, as I peered through the window.

Inside, the room was bare, save for a lamp and the large, lone figure of Solomon crouched in the corner. His back was to me, and he was squatting, rocking back and forth.

I shot a glance at Owen, who remained tight-lipped, still not looking at me. I frowned, and pressed my face closer to the window.

"Solomon?" I called gently through the door.

Immediately, Solomon froze. Several moments passed—enough time for me to start to call his name again—before his head whipped around so violently, I thought his neck would break from the speed.

But the face looking back at me was that of a stranger. Solomon's normally impassive face had morphed into one of unspeakable rage. His eyes rolled wildly in his skull while he gnashed his teeth together, spittle forming at the corners of his mouth. He had torn away the top part of his invisibility suit in the front, exposing his chest, which was covered with long crisscrossed bloody lines. It didn't take me long to put together that the wounds were self-inflicted. His fingers were red with blood, and it looked like he had been trying to claw his way into his own flesh.

His rolling eyes settled on me, and he snarled, causing me to flinch back. "Solomon?" I gasped, my voice tiny from the lump that had formed in my throat.

He snarled again and launched himself at the door so suddenly, I barely had a chance to take a step back before he impacted. The door shuddered in the frame, but held.

I covered my mouth with my hand, my eyes forming tears at the horror of seeing a man normally so cool and collected transformed into a monster. Turning to Owen, I breathed, "How?"

Owen's eyes filled with remorse. He opened his mouth to respond when the door frame shuddered again, forcing him to pause. "Outside," he said, pushing himself off the wall.

I followed him, feeling both eager and reluctant to leave. Solomon gave a low throaty roar as we departed, a crescendo of anger mingling with sadness. It felt like a knife straight to my heart, and it was with great reluctance that I continued following Owen, closing the door to the hallway behind me.

Owen was waiting on the platform, kicking his foot through a small puddle. I pushed the second door closed behind me and then sat down heavily on the steps.

"How?" I repeated, and Owen sighed, placing his hands on his hips.

"You have to understand, Violet. The pills… we were warned that there would be side effects before they were given to us."

I gaped at him, my confusion palpable. "I-I don't understand. Pills? What pills? What side effects?"

Owen kicked at the floor again, his lips twisting into a grimace. "The pills—the ones that Mr. Jenks invented to temporarily enhance regular humans. In the facility, our scientists, they… they refined the process."

It took a moment for his words to sink in. Once they finally did, I found myself standing, although I didn't remember making the motion to do so. An indescribable fury had flooded my senses and hijacked my brain. I watched myself cross over the wet floor. I felt my hand curl into a fist.

And then suddenly Owen was staggering back, clutching his jaw where I had punched him. My fist throbbed, and I shook it out, glaring at him.

"*How could you?*" I hissed, flexing my hand. Tears had escaped from my eyes, falling in hot trails down my cheeks and throat.

Owen stared at me, his expression infused with regret and pain. It wasn't enough—not by far.

"HOW COULD YOU?!" I bellowed, taking a step forward and raising a fist.

He flinched back, holding both his hands up. "I'm sorry!" he said, and I froze, my hands shaking. I clenched my teeth together, torn between hitting him again and backing off. He slowly lowered his hands, and I could see tears forming in his eyes too.

Frustrated by his acquiescence, I lowered my fist and stalked backward. I began to pace, trying to calm the anger pulsing in my heart. I took a quick breath in, followed by a long slow breath out. Then another. And then another.

It took several minutes for me to find a certain level of calmness. During that time, I tried moving past my initial question to find a more productive line of inquiry that would help me understand why they had done this.

Once I was ready, I turned back to Owen, who was standing where I had left him, his arms wrapped around himself. I had seen many faces of Owen since I had met him, but this was the first time I had seen him ashamed.

"Okay. Tell me what happened," I said, not bothering to keep the hard edge out of my voice.

"Solomon must have thought he had no choice.

He had almost a kilometer to run while carrying you and your gear. So… he took the pill."

"What did it enhance?" I asked.

"His strength."

I nodded slowly, furrowing my brows. "That would explain his anger."

It was Owen's turn to nod. "Yeah. Desmond gave them to us before the mission. I swear, Violet, I didn't know she was going to hand them out. Hell, I didn't even know she had been experimenting with the pill. She warned us that the side effects for us would be more pronounced than they were for the boys. They were given incremental doses over time—Solomon got a massive dose all at once." I shot him another hard, flat look, and he took a slow step back, away from me. "She told us not to take them unless it was a clear emergency."

I shook my head, as if trying to clear it from a punch. "Those pills should have never been handed out in the first place!" I said, my nostrils flaring. "Desmond said she would destroy them. She clearly lied."

Owen's face fell. "No. It's not like that, Violet. Desmond… she's going to be devastated by this. She loves Solomon—we all do. Nobody wanted this to happen. But if she didn't destroy them, then she had her reasons."

I fell quiet, swallowing hard. "It's my fault," I said

after a beat. Owen moved forward, his face reflecting his refusal of my statement. I held up a hand. "It's Desmond's fault too, for handing them out, but I'm not devoid of blame. I... I was certain you had left the laser behind."

"Of course it wasn't your fault, Violet. We lost communication, and... well... you were doing what you thought you had to. I know that if I, or Solomon, or anyone else were in your shoes, we would have done the same. How could we give up on a cure for the person we love? The answer is: We can't. Neither could you."

I moved back to the stairs and sat down. "What are we going to tell Meera?" I asked quietly, thinking of Solomon's mother.

Owen came to sit next to me. "She knew the risks of the mission. And with a little luck... who knows? Maybe the effects are just temporary. Hopefully, he won't have to be like this for long."

I heaved a sigh, my eyes finally drying up. "We can't take him out of the city, can we?"

Owen shook his head, his expression regretful. "No. We can't. But Thomas has promised that he will look after him while we're gone. And we'll hopefully be able to spare one of the scientists to come and examine him. Solomon will be all right until then, okay? You just have to give it some time and patience."

I laughed bitterly. "Time and patience? I'm not

exactly the patient type."

Owen's hand settled on my knee and I looked up at him. The two of us were sitting with our faces inches apart. It should have made the situation feel more intimate in some way. And yet it didn't, and Owen didn't make any inappropriate move one way or the other.

"You were patient for two weeks," he said, "waiting for this mission."

I laughed again, the sound brittle in my ears. "You have no idea," I replied, rubbing my temples. "You have no idea—I would've done anything, been nice to anyone, to get what I needed for Viggo. And while I don't think I would have abandoned you to die... I never trusted you enough to get the job done. I'm the reason Solomon felt he needed to take the steps he did. If I had just trusted you..."

My words hung in the air for several moments before Owen replied with a sigh, "I-I can understand, although I can't say I like it. But... you're doing the best you can, considering the circumstances. And, despite what happened to Solomon and Amber, we got what we came here to get. You have hope now, a very real hope, that you can touch. And maybe with what happened here... well, as dark as this is to say, maybe now you can learn to trust us."

He leaned forward and pressed his lips to my forehead, and I found myself leaning a shoulder against his. Owen wrapped his arms around me and hugged me. It felt weird, but kind of nice.

I wasn't sure how Owen had weighed into Desmond's decision to keep researching the pills, but I was still furious with her, and I planned to explain to her exactly how she messed up. Maybe it was my fault for making Solomon feel like he had to take that pill, but Desmond was the one who'd handed it to him.

Owen pulled back and smiled at me. "Don't tell your boyfriend about this when he wakes up," he said, and I managed a chuckle.

"Oh, I'm telling him," I said with a smile of my own. "He's going to eat you alive."

Owen rolled his eyes and stood up. "For the record, Violet, I am *totally* not into you."

I accepted the hand he offered, pulling myself to my feet. "Owen, you aren't even a blip on my radar," I replied, and he laughed, his laughter rich and genuine, dispelling the tension that had built, if only for a moment.

He looked at his watch and his shoulders dipped. Our moment of calm was shattered once again by the press of time. Wordlessly, we headed back to Thomas' lair, leaving Solomon alone in his prison.

CHAPTER 15

Violet

Amber groaned as we lifted her makeshift gurney up higher, jostling her.

"Sorry," I said for the umpteenth time, my arms straining to help lift her high above the putrid water flowing past us.

We had been moving her through the tunnels for ages, and the smell had gotten worse. With each minute we kept her down here, the chances of her developing a serious infection grew. We had done everything we could to stem the bleeding in her side, but she had gone incoherent with blood loss, and so pale that the normal rose tint of her lips had faded completely.

Owen and I pushed forward together, carefully placing our feet so that we didn't slip. Quinn grunted as he slid back a few feet on the platform, balancing the other end alone. Once she was up, I shifted over and grabbed Owen's side. He relinquished it as I did, and my arms strained, shaking under Amber's full weight.

Owen didn't waste any time—he slipped out of the water and quickly relieved me of the pressure, he and Quinn moving her further onto the platform and high above the water. I shook out my aching arms and then pushed myself out of the gunk.

Sweat was pouring off all of us, despite the cool air in here, and we were all breathing heavily.

"Do we need a break?" Owen asked.

Quinn and I looked at each other and shook our heads. We hadn't taken a break since we started, but we weren't going to stop until we got her aboveground and onto Alejandro's boat.

"How many more junctions?" I asked.

Owen gave me a nod, and I moved over to him, holding Amber so he could check the handheld. After a long moment, he groaned. "Three," he muttered.

I took another long slow breath and nodded. "Three, huh? Okay. We got this."

Quinn smiled at me and I shot him a smile in return. Owen quickly took back Amber's weight, and I moved over to Quinn's side to give him a break. Looking back at Owen, I gave a small jerk of my head toward the tunnel to our left.

Straining, we lifted her up and continued moving. It took us forty-five minutes to get to the junction, but we made it. We had to set her down after we got to the third and final platform and once we did, Owen handed me the pack off his back. Inside was the laser for Viggo, and Amber's and my costumes—the male ones.

"Help me get this on her," he said, pulling out the tweed coat and slacks for Amber.

"No padding?" I asked.

"No time..." He checked his watch and nodded, as if coming to a decision. "We're going to play this off like she's drunk and we're taking her home to her wife. Hopefully, no one will stop us, but we have to get her on her feet."

While he talked, he rummaged through my bag and pulled out a familiar-looking patch.

"That's adrenaline," I said, and he nodded.

"Just one patch—it'll get her on her feet and moving for long enough to get to the boat. After that, we'll let her lie down. It'll take us a day to get back into The Green, and another day to move her across the jungle, but I contacted Desmond—she's going to send us some help so we don't have to do it alone."

I paused while my mind raced through every conceivable problem we might face. "What about the red flies?"

"The team will be waiting for us with a clean suit

to put her in. As long as we neutralize the odor of the blood, we'll make it."

"Do you have any more of the blood patches? She needs more," I said as I began slipping her shirt off.

Amber moaned in protest, her eyelids fluttering. I carefully peeled off the patches on her neck and slapped the one that Owen handed me over the spot I had just removed the old one from before buttoning up her shirt.

Owen and Quinn were already down by her feet, helping each other slip the woolen pants over her legs. As soon as I was finished with the buttons, I moved down to help them pull her pants up past her knees and over her hips, then button the front. Owen helped pull her up into a sitting position, and Quinn and I grabbed her arms and pulled them through the sleeves of the jacket.

I gathered up the riot of curls at the top of her head, smoothing them down and placing the wig on her head. I pulled a few pins out of the bag and hastily fastened the short brown wig to her head before placing the cap on top. Quinn and Owen, meanwhile, had been applying the special glue to her face before affixing the beard.

After we were done, I took a step back to look at our handiwork. It was sloppy and rushed, but for the short walk to Alejandro's boat, it would have to do.

I looked at Owen. "Do it," I said, and he placed the

adrenaline patch on her chest, just under the neckline, so that her clothes and uniform would hide it.

Almost immediately, her eyes opened and she gave a gasp as she sat up, her hand gripping her side. She gazed at us groggily. "Where are we?" she slurred.

"We're almost at the dock, Amber," said Quinn soothingly, moving a few feet closer.

She dragged her gaze over to him and nodded, swallowing hard. "I feel awful," she said, as we helped her to her feet.

"Yeah, and you look it, too," I replied, quickly moving to pull on my own costume. Like Amber, I was going without the padding—it took too long to get on and we would be long gone before the wardens showed up, if things went according to plan.

Quinn moved over to the ladder, his own street clothes already on. "I'll go up first to check if it's clear."

Owen nodded, his fingers flying over his shirt as he buttoned it up. "We'll be good to go in three, right, Violet?"

I nodded absent-mindedly, fumbling with the front of my shirt.

Quinn quickly ascended as Amber wobbled to her feet.

"For the record, guys," she croaked, "don't ever get shot. It sucks."

Suddenly she doubled over and began retching.

There was a sickening sound of liquid hitting liquid, and I flinched. I had been in her shoes before—not with a gunshot wound, but when I had been bitten by a black centipede.

I gave up on my buttons halfway down and pulled on my coat, hastily fastening it at the waist. I smoothed down my hair and pulled the wig on, slipping a few pins in it to keep it secure. Applying the glue for the goatee without a mirror was difficult, but somehow I managed, although I could feel the glue drying in places that the fake hair didn't touch.

We couldn't use our invisibility suits, but now I wished we could. Well, technically two of us could— but Amber's, Solomon's, and mine had been damaged and wouldn't function now that the fabric was torn. So, we had decided on a ruse to get to the docks. Besides, Amber was in no condition to try to operate a suit. She could barely keep her eyes open.

Owen was already helping Amber to the ladder. His handheld chirped, and he pulled Amber close, letting her use his body as a stabilizer while he held up his forearm to check it. "Quinn says it's clear," he told us, pulling Amber upright.

She coughed and gasped as he did, but nodded weakly. "Great—the sooner I can lie down, the better," she said, giving us a small smile that didn't remotely break past the pain clouding her eyes.

"Don't worry," Owen grunted, as he placed her

hands on the ladder. "We'll get you there. And if you want to get there faster, you climb and don't stop. I'll be right behind you."

I tossed Owen's bag to him, which he caught one-handed, and slung my own over my shoulder.

Amber groaned, clutching at the rungs of the ladder as she slowly ascended. I admired her tenacity, and only hoped that I could be as tough as her if I was ever shot and not just grazed.

Owen was moving close behind Amber, using his free hand to help hold her up as she moved from rung to rung. I bounced on my toes, waiting for them to move high enough up for me to start climbing.

Eventually, Amber and Owen made it to the top. Quinn helped pull Amber up, and I made my way the ladder. For the fifteen or twenty seconds it took me to climb, it had taken Amber and Owen five solid minutes, and I was becoming more nervous.

The sewer entrance was nestled in the middle of hastily constructed warehouses near the waterfront. This was the closest insertion point to our destination—we needed to weave through the tiny narrow alleys to reach the docks. Owen and Quinn had already hoisted Amber up between them, her arms on their shoulders. Owen was giving her some last-minute instructions, making her promise to keep from groaning too loudly in pain.

I grunted as I began pushing the manhole closed

behind me. It took a minute for me to get it to move, but eventually I slid it over the hole and straightened. "I'll lead," I said, pulling out my handheld.

Owen nodded, his face strained. I pulled up the city map and studied it. It was mostly a straight shot, with only a few turns here and there. I nodded forward, and then began walking, moving toward the docks.

As we entered the main street, I motioned for them to stop, as throngs of people were shouting jubilantly and celebrating something. Frowning, I ducked back into the alley and turned to Owen. "There's some sort of party going on," I said.

Owen's gaze turned thoughtful and then he groaned, lifting his free hand to his forehead. "We had planned to be gone already, but… it's Foundation Day," he said, meeting my gaze.

Of course—Foundation Day was the Patrian holiday celebrating the founding of their city.

"What do we do?" I asked, meeting Owen's worried gaze.

His lips pursed. "We keep to the plan. We have to get Amber to the dock."

I gulped, not feeling secure about the plan—there were a lot more people in the street, which increased the odds of us being discovered significantly. But I didn't see a better option, so I nodded and moved back into the street.

Tension rolled through me as I began to push through the throngs of people. I kept my head down, avoiding any gazes that might be on me, and slowly wove a path through the milling crowd toward our destination.

CHAPTER 16

Violet

My neck itched in response to the hundreds of people in the street, as if dozens of eyes were on me. In reality, I suspected that nobody was paying attention to the four of us, but my irrational mind was paranoid.

Every time someone drew too close or turned to face us, I would hold my breath and alter my path slightly to avoid them. It made what should've been a relatively short walk slightly longer, but I didn't want to risk discovery. Amber's life was on the line, as was Viggo's, and I was determined to not lose either of them.

Just then, a slew of angry voices broke out to our left. I risked a glance over to see two men shouting at each other, their faces red and mottled with outrage. The men were clearly inebriated, and their friends were trying to pull them apart.

I started to change the angle of our path yet again when one of the men shoved the other directly into me. I stumbled back, and the man whirled around to face me.

"Sorry," I mumbled, before freezing. In my mad rush to get ready in the sewers, I had forgotten to take the Deepvox pills.

The man's eyes narrowed as he took me in. He was nearly twice my weight, and not from fat. His arms were thick and bound with muscles, his chest broad and wide. He looked at the crowd coalesced around us. I caught a glimpse of Owen and the others as they moved around it, taking advantage of the attention that the man and I were getting.

I moved to leave when he grabbed my arm. "Small little thing, ain't ya?" he declared. He was close enough for me to smell the foul stench of liquor on his breath, and I resisted the urge to gag. I looked at where his hand clutched my arm with bruising intensity, and then followed his arm up to his face.

He gave a feral smile and internally, I groaned. This man was clearly looking for a fight, and there was not going to be an easy or political way to extract myself. Around us, the crowd rippled as whispers were exchanged. I glanced back to where Owen and Quinn were standing with Amber. Owen shot me an inquisitive look, asking if I needed his help, and I gave a slow, barely perceptible shake of my head. The instant he got involved, the situation would explode.

I turned, facing the man. "Sir," I said, making my voice as deep as I could, "would you kindly let go of my arm? I'm just trying to help my mates home after a night of drinking. You understand, right?"

The man's expression morphed into one of confusion. He stared at me and then began to laugh, slapping his knee with his free hand.

"Look here, gents. We got us a bit of a spine in this little fish. What say we pulverize it?"

I saw his fist beginning to clench, felt as he tensed and shifted his weight in preparation to throw a punch. I didn't give him the chance. I snapped two quick jabs and an uppercut directly into his face with my free arm.

The man's head jerked back and he staggered, dragging me along with him. The heel of his boot caught the edge of the pavement, and before I knew it, he was dragging me to the ground.

I sprawled into him, caught off guard, but quickly pushed myself up, wresting my arm out of his grasp. As I straightened, someone in the crowd shouted, "That's not a man, that's a woman!" I reached up to my face to discover that my goatee had fallen off in the scuffle.

Excited whispers exploded from the crowd, and I used their shock as an opportunity to barge through them. I walked by Owen, Quinn, and Amber, hissing, "Get to the boat," before I heard someone from the crowd shouting, "Get her!"

Then I started running, leading the forming mob away from the three of them and deeper into the twisting warehouses. I could already hear several people in pursuit as I hooked a hard right down one of the narrow alleys.

I had bought myself only a matter of seconds before the whole crowd began the chase. I needed to get a bigger lead on them and lose them in the sprawling warehouse area, but it was going to be hard. Over fifty people had seen me, and by now, the news would be spreading like wildfire to the other people in the street. If I couldn't make it to the boat in time, I was as good as dead.

I kept an eye out as I ran, looking for somewhere, anywhere, I could hide or disappear from sight long enough to lose the group directly behind me. I hooked another hard turn—left this time—and followed the alley thirty feet before turning right again.

The road before me extended another forty feet before ending in a brick wall. For a second I panicked, but then I caught sight of a few stacked trash units. Without slowing down or pausing, I raced toward the wall and leapt up onto the trash containers, praying they were full. If they had been empty, my weight would've likely thrown them off balance, crashing me to the ground. Luckily, they weren't, and I quickly grabbed the top of the wall and pulled myself over.

As I slid down the other side, I caught a glimpse of the men chasing me and let go quickly, my feet hitting the ground. I heard them shouting at each other as I made a left turn into an adjoining alley. This alley was filled with small doors, which were beginning to open as the curious people who lived inside came out to see what the commotion was about.

I ducked and weaved through the people, barely losing any momentum. About halfway down the street, I saw what I needed—a ladder hanging off one of the taller warehouse buildings. As quickly as I could, I moved toward it and jumped, grabbing the rusting ladder with one hand.

My arms were still aching from earlier, but I pulled myself up and climbed to the roof. I had just swung one leg over the ledge when the pack of men chasing me finally caught up. I pressed my cheek to the rooftop and held my breath, praying they didn't look up.

Their footsteps thundered on the pavement below me without stopping, and I exhaled. Pulling my backpack around, I grabbed the subvocalizing caller and earbud from where I had packed them earlier. Thomas had assured us they were still functional, and I had to hope that Owen had already put his on during the commotion and was waiting to hear from me.

Owen? I called.

Yeah. Where are you? Are you okay?

I pulled out the handheld from where I had tucked it in my pocket and brought up my location, studying the map.

I'm about ten minutes from the boat. How are you guys doing?

He grunted. *We're about three minutes out. Your distraction has pretty much cleared the way, but…*

Am I going to be able to make it?

Yeah.

I scanned the streets. More and more people were starting to fill them, with packs of men shouting something at each other.

I can't use the streets. They're alerting everyone.

The sewers are out too—you'll fall into the river if you're not careful.

I studied the rooftops—most of them were pressed together, with barely a foot of space between them. I stood up.

I-I've got an idea. If it works, I'll get to you a lot faster.

Okay—I'll hold the boat as long as I can. Just get to the docks fast.

Slinging my backpack once again over my shoulders, I tightened the straps. The roofs were slanted, but not steep. If I was careful and watched my footing, I should be able to run across the rooftops.

Even as I had the thought, a wave of dizziness overwhelmed me, and I carefully lowered myself back down again. Tilting my head up so that my jaw ran parallel to the roof, I focused my gaze on the horizon. It was a trick that I used every time I went down to the lowest level of the facility. There was no floor there— just a deep pit of open space that threatened to swallow me up. Yet, even there, I could count on a handrail and a level walking surface.

Taking a measured breath, I willed myself to stand, ignoring the precarious flip-flopping of my stomach as I stared out over the rooftops in front of me. I summoned up an image of Viggo, picturing him in my shoes, and then exhaled, taking a slow step forward. Then another.

Cautiously, I moved a few feet down the ridge of the roof, my arms extended to help me keep balance. The smoke coming from the chimneys of people's houses made the air a little polluted, but if I put enough distance between them and myself, I'd be okay.

As long as I didn't look down.

I eyed the gap between this warehouse and the roof of the building a few feet below it. The gap was about a foot and a half wide—I could step across it if I wanted to... Before my rational mind could register that fact, I started running. I was already across the gap by the time it caught up, moving at a fast jog across the rooftops. I leapt over the small gaps between houses, the fear in my throat morphing into a sense of exhilaration as I picked up speed. Running on the streets or through The Green had nothing on this—it was exciting and dangerous, causing my adrenaline to pump and my heart to soar.

I saw the wide gap as I approached it, my eyes glimpsing the pavement below. It was likely one of the bigger streets. I thought my vertigo would kick in and I slowed in anticipation to the dizziness, but when it didn't manifest, I grinned, pouring on more speed. I approached the gap, gathered myself, and leapt out into the void between the two buildings, resisting the urge to whoop when my boots planted on the other side.

I continued picking my way across the rooftops at a high pace, slowing down only when I made it to the docks. I walked up to the edge of the roof and scanned the docks on the pier. I could make out Alejandro's boat about a hundred feet away. Looking at the area immediately below me, I saw stacks of crates I could climb down.

Owen, I see you and the boat. I'm on my way to you—start casting off.

Got it, he replied.

I watched as he and Alejandro started throwing lines off the boat and began to climb down the crates when a flood of people erupted from the alley on my right.

"There she is!" someone shouted and I lost my grip, crashing through a crate.

I was stunned for a moment but I sat up quickly, brushing off pieces of wood. The crowd began to close in, and I leapt to my feet, sprinting for Alejandro's boat.

There was a crack of a gunshot, and I winced, veering left, and then right.

Owen was frantically waving me forward, and I saw the glint of the gun in his hand as he leveled it at the crowd.

Don't, I implored him over the subvocalizer. He lowered his gun a fraction of an inch and I sprinted faster, my arms and legs a blur. My lungs were heaving from the strain, and I could see the boat drifting further and further away.

With a roar, I planted a foot on one of the mooring beams on the dock and leapt with all my strength toward the boat. I grabbed hold of the railing, my body slamming hard into the hull, the murky water of the river churning barely a foot under my feet.

I gasped for air as Owen leaned over, grabbing my wrists and yanking hard. I pulled myself up, helping him assist me. Within seconds, I was sprawled out on the deck with Owen on his knees beside me, his chest heaving.

I ripped off my collar and looked at him, still struggling to catch my breath. "That... was... fun," I managed.

He rolled his eyes and leaned back heavily onto his hands. "You have... a weird definition... of fun."

I let out a laugh as Alejandro sailed us into the night.

CHAPTER 17

Viggo

Three days later

Arhythmic beeping caught my attention. It was high-pitched and constant, like a whining drumbeat that never changed. It was disturbing my well-deserved sleep, forcing me to rise to consciousness.

I cracked open my eyes and tried to look around the room. A sudden fit of coughing overcame me, causing me to awaken even further. Someone murmured something gentle that I couldn't quite make out. Something was pressed to my lips, and I felt cool liquid pass through them, into my mouth.

It took me a moment to realize it was water, and

when I did, I realized how dry my throat was, and how desperately I wanted a drink. I began sucking down mouthful after mouthful until the container was removed. I groaned in dismay, wanting more than I had gotten, but there was a gentle shushing, and I felt my head being lowered.

Suddenly, I was exhausted. I felt the tension drain out of me as the dark reclaimed me.

The next time the beeping woke me up, I felt more like myself. My first memory, as brief as it was, had prepared me for what to expect next.

As I peeled back my eyelids, I did so in small cracks, letting the bright light in slowly. It took an annoyingly long time, but after a while, I could make out shapes and colors. I saw the IV running from my hand, and followed the line up to a clear bag holding what looked like water, but which I knew must be a saline solution.

I inhaled a slow, shallow breath, feeling a sharp ache in my side as I did so. Looking around, I saw a woman sitting in the corner of the room, looking at some papers. I licked my lips, feeling inordinately dry again, and stared at her.

"Wa—" I tried to say, but my voice came out raw, practically silent. I tried to gather some saliva in my mouth, but there was practically none. Looking over at the woman, I coughed. She looked up, her blue eyes growing wide. "Water," I breathed, and she immediately stood, moving over to the tray beside me.

I watched as she poured water out of a yellow pitcher into a cup, and then kept a steady eye on the cup as it traveled from the tray to my mouth. I greedily drank, trails of it sluicing from the corners of my mouth.

I panted when it was finished. The woman lowered her hand, her brows drawing together in an inquisitive stare. I nodded, watching as she poured me another cup and held it to my lips.

I flexed my hands while I drank, and realized I could move my arms, if I moved slowly. My arms and legs felt heavy and weak at the same time, a languidness that could only be explained by lack of use. I slowly reached up and claimed the cup from her, and she gave me an encouraging smile and a nod.

"I'm glad to see you're recuperating so quickly, Mr. Croft," she said cheerily.

I pulled the cup away from my lips, gauging the saliva ratio in my mouth. "Who are you? Where is Violet? What do you want?"

The woman smiled and stood up. "I'm Dr. Elizabeth Tierney. Violet is downstairs. As for what I want... well... if you could just keep drinking water, then that'd be a great start."

I frowned as she poured more water into my cup. "Not who are you," I said after a long sip. "I don't care about your name. Who are you with? Am I a prisoner? I need to see Violet. Get her now."

Dr. Tierney took a step back. "Okay. I'll send a runner down to Desmond's office to let them know you're all right."

I watched her as she crossed over to the door and opened it, speaking with someone on the other side in a hushed voice. I was suspicious by nature, and looked around for anything I could use as a weapon if need be.

I toyed with the idea of pretending to go back to sleep. That way, if someone other than Violet walked in, I would know without raising any alarms. Dr. Tierney had closed the door and returned to her chair, burying her head in files and avoiding my gaze. I watched her for several minutes, still toying with the idea of faking sleep, when a whirlwind of arms, legs, dark hair, and a delightful set of gray eyes burst into the room.

I felt my face break into a smile against my own volition. Violet gave a little cry and launched herself at me. I flinched, but she pulled back short and then slowly slid her hands over my shoulders. I could feel the heat of them through the thin cotton hospital gown they had given me.

"Vi—" I said, my voice cracking.

She smiled, her eyes brimming with tears. She leaned close, bringing her forehead to mine. "Saved your life," she breathed across my face.

A smile bloomed on my lips at her quip, and I reached for her head, sliding my palm against her soft cheek. "I missed you," I whispered, dismissing the trembling in my arms.

She gave me a small, sweet smile, one that made my heart ache, and pressed her lips to the palm of my hand. "I missed you too," she croaked.

I pulled her head closer and claimed her lips in a kiss. I had no idea how long I had been in this hospital bed. I didn't know if I or my breath stank, and I didn't even know if they had shaved me.

Yet none of that mattered as soon as my lips pressed to hers. I felt her soft surrender as she leaned into me, and I kissed her like she was the air I needed to breathe.

She gave a low moan, and I slid my tongue between her lips, caressing hers with my own. If I had died right there, it would have been worth it. To feel her fingers sliding through my hair, as if she couldn't believe I was finally back in her arms.

I groaned, wanting to feel her more fully against me, remembering the scent of her skin from when she had first kissed me, but as I tugged at her, she resisted.

Slowly, tenderly, she broke the kiss, pressing smaller kisses against my lips, my jaw, and my cheeks, before resting her forehead against my own again.

"What happened?" I asked.

Violet settled a hip on the bed beside me. "Well, how much do you remember?" she asked.

I licked my lips, which had become parched yet again. Violet noticed, and immediately filled the empty cup that Dr. Tierney had left on the tray next to the bed. I reached for it, my hands shaking.

I felt Violet's eyes as they drifted to my hands. She gently used her free hand to push them away, and then leaned forward, pressing the rim of the cup to my lips. I frowned, irritated that I was as weak as a newborn kitten. I considered turning away from the cup, but I refrained because my need to drink was overpowering, and it wasn't Violet's fault I was so weak. She was just trying to help me.

I took several long pulls from the cup, nearly draining it, and then leaned back in the pillow, considering her question.

"I… was shot," I said slowly, untangling my hazy and confused recollection of what happened in the lab with the twin princesses.

Violet nodded, setting the cup back on the table with a hollow click. She peeled back the right side of my hospital gown over my shoulder, and I stared at the puckered, half-healed pink scar sitting just next to my shoulder socket, under the collarbone. An inch to the left, and it would've nicked an artery. Two inches, and it would have torn through my lungs.

Still… the wound was doing remarkably well, considering how long…

My thoughts faltered as I realized I had no idea how long I had been unconscious. Judging by the wound, much longer than I thought. I gave Violet a probing look as she pulled the fabric back up, covering the scar.

"Twenty-one days," she said, guessing the question that must be running through my mind.

I let out a slow breath, my mind trying to comprehend. "I… I don't understand," I whispered. Her face was sympathetic as she reached out to take my hand. "How could a gunshot…"

"It wasn't the gunshot, you idiot," she admonished, a small smile playing on her lips. "It was the mega dose of adrenaline. You… you caused a tear in your heart."

"Several," chimed in Dr. Tierney from behind us.

Violet pushed a lock of hair out of her face, and gave an exaggerated eye roll that only I could see. I knew she was trying to be funny, but it wasn't funny. I stared up at her, and the humor bled from her expression. Her gaze drifted down to the blanket.

"Sorry," she said.

I frowned and took a deep breath, trying to sort through the tremulous emotions I was experiencing. "What happened exactly?" I asked after a few seconds.

"They had to put you into a medical coma, to keep your heart rate low. It prevented the muscles from giving out or tearing more, and bought us some time to fetch a surgical instrument we needed to repair the tears."

My hand drifted up to touch my chest, as if reassuring myself that my heart was still beating, just inches under the skin and muscles. Violet's hand came up and settled gently over mine. I gripped a few of her fingers tightly, meeting her eyes.

"Who's they?" I asked.

Violet bit her lower lip, and had opened her mouth to respond when three things happened at once—the lights flickered and then dimmed. A red pulsating light activated over the door, and a loud klaxon poured through a speaker located in the ceiling of the room.

"Attention, attention," a robotic voice boomed. "Failure to input classified code within timeframe. Protocol three dash seven enacted. Personnel have ten minutes to comply."

I blinked and barely had time to look at Violet in confusion as the door behind her swung open and a blond-haired man I didn't recognize poked his head in.

"Violet, Desmond is on the radio—she needs you and me to report to her now."

Violet turned to the man. "Go, I'll catch up."

The man nodded back and then disappeared. The siren filled the silence between us as she swung back to me.

"Who was that?" I demanded. "What's going on?"

"That was Owen. And I'm not sure what's going on yet, but I'll go find –"

I had already started moving, pulling the blanket off my body. My legs were stiff and ached as I swung them over to the side of the bed. I was shocked at how damn weak I felt. As I placed my feet on the floor, Dr. Tierney appeared next to me, a firm hand on my chest.

"Mr. Croft, no," she said, taking a step closer to me as she noted my weakness, making it more difficult for me to stand up. I batted her hand to the side. Or rather, I attempted to—I was barely able to move her arm an inch.

"Mr. Croft," she said primly, her lips a thin line. "I spent a rather tedious six hours sealing all of those holes in your heart. Six. So, I expect you to lie down and relax, not get up too soon and destroy my hard work within minutes."

I looked at Violet, and she crossed her arms, radiating her own displeasure.

Sensing my inevitable defeat, I let out an irritated growl, swung my legs back in the bed, and flopped back on the pillows. Dr. Tierney gave me a nod and then moved back to her desk, mumbling something under her breath. I caught the word *arrogant*, and sighed, swiveling my head toward Violet.

Her face had softened slightly, and she had relaxed her shoulders.

"I'm sorry, Viggo," she said, closing the gap between us. She pressed her thumb to the lines across my forehead, massaging them. I blew out and tried to relax. The alarm bells had stopped as I had been trying to get up.

Violet gazed at me earnestly, and I mustered a smile for her. "Go," I muttered. "I'll…uh, be here when you get back."

She leaned down and kissed my lips. "Thank you. Don't worry—I'll be back soon and I promise I'll fill you in on everything."

I watched her back away, keeping her eyes on me, before she whirled around and hurried out of the door.

I heaved a sigh and looked at Dr. Tierney.

"So, how long do I have to rest?" I asked, dreading the answer.

CHAPTER 18

Violet

I burst into Desmond's office, my breathing coming in rasps. Desmond was on her handheld, talking to a blurry image. I heard a voice piping through it, but it took me a moment to register that it was Thomas.

"It's bad, Des. It looks like the Matrians rigged the support beams on the bottom level with enough explosive to collapse all the levels. This is why they haven't come—they haven't needed to."

Desmond's frown intensified. "How were they able to activate it? You told me this place didn't share a direct line with them."

"They didn't need to have a direct line—apparently there's a code that needs to be input monthly. No code was ever entered, so it triggered the protocol."

Cursing, Desmond lowered the handheld, her other hand clenched. She exhaled, then took a deep breath in, relaxing the tight muscles in her face. She slowly raised the handheld back up to her mouth and spoke with deliberate words.

"Tell me you have a way to stop this," she said.

"Plug me into the network there."

Desmond hurried over to the computer and I stepped over to where Owen was standing. His mouth was turned downward in a pensive frown.

"What's going on?" I whispered. "I feel like I missed the first part of this. The place is rigged to blow?"

Owen bobbed his head up and down a few times. "We kept asking that same question you were asking in The Green that one night: Why hasn't anyone come to do something with the base? Now we know why— they were just letting the clock on it run out."

I felt the blood drain from my face.

"I'm reading the code here, and it's bad," Thomas said. "Once the window to input the code is missed, the computer stops receiving any messages from the mainframe. There are also messages set to be sent when the detonator activates, so that they know when it went off."

Desmond placed both fists on the desk. "Thomas, I have over a thousand people here whom I cannot evacuate and a little over five minutes for you to find another solution. We are here—is there anything we can physically do to stop it?"

"I'm way ahead of you, Des—I pulled up the blueprints and schematics, and I have been isolating the electrical lines. There's a way we can stop the explosion, while simultaneously letting the detonator go off, so the powers that be will think the building has been destroyed, but it's tricky."

"Tell us what to do, Thomas," Owen said. "We'll get it done."

"You need to get to the main electrical station that's under the lowest level. There's a stairwell that leads down to it from—"

I was already moving. I snatched one of the radios from the desk and clicked it over to three as I headed toward the door. I held up three fingers as I went by, and watched as Owen grabbed another radio and followed.

I ran, knowing that there wasn't enough time to walk. I remembered the room that Thomas was describing well, although I hadn't known it was an electrical station then. But it was the only room that sat somewhere under the pit, so therefore, it was the only logical place to go. I trusted Desmond to get the details of what we needed to do, and Owen would help me to execute them.

I ran fast, only pausing long enough to open the doors. Owen quickly caught up with me, and together we entered the lowest level, our rapid footsteps clattering down the catwalk. I kept an eye on the numbers, and then took a left when I spotted the correct row.

Ahead of us, the catwalk extended to the wall where a gray door stood, barely lit by a yellow light.

I slowed as I reached the door and pulled it open. Owen darted past me down the stairwell, his boots clomping loudly. I clamored down after him. We likely had around two minutes left. We had to hope that Thomas' instructions were simple.

We made it down to the lowest landing, and Owen didn't hesitate. He threw open the door and rushed inside. Winded, we were both sweating profusely.

I held up the radio to my mouth and clicked the button. "Desmond, we're here. What do we do?"

Her response was immediate. "Find the main console—lots of buttons and levers—go around to the back and pry it open."

Owen scrambled behind the giant rectangular control box, and I heard the sound of metal bending and flexing. I staggered behind him and stared in horror at the multitude of hanging wires.

"Got it—but there are a lot of wires in here."

"Ignore them, pull out the back panel. There should be three electrical cords running through it. You need to cut the middle one, at the same time that Owen disconnects the circuit… one-seventy-one through one-seventy-eight. It's on the opposite wall."

I looked at Owen who was already pulling the panel out, pushing the bundle of dangling wires to one side. I moved over to the opposite wall and opened the gunmetal gray cover, looking at the circuit breakers. My mouth moved as I sought out the numbers.

"Got it," I called, my voice hoarse, but loud.

Owen grunted, and then shouted back, "Got mine. On one, okay?"

"Okay," I replied, wiping my sweaty hands on my pants before lifting them to the row. I assumed all seven circuits needed to be flipped at once, so I shoved the radio between my knees, allowing me use of both hands.

"Three... two... ONE!" Owen shouted. I slammed the switches down at the same time I heard the pop of electricity, followed by Owen's curse. I snatched the radio from between my legs and held it up to my mouth.

"We did it," I radioed. "Desmond—are we good?"

There was a long pause, followed by Desmond's voice, relief evident in it. "We're good. Close, though— we were thirty-six seconds from detonation... Good job."

I let out the breath I'd been holding and allowed myself to sag. I sat down hard on the floor, my legs, which had been rock solid moments ago, turning into twin columns of pure jelly. Owen grunted and slid out from the panel, his hair sticking up slightly.

I stared at him and laughter involuntarily bubbled up out of my chest. Owen gaped at me as I laughed, and then broke out into similar laughter, his eyes twinkling in the shared unexpected joy of still being alive.

We stayed there like that for a while, until we felt confident that our legs would support our long climb back to Desmond's office.

Half an hour later, Desmond's firm grip was on my hand. "Thank you, Violet," she breathed, pumping my hand an extra time.

I bit my tongue and returned her hand shake.

Since we had returned from Patrus, I had been trying to get some face to face time with Desmond to ask her why she had lied to me regarding Mr. Jenks' pills that she had promised to destroy. I knew that Owen had given her the low down, and I had sent Desmond numerous requests to talk, but they'd all been denied.

Now that I was in her office with her, I wasn't leaving until she answered my damn questions.

Desmond had relinquished her hold on my hand and turned to Owen to shake his. He smiled broadly as she pulled him in for a hug, whispering a *thank you* in his ear. Then Desmond leaned back against her desk, relaxing.

I watched her curiously as she picked up her handheld and held it up to her face. "Thomas, I've got Violet and Owen here," she said after he came online.

"Good job, you two. That was close!" Thomas said, relief thick in his voice.

Owen replied for us. "Thanks Thomas, especially on the clear instructions. How did you know what to—"

"Electronics are my specialty—besides, they didn't build it that well. I guess when they built it to explode, they never considered people might be inside who would want to stop it."

Owen and Desmond nodded in agreement, but I frowned. That seemed like a pretty big scenario to overlook. I mean... I knew that the facility was buried in The Green, but surely they had considered the possibility of a human incursion on their base. Or that maybe one day the boys would break free.

"We just need to be thankful for the lack of Matrian foresight," Desmond said. "In my day, we would have rigged that thing to be unstoppable. Clearly my successors aren't nearly as thoughtful as I am... Thomas," she went on. "I want you to dig through the blueprints and find every explosive location in the base, then send me a report on how to safely remove them. I want this place free of any advantage to them that would do us harm."

"I'm already on it, Des. I'll have it for you in three hours or less."

"Good," she replied, before hanging up.

Then she turned her attention back to Owen and me. Standing up, she inclined her head toward us. "I'll let you both know what Thomas finds, if you want to be part of the team that helps do the disconnecting. I'd understand if you didn't want to, however—you did just save us, after all. That entitles you to a little—"

"Won't be necessary," interrupted Owen, who had straightened to his full height. "It doesn't merit us to anything."

Desmond shot Owen a winning smile and nodded. "All right then. I'll send a runner for you when Thomas gets the report to me."

Owen nodded and turned at her clear dismissal, while Desmond went to sit behind the desk, her hands scrolling through various files on her handheld. Owen stopped at the door when he realized I wasn't following.

"Violet," he hissed, and I met his gaze.

"I need to have a chat with Desmond," I announced, causing Desmond to glance up at me.

"Owen, it's all right," she said. "I've… I've been putting this chat off. I'll see you later."

Owen gave us both a dubious look, but acquiesced, drawing the door closed behind him. I turned and stared down at Desmond whose mouth was drawn tight.

"I already know what you want to talk about, Violet, and I am sorry for putting you off, but—"

"How *could* you," I said through clenched teeth, cutting Desmond off.

She froze, her mouth still open to speak, and then leaned back in her chair, giving me a stern look.

"I made the decision because it was the right one to make," she said.

"We were right here in this office when you agreed—"

"We discussed it, Violet, and I told you I agreed with you *in principle*," Desmond snapped. I shot her a contemptuous look and she tossed the pen in her hand on the desk with a clatter. "I'm sorry you disagree, but the truth is that if this is the enemy's weapon, then we have to utilize it or be destroyed. It is an arms race, albeit a genetic one, and we are *losing*."

"But Solomon –"

"Solomon knew what he was doing. He knew the risks and he did it anyway. Let me ask you this—if your roles had been reversed, if you knew your partner on a mission was about to rush headlong and needlessly into death, would you try to stop him?"

"Of course I would, but that doesn't mean I'd need some super pill to do it!"

She shot me an acerbic look and shook her head. "Now you're just being stubborn. Let's imagine it's your young Mr. Croft. Only he isn't about to do something stupid—he's been hurt. He's got nearly fifty pounds of pure muscle on you—all dead weight—and the enemy is closing in. The only options are to take a pill that might drive you insane, leave him behind, or both get caught and executed. Would you do it for him?"

"Of course I would, but that doesn't mean—"

"Oh, I am quite positive he wouldn't like it, Ms. Bates. I am also quite certain he would resent it. But that doesn't change the fact that you would still do it. So while you're standing there preaching to me about what we can and cannot do, I would remind you of three things. The first is—you are no better than us. We do what we have to, to survive. The second is that you aren't part of this group. Your hesitancy to join has painted a very clear picture that as soon as your Mr. Croft is better, you will be leaving. But the last is this—I have offered you shelter, medical supplies, food… everything you need and then some. And asked for nothing in return—save the possibility of you joining a group devoted to destroying the very thing you are on the run from—and that still hasn't been enough to afford your respect. As far as I'm concerned, you are ungrateful, rude, and manipulative, and while I appreciate what you did today, it certainly doesn't merit this level of scrutiny and condescension."

I found myself speechless in the face of her passionately delivered put-down, unable to find a

response to what she was saying. My anger had gradu-
ally diminished as she was talking, the wind from my
argument evaporating.

Desmond leaned forward and snatched up her
handheld, then swiveled her chair around, presenting
me with her back in a clear and obvious dismissal.

Silently, I left, closing the door behind me with
a definitive click. Resting my back against the door,
I felt a surge of worry. I had just majorly pissed off
Desmond, and what unnerved me even more was the
deep dark blossoming of an idea that Desmond might
have been right. About everything.

CHAPTER 19

Viggo

I was deep in thought when Violet finally returned, nearly an hour and a half after she had left. She had changed clothes, and her skin was pink and her hair damp, like she had just taken a shower.

"I'm sorry," she murmured as she entered. She came to sit down on the edge of the bed. Her demeanor was different than before. She looked serious and distracted.

"What happened?" I asked, my attention turning away from my own problems and devoting itself to her.

She gave a slow blink, and then dragged her gaze back over to mine. "Do you think I'm rude? Or ungrateful?"

I frowned, unable to follow her. "No, why would you ask that?"

Violet brought her legs up and stretched out next to me, being careful not to pull on any of the leads or jostle me in any way. I made room for her anyway, shifting on the bed to give her more space. She shot me a grateful glance, and I became aware of how tired she looked.

I adjusted the pillow so that both of us could rest our heads on it, and then lay back down, my muscles trembling from the exhaustion that simple sequence of movements cost me.

She reached for my hand and threaded her fingers through mine.

"Vi... talk to me. What's wrong?"

A smile formed on her lips. "I'm... just really happy you're awake," she said. Untangling my fingers from hers, I cupped her cheek.

"Me too—although I am less than pleased with Dr. Tierney's medical advice."

"What'd she say?" Violet asked, stroking my knuckles with her thumb.

I sighed. I gently pulled my hand from hers and shifted my weight to the back of my hip, turning my head to the ceiling. "That it's going to take four to six weeks to recover my strength. Minimum."

The words came out frostier than I intended them to, but I was exceptionally frustrated by the situation.

I had only been down for twenty-odd days... and now it was going to take just as many or more to recover.

I still had no idea who these people were and where they came from—Violet had left before she could tell me. It was clear she was working with them, but was it all a ruse, or had she joined their cause?

The questions swirling in my head weren't just directed at the people who were here or the situation we were in. They were also directed at myself, and had started building since the moment Dr. Tierney announced how long it would take to get my full strength back—if I *could* get it back in the first place.

The *could* sent a burst of anger through me. I had been in my prime, capable of holding my own in a fight with someone who had super strength when I was wounded. Now what was I? A crippled ex-fighter who could only slow Violet down?

It disturbed me to no end knowing that whatever this situation was, Violet was facing it without me. Would that be our future—her racing off to some other adventure and leaving me behind?

The logical part of my mind reasoned with me. It reminded me that Violet hadn't left yet, and, gauging from her earlier quips about saving my life and securing a surgical instrument, she had actively gone out of her way to save me.

Suddenly, I was bone-weary exhausted. I rolled back toward Violet, who was looking at me in concern.

Swallowing, I shook my head.

"Don't worry about it," I urged, not wanting to disturb her with my own broken ego. What I was going through was my problem, not hers.

Trust is a powerful thing, I realized as I watched her concern morph away, replaced completely with a warm contentment. She didn't dig any deeper, just trusted my judgement that she didn't have to worry.

It made me feel even worse than before, like I was lying to her. Even though I wasn't—not really. Getting back on my feet and into fighting form was my responsibility. I just had to put in the work. And once I was back on my feet, I would feel better. Once I was able to keep up with her again, it would all work out.

I forced a smile and settled my hand on her shoulder. "So how was your day, dear?" I asked, making my voice light and teasing.

She smirked at my comment, which sent another guilty feeling through me as she began to recount the events that took place after I'd been shot. I listened as intently as I could, but soon, my eyelids became heavier and heavier, and sleep reclaimed me.

Several hours later, my eyelids fluttered open as the bed dipped and moved, jostling me. Opening my eyes, I saw Violet standing up, stretching silently.

"Wha—?" I asked, groggy and confused.

"You drifted off," she whispered. "I napped with you for a while, but I'm late meeting Tim. I'm taking him to the cafeteria for dinner."

I tried to clear the cobwebs from my head. "Do you want me to come with you?" I asked, trying to force myself into a sitting position. Every limb in my body still felt like it was asleep, even my brain. It was hard understanding what was being said, and it took my mind even longer to formulate a response.

Violet chuckled as she shook her head. "Viggo, you can barely keep your eyes open," she whispered. "Besides, walking down several flights of stairs is going against doctor's orders. You've got to build up to it. I promise I'll bring Tim to you tomorrow."

"No," I said, my mind revolting at the thought. Violet stepped back, cocking her head at me, and I realized my response had been given more vehemently than I'd wanted. "Sorry," I said sheepishly. "I just… don't want to meet the only male of your family before I can stand on my own two legs without help. You know… like a man."

Violet's eyes narrowed and she frowned. "That's a little… misogynistic."

I clenched my teeth in frustration. "That's not what I meant. I just… I want to be upright, you know?"

"I… can understand that," she said, but the

reluctant quality of her tone told me that she was just placating me. Irritated, I leaned back into the pillow, debating whether it was worth it to try to explain. I ultimately dismissed the idea, reminding myself once again: it wasn't her burden to bear.

"You're right. I'm being dumb. Of course I would love to meet your brother."

The confused look in her eyes softened to a mask of empathy. "No, you're right. I was… reading too much into the comment. I don't actually know what you're going through, but I can respect your wish to meet Tim on your own two feet. And… I just want you to know, you aren't going through this alone. I'm going to be with you every step of the way."

I really wasn't sure that I wanted Violet in the room with me while I was going through the physical therapy, seeing me struggle just to stand upright. But as I looked into her shimmering gray eyes, I couldn't muster up the words to ask her not to come. She looked so hopeful, so bright, so… optimistic.

"That'd be great," I rasped.

She beamed at me and then stooped over, planting a kiss on my forehead. "Okay, well… I'll see you tomorrow. The doc said you'll probably sleep through the night. Unless… do you want me to come back after dinner?"

I shook my head and feigned a yawn. "No. She's probably right. Enjoy your dinner with your brother, okay?"

Violet smiled again, and then let herself out, giving me a little wave as she closed the door. I held up my own hand, and then dropped it after I heard her footsteps disappear down the hall.

Sliding my hands down my face, I sank back down in the mattress and listened to the steady beeps coming from the machine connected to my heart. It would be hours before I'd sleep again.

CHAPTER 20

Viggo

The next day, Dr. Tierney arrived early in the morning—her attitude too chipper for me to do anything other than groan and demand coffee. With her were two people I had never seen before, one teenage boy, probably fifteen or sixteen, and a rounder middle-aged woman with a stern face and no-nonsense attitude.

Between the three of them, they carried several metal poles—two apiece, at various lengths. I sipped the water that Dr. Tierney handed me in lieu of coffee and watched the two strangers as they began joining the poles together by screwing one end into the other.

The boy on the floor kept shooting furtive glances at me, but I ignored them, drinking my water as if I didn't have a care in the world. After a few minutes, it became clear that what they were building was intended for me—as they wound long bits of fabric around the two long bars on the top.

They bolted the bottom ones to the floor, and then gave them a few tentative shakes before the younger boy grabbed the bars and lifted his feet off the floor, testing them under his weight. He dropped back down and gave a satisfied nod to the older woman, who ruffled his hair before shooing him out of the room.

He laughed, scampering toward the door, where he slammed into Violet as she stepped into the room. She made a sound as his shoulder connected with her, tossing her arms up to stabilize herself. There came a wet splashing sound, and I detected a familiar bitter smell.

Sitting up, I saw most of the coffee in the mug she was carrying had splashed against the doorframe and in the hall behind her, but some of it was dripping from her face as she stared at the youngster in annoyance.

"Quinn!" she snapped, sweeping the remains of the coffee from her face.

The boy cringed. "Sorry, Violet."

She thrust the now empty mug against his chest. "Please see if you can track down some more coffee," she said. She reached over and grabbed a fresh towel from the table next to her, running it over her face and hands.

"Violet," Quinn started to say, but she silenced him with a gaze, her lips drawing tight.

He sighed, his shoulders slumping. The older woman behind him who had been watching the scene unfold marched up to him and clapped him on the shoulder. "I've actually got a wee bit tucked away somewhere," she said. "I'd be more than happy to brew up some more."

Violet's expression warmed as she looked at the older woman. "Thank you, Meera... Any news on Solomon?"

The woman shook her head and swallowed. "No change. No sign."

Violet's face fell to one of sympathy, but I also detected a flash of guilt. "Just... let me know, okay?"

Meera nodded, wrapping her arm around Quinn. "I will," she promised as she pulled the lad outside.

Violet watched them go, and then turned back to me with a smile. "Hey you," she said, her voice soft.

I smiled back. "You brought me coffee?"

She chuckled. "Tried to."

"I appreciate it. Any chance there's any still on your face?"

She walked up and leaned over me. "Care to check?" she asked.

I grinned, sliding my hand around the back of her neck before pulling her down to meet my lips. There was no coffee left on her, but her lips alone were a better tonic than any cup of coffee. I immediately found myself feeling more aware—although it was only of her.

We broke the kiss after a few seconds, and she sat down on the bed next to me. "Doctor Tierney said they're going to start your physical therapy today. It's why I brought you the coffee. I figured you might want a pick-me-up."

"Ms. Bates, coffee is not recommended for Mr. Croft at this time—we need to give the scar tissue on his heart some time to heal before we start artificially stimulating it with caffeine," commented Dr. Tierney from the other side of the room.

Violet sighed and this time I laughed, causing her to smile.

"So, what are you going to do today?" I asked casually.

Violet straightened her back with a considering look. "Well, I kept my morning open so I could be here with you for this. I'm going to have lunch with Tim—I'm working with him to try to get him comfortable around larger groups of people. After that... you... some gardening... then you... maybe some cleaning... then you... and then dinner, shower, and bed—with some more you scheduled somewhere in the middle of those last three items."

I kept my face neutral, but as she described her plan I felt guilty again. She was devoting all of this time to me instead of doing whatever she wanted to do, or spending more time with her brother. It wasn't fair to her, but I didn't know how to tell her without making it seem like I was trying to get rid of her.

I wanted her to come visit me... but the thought of her watching and shouting encouragements while we did whatever pathetic exercises that Dr. Tierney was about to run me through didn't fill me with a sense of confidence. It made me feel insecure.

Violet cocked her head at me. "You okay?"

I nodded, plastering a smile on my face. "I'm okay. I'm just worried that there might be more important things you need to be doing, and I'm keeping you from them."

Violet leaned closer. "Nothing's more important than being here for you, and helping you get better," she declared, giving me another kiss.

As her mouth touched mine, I knew it was better to let it go. I didn't want her to think I was ungrateful for the support she was giving me. I just wished I could find the right words that would encourage her to let me do this alone.

"So, what exactly can we expect today, Doc?" she asked, leaping off the bed. I watched her walk, envying how she could do it so casually. The emotion caught me by surprise. I shouldn't be jealous of her ability to do something as simple as walking.

"Nothing too extreme today," the doctor said.

"We're going to work out his legs, which have suffered some mild atrophy from the duration of his coma. It's going to be a few days before we can build up to assisted walking. For today, just getting back some flexibility and mild re-strengthening."

I frowned. "We aren't going to try walking today? Then why did you have that set up?" I asked, nodding toward the makeshift handrails.

Dr. Tierney smiled at me, setting the pen she was holding down on the table. "For convenience's sake," she said, standing up. "Are you ready to get started?"

I glowered at her, until I saw the naked hope and sparkling eagerness in Violet's eyes. I swallowed my frustration and nodded.

Dr. Tierney approached the bed, Violet at her heels. The doctor grabbed my blanket and tossed it back, revealing my stupid hospital gown and my legs.

My legs looked… thinner and less muscular. Not much, but weeks of no activity had left their mark.

"All right, Mr. Croft. All I want you to do is lift your left leg off the bed and hold it for as long as you can."

Taking a deep breath, I focused on my left leg, lifting it as high as it would go. I got about a foot off the bed before my muscles began to protest the move. I gritted my teeth, straining hard, but I could only manage another inch before it was too painful. Clutching the sheets, I felt a tremor roll down my thigh and into my calf as I tried to hold it up.

I released my breath and let my leg collapse back on the mattress. I had started to sweat, which unnerved me, and I felt like that little bit of movement had drained me of more energy than I had to spare. I met Violet's gaze and then looked away, humiliated.

"That was very good, Mr. Croft," Dr. Tierney announced with a sickly sweet smile. She pulled a pen out of her pocket and grabbed the file at the end of my bed, jotting a few notes. "Five seconds is an excellent start," she added, clicking the pen. She lowered the chart and turned back to me. "Now for the other one."

I tensed my jaw and concentrated on repeating the move with my other leg. I got it slightly higher off the bed before the pain set in, but I fought it off, determined to hold it up longer. The shaking started almost immediately, but I ignored it, trying to will my leg to stay up. Just like before, however, the pain became unbearable. It fell back to the bed and I loosened, panting.

Dr. Tierney nodded again in satisfaction and scribbled another note. "Two extra seconds on that leg—it's very promising. Now, try to lift your knee up to your chest and hold it."

Aggravated, I looked at her. "Is that all we're going to be doing today? Holding my legs up?"

Still smiling, the woman crossed her arms and shot me a look. "What did you expect? Squats?"

Defeated, I slumped back into the pillows and forced myself to look at Violet. Her face had once again turned sympathetic, and as much as I cared about her, looking at her was making me angrier. I didn't want her sympathy. I wasn't even sure I wanted her here.

I forced my mind back to the task at hand. Groaning, I lifted my thigh toward my chest. I could only work it up to a forty-degree angle before the muscle spasms and discomfort started. Biting my lip, I focused on my breathing. I forced myself to breathe slowly, in and out of my nose. I was only able to hold the position for a few seconds before the pain forced me to drop my thigh.

"Excellent! And the other?"

Exhaling, I started to lift it when there was a sharp knock at the door.

Violet looked at me and then Dr. Tierney, and I relaxed my leg back on the bed, both grateful and irritated by the interruption.

"Yes?" Dr. Tierney called, turning toward the door.

The door swung open, revealing the same blond man who had called for Violet before. I thought Violet mentioned his name was Owen, but there were a few holes in her story that were a result of me falling asleep during parts of it.

"Hey Owen," Violet said cheerfully. "What's up?"

"Hey Violet," he greeted, looking slightly bashful. "I know that you slated this time for Viggo," he nodded at me as he said my name, and I held up my hand in return. "But Thomas and Desmond have that list for us, and Des is kind of in a fit to get it done sooner rather than later, so…"

"Oh," Violet said, turning back to glance at me, her face indecisive. "Uh… Sorry, Owen. Viggo takes priority right now. Ask Quinn to help you."

"Quinn," he replied flatly, looking dubious. "He's so…." And then he rolled his eyes and made an excited face, and Violet laughed.

I zeroed in on that laugh and Owen's face, a wave of jealousy crashing over me. I suddenly felt like I had the strength to get out of bed and smash my fist into his jaw, and I even started to sit up but was forestalled by Dr. Tierney's hand on my chest, as well as the pain that was still radiating in my thighs from the simple exercises.

Violet hadn't noticed, but Owen had, and he shifted nervously. "Okay, well. If you find some time later…?"

Violet nodded, her dark hair bouncing. "All right, Owen. Please be careful."

I tried to read the nuance of her voice as she said it, trying to get a feel if there was something more there, but she said it casually, as if he were a friend. Owen raised his hand and then left.

Violet turned back to me. "Ready for the next exercise?" she asked, clapping her hands together.

I frowned at her. "Who was that?" I asked, hating the tone of my voice as I said it. I was too old to be jealous like this, but I couldn't seem to be getting anything right.

Violet gave me a confused smile, and I could tell she had picked up that something was wrong. "That was Owen. He's one of the people who went with me to Patrus to get the laser for you."

The words registered, causing me to falter. "Oh. He seemed...uh, nice."

Cocking her head at me, Violet's gaze twinkled as realization dawned. I suppressed a groan. "Oh my God... you're jealous!" she announced. "Of Owen!"

I flicked my attention over to Dr. Tierney, who took a slow and exaggerated step back and walked away, her face a careful mask of neutrality.

I felt my cheeks grow hot in embarrassment.

"No," I insisted, and Violet shook her head, refuting my statement with her disbelieving gaze.

"You are! Aww, that is adorable."

I felt a flash of irritation at her adjective of choice but rolled my eyes. "Okay. I'm sorry—I did... feel... a moment of jealousy," I admitted, unable to meet her eyes. "It's just... he took you away yesterday and now he came for you again today... and I've just missed so much over the past two weeks that it's hard to take in all of these changes at once. I'm having a hard time processing."

I risked a glance at Violet and saw total understanding. She reached out to cup my cheek, her thumb stroking my stubble. "It's okay," she said. "I get it. I know it's a lot to take in, but I'm here. Okay?"

I nodded, some of my negative feelings dissipating, before my lips turned upward. "I really do appreciate it, but as I said before, if there *is* somewhere you need to be or something you need to do… then you should do it. I'll be okay here with Dr. Tierney."

Violet's eyebrows drew together and she slowly lowered her hand from my face. "You… want me to go?" she asked.

"No! Of course not. I'm not saying that at all. I just… I don't want you to waste your time—doesn't that make sense?"

Violet's frown deepened, and I sighed, my earlier frustration returning. "I didn't mean to imply that I'm not important to you," I said, picking at a loose string on my hospital gown. "I just meant that—"

"It's okay, I think I understand," Violet murmured. "I mean, I don't totally understand, but if you think I should go and help Owen, then I will."

I let out the breath I was holding and jumped on the out she was offering me. "I do. I can tell you've come to care about the people here, so if there's something you need to do to help them, then do it… you, uh, know where to find me."

The last part I added in a dry tone, and it had the desired effect of wiping away Violet's frown and getting her to chuckle. "Okay," she acquiesced, leaning forward to land a kiss on my forehead. "But if you need anything, or if you just want to see me, then—"

"I promise I will tell Dr. Tierney."

"Okay... I'll see you as soon as I'm done," she promised before leaving.

I watched her go, the smile fading from my lips, and turned to Dr. Tierney.

"Is there any way... you could... ask Violet not to come for my physical therapy appointments?" I asked with considerable effort as I met the doctor's gaze, feeling every bit the coward in that moment.

CHAPTER 21

Violet

The conversation with Viggo had been a bit odd, and I could sense there was something off with him, so retreating had seemed like the best course of action. I might have been reading too much into things—after all, he was just getting back on his feet in a manner of speaking, and had a lot of history to catch up on.

As I walked down to the next level, I tried to imagine what it would be like to be in his shoes. I wouldn't react well to all the changes either. It had to be frustrating, waking up in a place you knew next to nothing about, surrounded by and dependent on strangers.

I let out a sigh. As it stood, I didn't really know how much longer we were going to be able to stay here. I had clearly angered Desmond with my line of questioning from yesterday, and when I woke up this morning, I realized I regretted approaching her the way I did. I had been downright antagonistic toward her, when I had no right to be.

She was correct—she didn't have to conform to my ideology, just as I didn't have to conform to hers. In retrospect, I could kind of see her point about Mr. Jenks' pills and using them, but I still felt fairly certain that I wouldn't take them. Still, she had made a good point with the arms race comment, and I couldn't find fault in her logic.

I just found fault with the science behind the pill. It was emotional, pure and simple; emotional reactions didn't win battles, and they certainly wouldn't help Desmond win her war. And it was clear that she was in it to win, although how she planned to do that was still beyond me.

I was in the process of stepping through the door connecting the stairs to the second level, when the sound of running feet hurtling toward me caught my attention. I looked up and saw Quinn racing toward me, his eyes wide and feverish.

"Violet," he panted, sliding to a stop, his arms windmilling to keep him from losing his balance. Reaching out, I grabbed his shoulders and steadied him. His cheeks were flushed from exertion. He also looked afraid.

"What's wrong?" I half asked, half demanded and he pointed behind him.

"It's your brother! He's gone… crazy, tearing up the cafeteria and… hey!"

I had already pushed past him, my heart in my throat. The cafeteria was another two levels down, and I had to race through each level to get there. I shut everything off and ran, hoping that it wasn't as bad as Quinn was making it sound.

The only word I could find to describe the wreckage before me was devastation. The room was a disaster—tables knocked over and chairs shattered in an impressive yet terrifying display of anger. And in the center of it all stood a wild-eyed heaving young man with the same dark hair and gray eyes as me.

He stood over an unconscious person, his fists clenching and unclenching. Everyone else had scattered and fled, except for a few ducking down behind upturned tables. I saw Meera and Nissa—a little girl whose mother had joined up with the Liberators and then died while on a mission. They were crouching behind a counter in the kitchen area, and I carefully noted the knife in Meera's hand and the way she was looking at my brother.

This was bad.

I stepped out from the doorframe and into the room, looking at my brother.

"Hey, Tim," I said, struggling to keep my tone light and soft.

Tim looked at me, watching me warily as I moved closer to him. From the corner of my eye, I spotted Quinn dart in and move slowly toward a group of people cowering behind a table, beckoning them over. I met his glance and gave him a quick nod, approving of him getting people out, before refocusing on my brother.

He had switched his focus to Quinn, his expression dark and thunderous. I could see the tension contained in his muscles, the malicious intent in his eyes.

"Tim," I called, and he turned back to me, much to my relief. "Look at me, baby brother. It's okay. It's going to be okay. I just need you to take a step back, so I can check on Henrik."

Henrik was a defense instructor. He was older, in his late forties or early fifties, and a retired warden from Patrus. His son had married a Matrian woman and elected to move there. Henrik had gone with him, not willing to lose the last bit of his family due to political differences. His son and daughter-in-law had a baby boy, but when his only grandchild later failed the test and was taken from them... well, it hadn't been pretty. His daughter-in-law had been unable to cope with the loss of her child and committed suicide, and shortly thereafter Henrik's son followed, unable to cope with the loss of his wife and their child.

As I stared at his unconscious form at Tim's feet, I felt relieved to see that his chest was still moving, although the blood streaming from his nose and mouth wasn't very reassuring. Tim took another slow step back as I moved closer, keeping my hands up and my face calm. Kneeling, I placed two fingers on Henrik's neck. There was a steady beat there.

I nodded to Tim and gave him a reassuring smile. "He's okay, Tim, but we need to get him to the doctor. Can I ask some of the others to come help carry him? Will that be okay?"

Tim gave me a long hard stare and then nodded once. Turning back to the door, I waved over the others who were lurking just outside the doorframe.

"Slow movements," I said calmly. "Nothing fast, no aggression, okay?"

Several people crept back in and helped gather up Henrik. I kept myself between them and Tim, my gaze on Tim. "See?" I said, taking another step closer. "It's okay. No one's going to hurt you, I promise. We just need you to calm down."

Tim gave a slow blink, the anger in his face slowly draining. He shook his head, as if to clear it, and then looked around the room, his face morphing to one of confusion and horror. I winced as I watched him slowly realize what he had done during his fit.

His eyes found mine, and my heart slowly broke, seeing the unshed tears threatening to spill from them.

"Violet?" he asked so softly, the sound was barely audible.

"It's okay, Tim. It's going to be okay," I promised.

Tim took a deep shaking breath, his legs and arms trembling. He moved toward me, and I felt even more relief wash over me. It was over and done with, for now.

Just then a blur came up behind my brother; a figure leaping on his back and wrapping two arms around his neck, holding tight.

"I've got him Violet!" Quinn shouted, his head appearing from behind Tim's shoulder.

"Quinn! NO!" I yelled, but it was too late.

Tim's sad face darkened again in anger, and he roared, lashing out with his limbs. He caught me by surprise as he did, the back of his hand cracking hard and unexpectedly across my face. I staggered from the force of the blow and tripped, grunting as I fell hard on my right shoulder. I grabbed at it for a moment, waves of pain shooting through my jaw and side, before pushing myself off the floor.

I climbed to my feet in time to see Tim grab Quinn and fling him across the room. Quinn didn't go far, but I cringed at his cry of pain as he hit the flat edge of an overturned table.

I staggered over to Tim, still clutching my

shoulder. "Tim," I cried, and he whirled, his fists already moving. I ducked the first blow and sidestepped the second one, but his third punch made it through, striking me directly on my already throbbing shoulder.

I hissed in pain as I fell to one knee. Tim rose over me, like a titan about to reign hellfire down on the earth, when something came between us.

Looking up, I was shocked to see that it was Desmond.

"Desmond," I coughed, trying to struggle back to my feet in spite of the overwhelming pain I was in.

She ignored me, her focus completely on Tim. He roared at her, spittle flying everywhere, before lashing out wildly. Desmond... I couldn't begin to describe how graceful she was. She flowed like water around each blow, easily sidestepping and dodging, with minimal use of energy.

My jaw dropped as I watched her move, biding her time, waiting for the right moment to strike. When she did, it was in an unexpected way: She grabbed something from a pocket in her suit. I had just enough time to register that it was a syringe, before she pulled the cap off of it with her teeth, stepped inside my brother's guard, and jammed it into his neck, compressing the plunger.

My brother reared back, slapping one hand to his neck, and stumbled. Desmond spat the cap into her hand and recapped the needle on the syringe calmly, as if this were an everyday occurrence, before returning her focus to my brother.

Tim had sagged to his knees, gaping at her, before slumping to the ground, unconscious.

I rushed over to him, crawling through the debris, panic a thick taste in my mouth. I quickly put my fingers to his neck, and nearly cried in relief to feel his heartbeat alive under my fingertips.

I whirled on Desmond to find her already giving orders in a soft yet commanding tone.

"Have Dr. Tierney come here immediately to check on young Mr. Bates and everyone who is injured. I want statements from everyone about what happened here today within an hour. No one is to leave until I get to the bottom of this event."

Several people peeled off to follow her orders. Desmond turned, rubbing her temples lightly. When she saw me staring at her, she dropped her hands.

"Are you okay?" she asked.

I licked my lips and swallowed the excess saliva that had built up. The pain in my shoulder had faded some, and my jaw ached down to the bone, but I nodded. "I'm okay," I said, climbing ungracefully to my feet. "What did you do to my brother?"

"I gave him a sedative," she replied.

"So what, you were just carrying that around waiting for him to explode like that?" I couldn't help but ask, clenching my fists. Desmond had never hidden her compunctions about having my brother around; it was why she insisted that he be shadowed by a Liberator guard whenever he left our room.

Desmond's lips flattened to a thin line, her eyebrows almost touching her hairline. "Ms. Bates," she said, her tone clipped. "That is the second time in less than twenty-four hours that you have been disrespectful and rude to me. While it is understandable that you are upset at the moment, you would do well to remember that had I not shown up, your brother may have killed you and young Mr. Hughes over there." I looked over to where Quinn was now sitting slumped against the table, his hand clutching his stomach as his face turned an interesting shade of green.

"Now," continued Desmond, her voice dangerously low. "I understand that you have trust issues with authority figures, so allow me to answer your question. No, I have not been carrying a syringe in my pocket with the expectation of your brother losing control. I was notified that he was in a rage, and grabbed a sedative from the lab just in case."

Once again, Desmond's argument served to suck the fire out of me, leaving the remnants of a sputtering coal of embarrassment that lodged in my throat.

"Sorry," I mumbled after a few seconds.

Desmond sighed loudly and brought her hands in front of her, lacing the fingers together. "No, I'm sorry, Violet. As I said, I recognize that you have severe trust issues, and perhaps I came down a little too hard on you yesterday. I felt... bad after our conversation. I regret giving you the impression that I would have the pills destroyed, and should have perhaps notified you of my decision not to. I'm not used to having people question my orders. The circumstances that brought us together are unique, and merit special consideration in some matters."

I nodded, taken aback by her apology. "Thanks," was all I could think to say.

She placed a hand on my shoulder. "Which is why we need to talk about your brother," she said, her face grim.

I looked down at where Tim was lying on the floor. "What about him?"

Desmond gave me a steady look, and then half turned, allowing me to gaze out on the wreckage. Looking at the injured people in the room, I saw the confusion and anger in their faces.

"What do you propose?" I pressed, my heart beating painfully against my chest.

She turned back to me, a sad look on her face. "He can't be allowed to roam around the facility anymore," she said, her voice and eyes sympathetic.

I closed my eyes and felt a tear slip from under

my eyelid and fall down my cheek. I took a deep, shuddering breath, trying to resist the painful reality of what Desmond was trying to say, and nodded.

"I understand," I said, even as I hated myself for it.

CHAPTER 22

Violet

I was physically and emotionally drained as I trudged up the stairs. I had spent the last three hours doing everything I could to help clear the wreckage that my brother had caused, and it still didn't seem like I had done enough to help.

After a long discussion with Desmond, we had decided that, for the time being, my brother was to remain confined to the room downstairs that had been used for Viggo's interrogation. Tim wasn't allowed to leave without me and one other Liberator to go with him, and even then, he could only go with special permission from Desmond.

Owen and Quinn had helped me carry him downstairs, and Quinn had been kind enough to offer to go upstairs and get Samuel and the blankets Tim had been using to form his little nest on the floor. I had been surprised at his offer, and told him not to worry about it, but he insisted. Owen told me that it was because Quinn felt guilty—he had reacted to Tim's step toward me as an act of aggression, and had been trying to stop Tim from hurting me. I guessed I couldn't blame him. A part of me wanted to, though.

I had pushed that part aside—there was no blaming anyone. The reports that came in were that my brother had slipped down to grab a snack. Apparently Henrik had approached him, and said a few words to him—no one was sure what though—but apparently Tim had been smiling a little bit.

Until Henrik clapped him on the shoulder. The reports around this were murky—some people said it was a light punch, others said that Henrik was picking something off Tim's shirt. Everyone agreed that Henrik had touched him, and that's what had triggered the violent reaction in Tim.

I ran a hand over my face. Tim's condition made him physically hurt when anyone touched him. Apparently it was called synesthesia, a genetic disorder that confused the senses, and in Tim's case, made touch cause physical pain. I could just imagine what had happened to Tim, and how confused it would make him when he woke up.

Dr. Tierney had assured me I had a few hours

before that happened, which was why I was making my way back upstairs. I needed something positive at the moment, and there was only one face in the world that could make me feel better—even if it was attached to a dry sense of humor and a surly disposition.

I stepped through the door on the top level and saw Dr. Tierney closing the door to one of the patient's rooms. I raised my hand—the left one, not the right because it still hurt—and approached her. "Hey Doc. How is everyone?"

Dr. Tierney mustered up a smile. "Everyone's going to be okay," she said. Her eyes moved to where I was awkwardly cradling my shoulder. "How are you?"

I gave her a half shrug. "I didn't want to bother you. I think it's fine—it doesn't feel dislocated."

Her eyebrow arched and she looked impressed. "You've dislocated a limb before?" she inquired.

"Once, during a sparring match. My opponent slammed me against a wall to try to get me off her back. At one point... my body went left, shoulder right."

She made a face at that, and then gestured for me to follow her into one of the empty side rooms. I sat down on the gurney as she pulled her handheld out of one pocket and a small medical scanning ring out of the other. She ran the scanning ring over my shoulder, and then looked at her handheld for the results.

"How's Amber?" I asked, remembering that I had

meant to inquire about her this morning.

Dr. Tierney nodded without taking her eyes off the digital image the scan had produced. "She's much better today. Was able to keep down some food. I'll have her walking in a few days."

"And Viggo? How did his physical therapy go?"

Dr. Tierney frowned and lowered her handheld. "Violet," she said, and then hesitated.

I widened my eyes. "What is it? Is the scan okay?"

She fidgeted back and forth a few seconds and then sighed in irritation. "Mr. Croft asked me to ask you if you would stay away from his physical therapy sessions."

I suddenly felt very small and extremely confused.

"What?" I asked, needing her to repeat it.

She rolled her eyes toward the ceiling. "Before you jump off the deep end, you need to understand a few things, okay?"

"Like what?"

"Mr. Croft is… well… he's feeling pretty poorly about himself right now. He's embarrassed about all of his physical therapy, and he's—wait, where are you going?"

I had jumped off the table and was halfway to the door when she asked the question. I grabbed the door knob and threw open the door. "I'm going to get it from the source!" I shouted as I walked the short distance to Viggo's door. I threw it open and strode inside, determined to get to the bottom of this.

"What the hell, Viggo?" I exploded.

Viggo fixed his gaze on the blanket, his jaw twitching in irritation. I folded my arms over my chest and waited.

"Violet, please…" said Dr. Tierney as she arrived at the door.

Viggo shot her a glance so vicious, if he'd had any form of telepathic power, she would have died immediately.

"Oh no, don't blame her!" I said. "You put her in the middle of this. So explain to me why you don't want me to come see you while you're here!"

Viggo cleared his throat at the sound of my shouting resounding off the walls. "Could you close the door, please?" he asked, his tone tight.

Gritting my teeth, I turned around and calmly closed the door in Dr. Tierney's face. I took the moment to collect myself, taking hold of the hurt I was feeling and gently pulling it back, one deep breath at a time.

As I swung back around, I met his eyes. "I'm sorry I shouted," I said after a moment. *I'm just under a lot of stress right now.*

Viggo nodded slowly, accepting my apology. I waited for him to say something, but he was stubbornly staring at his blanket again.

"Viggo, c'mon. What is going on?"

He hesitated. "I can't have you here," he said quietly. "Not during this."

"But why?" I asked, exasperated. "I only want to help you. Support you."

"I don't want you to see me like this," he said, his voice rising as he met my gaze, his green eyes iced over.

I reeled back, confused. "Like what? Sick? Like you saw me in The Green?"

He shook his head. "That was different."

"How? How was it different?"

"Well, for one thing, you could walk right after."

I gaped at him for a moment. "I fail to understand how that connects."

Viggo made a frustrated sound in his throat. "Violet, you just... you don't understand."

"But I'm here now, so make me understand. Please, Viggo, I would do anything you ask, but you've gotta give me a reason."

"I just did," he said.

"What... is this an ego thing? Dr. Tierney said that you were feeling sensitive to this but..."

"No, Violet, it is not an *ego* thing, okay?! So just back off and give me some space!"

I recoiled at the defensiveness in his voice.

I had never heard Viggo speak like that to anyone, let alone me. He had always been cool and collected, letting his logic win out over his emotions. But the

Viggo in front of me wasn't doing any of that.

It felt like I was looking at a stranger.

And it hurt. It hurt badly.

I breathed in, my eyes growing hot. And just like that, I was mad again.

"All right," I said softly, my voice thick with emotion. "You want space? I'll give you space. You can take the whole damn base."

With that, I turned and stalked out.

CHAPTER 23

Viggo

One week later

"**N**ext leg, Mr. Croft," ordered Dr. Tierney.

I slowly exhaled, lowering my left leg down and obediently raising my right, straining to keep it off the bed. Dr. Tierney had told me that if I could hold my legs up for forty-five seconds, she would let me try to walk today, and I was sick to death of lying down.

I had been progressing in leaps and bounds this past week, and was beginning to feel more optimistic about my recovery time, but it was still frustrating. Especially since it had been a week, and Violet still hadn't come by to see me.

Not that I could blame her—I had been an unmit-
igated jerk to her. It wasn't her fault that I was having
a hard time coping with the transition after surgery.
It had just taken me a little bit to process what I was
feeling, and a lot of reminding myself that I could get
better—that I *would* get better.

Now I was more than determined: If she wouldn't
come to me, I was going to go to her. Under the power
of my own two feet.

And then I was going to make it up to her, even
if I had to apologize three hundred times a day for a
year.

The entire process had been miserable without
her. I wished I had realized it sooner, but having her
around would have made it more worthwhile. Because
while I knew I felt good at my own successes, nothing
would've beat seeing the pride in her eyes. Her happiness at my progression might even have spurred me
on faster.

My right leg started shaking but I held it steady,
waiting for the doctor to give me the go-ahead to lower it.

"And now," she announced, clicking her pen.

I lowered my leg to the bed quickly and shook
both legs back and forth, trying to ease the burn in
them. I sat up on my forearms and looked at her. "So?"

"We'll give your legs a bit of rest, and then get you

started on the rails," she announced.

I grinned in genuine pleasure. "Thanks, Doc," I said.

"Oh, don't thank me yet. I get to be there when you go walking back to Violet. I am going to enjoy that particular evisceration. I might even patch you up afterward."

She said this with a wink, but I sighed, resting back on my hands. "I know, I know. I was an arrogant, self-centered... Patrian."

"Yes, yes you were," she agreed amiably as she sashayed back to her desk.

She had been pretty vocal about reminding me of all my shortcomings, but in spite of that, I had come to like Dr. Tierney. With Violet so angry at me, I had come to rely on the doctor for information and conversation. No one else came to visit me—I had yet to even meet the mysterious Desmond who apparently led these people. I had gathered that she was supposed to be brilliant but beyond that, I knew more about the doctor, Owen, Quinn, and some girl named Amber I had yet to meet, than I knew about Desmond. She was an enigma, and I was looking forward to meeting her and getting to the heart of the matter.

After I patched things up with Violet, of course.

There was a sharp knock at the door, and Dr. Tierney went to open it. I saw Owen and an older woman with grey hair in the hallway through the window—anyone else who might be there was being blocked by the doctor's body.

The doctor spoke in a soft tone, and then stepped aside to let a young man I hadn't seen before enter. I froze when I realized he had gray eyes, just like Violet's.

Suddenly nervous, I pushed myself up to a sitting position so that I could see the boy better. He stared at me, and then stepped into the room slowly, taking care not to brush against anything. Owen and the woman stayed in the hall, and Dr. Tierney stepped into it, closing the door behind her.

I stared at the boy I was certain was Timothy Bates, unsure of what to say.

"Hello," he murmured.

"Hello," I replied. "You... you must be Tim."

Tim nodded and took a step toward me. "Sick," he said, nodding toward the machine.

It was my turn to nod. "Yes, but getting better."

"Lucky," he replied, tilting his gaze around the room.

I frowned and leaned forward. His head snapped back to me, eyes studying me intently. "Why?" he asked finally, and my frown intensified in confusion.

"Why what?"

He gave me an irritated look. "Violet—why?"

Comprehension dawned on me and I blew out.

This was... not going to be easy.

"Tim, it's… complicated," I hedged.

Tim frowned and then shook his head. "Love?"

I stalled, clueless as to how to answer the question. The feelings I felt for Violet were deep… and complicated. I didn't know where we'd stood before my little tantrum, and I was even more uncertain now.

"I… uh." I gulped. "I care a lot for your sister," I managed, and he nodded.

"Good," he replied. "Tell her."

I let out a breath and shook my head. "It's not so… simple," I replied and he shook his head.

"No. Tell her. Say sorry. It's enough."

"That's what I'm planning to do," I protested. "I'm just trying to get my feet under me so I can do it."

Tim frowned, then shook his head again, more vigorously this time. "No. Now. She's… sad."

"But I—"

"Violet talks about you," Tim said, interrupting me. "Told me stories. 'Viggo is brave, Tim. He's so good, so kind, so caring. Treats me like a person.'" Tim's eyes met mine, and I could see tears in them. "Not a person," he whispered, touching his chest with his fingers. "Monster. But you… you're… a person. She's a person. She needs you. You need her. So, now!"

I opened my mouth to reply, but the words stuck in my throat as he abruptly turned and walked out of the room. I watched as he stopped in front of the older woman. She asked him something and he nodded, holding his head high. Then the older woman flashed a glance at me, and I gaped at her... This was Desmond. The resemblance between her and Lee was too clear to me as I caught sight of her eyes.

She said something to Owen, who then left with Tim. Desmond let herself in and I settled back into my pillows, studying her.

"Mr. Croft, we haven't met yet, but I'm—"

"Desmond Bertrand," I announced for her, and she smiled, the lines beside her eyes crinkling.

"Indeed. How are you feeling?"

"Pretty good, considering I'm being taken care of by a woman whose son tried to set me up for a bombing I had no knowledge of."

Desmond frowned. "Mr. Croft, please, I've explained to Violet..."

I waved my hand. "Whatever. Regardless, you offered haven to Violet, myself, her brother, and... no, probably not Ms. Dale, and we're all awesome friends now, right?"

Desmond smirked, her eyes glistening with laughter. "I knew I'd like you," she remarked.

"Interesting thing, hindsight, huh?"

There was a flash of something behind her eyes and her face tightened. "Mr. Croft, I had no idea you and Ms. Bates were malcontents. You were just pieces to me—and unfortunately for you, you were expendable. However, given the situation, I have done my best to make amends. I hope you'll consider that the next time your patronizing streak manifests."

I narrowed my gaze at her. "You have this blunt thing down, don't you?"

"I'm not sure I follow."

"The act, right? It's bold, but then again, you've got a lot of guts."

Desmond looked unfazed under my scrutiny, and that in itself was telling. Most people who were bad liars would start to protest. But she was schooled, careful and precise. She could slip in and out of the role, but only when it suited her. It took a keen eye to pick up on the signs, but they were there.

In the way that she opened her mouth to retort before slowly closing it and forming a tight smile. In the calculating gaze that she leveled at me as she ran through the options that would be most effective on me. She was so smooth, so collected about it, it was a wonder that I had even picked up on it. But I had, although I wasn't sure what it meant yet.

"It was a pleasure to meet you, Mr. Croft. I do hope to see you up and walking soon," she said after a moment. "If you need anything, please don't hesitate to ask."

I shot her a smile that was as fake as King

Maxen's and watched her leave, calm and collected. Dr. Tierney came back in and looked at me expectantly.

"Can I get a piece of paper and a pen?" I asked.

"Of course," she replied.

CHAPTER 24

Violet

I was dangling between two thin lines, trying desperately not to wet myself as I carefully examined the explosive device in front of me. I did my best to ignore the vast darkness below, taking care to focus the flashlight on my helmet on the massive concrete pillar in front of me. The bomb removal task was taking longer than anyone had thought, but that was because of the sheer volume of explosives the Matrians had rigged the facility with.

I had been assured several times that the two lines would hold me, and that if the lead line broke, I would still have the back-up line to catch my weight. Plus, there was a man waiting on the catwalk above with the electronic winch ready to go.

To be honest, when I found out about this particular detail of the job, I had been beyond hesitant to take it. But with my brother being cold and non-communicative, and with Viggo doing… whatever it was he was doing, I needed the distraction, and this one promised hours of work, as well as a bone-jarring fear that could keep my mind off anything.

Except it wasn't really working. Even as I swung in the air, trying to pry a detonator out of the sculpted explosive, I still found my thoughts drifting to Viggo. I wasn't even angry at him anymore—not really. I was worried about him.

I had no idea how he was doing, and it bothered me. I kept trying to remind myself that he didn't want me there, but it didn't matter. I couldn't stop wondering if he was eating well, or how his exercising was going.

"Hey, Violet!" came a shout from above and I lowered my arms, tilting my head up to see Owen being lowered down slowly *face down*. A wave of vertigo hit me and I shook my head, focusing my gaze back on the wall.

"You're insane," I said, turning back to the silver pin jutting out of the mound of brown explosive clay.

"Says the girl tinkering with a bomb," he replied, coming to a stop next to me.

"What are you doing down here?" I asked as I slowly pulled the detonator pin out. I carefully wiped it off using a cloth clipped to my belt and then put it in a small bag that was attached to my harness.

"Looking for you, actually. Well, that and I came to help. But... I... uh... have some news that you really aren't going to like."

I frowned as I pulled out my knife, carefully sliding it under the soft clay-like explosive. "Maybe you shouldn't tell me when I'm playing with this crap," I said as I began to pry it from the cement.

"You need to hear about it now before you see it later."

I paused and turned toward him. "What?"

"Your brother asked to be moved back to the cells."

"What?!" I exclaimed, cringing when the sound of my voice reverberated back from the walls loudly. I waited for it to fade before turning back to Owen. "What?" I asked more softly, but twice as insistently.

Owen flinched and fidgeted on his rope line, the rope creaking ominously under his weight. I tensed, but the line continued to hold. "Before you get upset, let me remind you that it was at his request."

"Who did he ask?"

"Desmond."

My throat constricted. "Did... Did he give a reason why?"

"You're going to have to ask him that. I wasn't present at the time."

I rested my head against the rope line, trying to process the disappointment and hurt I was feeling. I didn't know why I hadn't seen this coming. Every time I tried to interact with Tim, he had been cold, distant. I knew he was trying to keep his distance because he was worried about hurting me again, but I had tried everything to convince him that I was okay.

The problem was that Tim had lost hope in himself since that day in the cafeteria. He had been making some progress—he had been speaking more, smiling more, and was even more willing to interact with people, for a short time, anyway. But since he had lost it with Henrik, his confidence had been shattered, and I didn't know how to get it back.

"I hate Mr. Jenks," I hissed suddenly, my mind zeroing in on the culprit of the wrongdoing my brother had suffered.

"That's an interesting thing to say," said Owen, and I looked up at him in surprise. I had almost forgotten he was still there; I had receded so deeply into my own thoughts.

"What do you mean?" I asked him.

"Did I ever tell you I was shot?" he said, his voice light and conversational.

I blinked, surprised at the change in topic. "Uh… no?"

"Because I was. On my first mission, actually."

"How bad?"

"It tore through my liver and ruptured my spleen."
I watched him closely, not sure of what to say or how
this related to Mr. Jenks. "The spleen I could do without," Owen went on, "but the liver... well... that's a
different story. I had to be on dialysis for days while
the doctors figured out what to do. Couldn't get a
transplant—we didn't have the equipment or a donor.
But... it turned out Matrus had developed a simple
cure."

"The bio implant?" I replied and he smiled.

"Yeah. Stem cells that could be attached and pro-
grammed to repair damaged flesh. Can't be used on
certain organs, like the heart, lungs, or brain, but it was
a... miracle cure for lack of a better word. Desmond
got it for me."

I still felt confused. "Why are you telling me this?"

"Do you know who developed it?"

I shook my head.

"Mr. Jenks."

"Oh," I murmured.

"Yeah, *oh*. It's kind of a crappy feeling, knowing
that the one person who is responsible for destroying so many loved ones is ultimately the person who
saved my life."

His reply swirled in my mind as I tried to make
sense of it all. "Why are you telling me this?" I asked
again.

"You want to blame Mr. Jenks for your brother,

and I get that—he did some bad stuff to him. But Violet... no person is ever the villain in their own mind. They're just people who got confused between point A and point B."

His point was clear now, and I spent some time considering it in silence, continuing my job of prying the substance off the wall. Owen worked quietly behind me, and then chuckled suddenly.

"What?" I asked as the sticky stuff finally came off with a wet sucking noise. I carefully smashed it into a ball and then placed it in another bag.

"I was just thinking that it's too bad he isn't around—I bet we could've kidnapped him and made him make some sort of miracle drug to help the boys."

His words rattled around in my head, and then I felt a lightbulb switch on.

"Maybe not him..." I said thoughtfully.

Owen shot me a curious look, but I was already on the radio requesting to be brought back up. I clipped the radio back to my belt and looked at Owen, already starting to rise. "Thanks for the idea," I called. "I'll tell you about it later."

An hour later, I was pacing in front of Desmond's office, waiting for her to finish her meeting. Inside the office, a man I had never seen before was shaking

Desmond's hand. He had come in from The Green a few hours ago—which had the entire group buzzing. There were mentions of the name Dobin whispered in hushed tones—not that I had been paying much attention; my mind was focused on the vial in my hand and the implications it might have for Tim, Solomon, and the rest of the boys.

The door swung open and the strange man stepped out. I froze in the middle of my pacing, my booted foot landing heavily on the floor, making a dull sound. The man turned his head toward me and stared at me with a heavy gaze, his dark eyes glittering.

He was in his late thirties, but he was fit—not bulky, but in shape. He was taller than me by about four inches, and his dark hair was shaved close to his head. White was beginning to bleed through at his temples. He wore a beard that was closely trimmed, and his mouth was turned down in what appeared to be a perpetual frown.

The two of us stared at each other. I was distinctly uncomfortable with his scrutiny of me, but something about how he looked at me warned me to keep my gaze on him. My instincts were telling me that this was a dangerous man, one capable of deep violence. Like many predators, he seemed like he would respond to weakness, so my only call was to be calm and display a casual confidence.

I felt the seconds march by as we regarded each

other. It took everything not to exhale in relief as he turned away, heading for the door. I watched him closely as he opened it and stepped through. I kept my gaze on the door until it had closed.

Then I exhaled. Turning my eyes back to Desmond, I could see her standing in front of the glass, her arms crossed and her eyes watching me. They surveyed me up and down, seemingly assessing my posture. I straightened my spine and met her gaze evenly.

We hadn't talked since the incident in the cafeteria, but I didn't get the sense she was angry with me—just busy. However, I really wanted her to make time for me. She waved her hand for me to enter and I sprang forward, eager to share my idea.

"What can I do for you, Violet?" she asked, and I crossed the room, hurriedly setting the vial of pills on her desk.

She frowned in confusion. "What's this?"

I dropped down in a chair and leaned forward. "It's Benuxupane," I said, rubbing my hands together.

She narrowed her eyes at the pills, considering them. "Why are you showing me this?" she asked.

"I know that Lee must have told you about them, what they did?"

"He told me the intention—suppressing emotions. I fail to see how—" She paused, and I saw the realization dawning in her eyes.

"I think that, somehow, King Maxen found out about the flaws in Mr. Jenks' process," I said eagerly, scooting forward in the chair until I was a few inches short of falling. "I'm not sure how—maybe he also got some of the classified documents. Anyway, instead of wasting the time to perfect the process, he was going to replicate it, and use the Benuxupane to counter the effects."

Desmond looked dubious. "How could you know that?" she asked.

"I don't. But it's the only reason I could come up with for their development. It makes sense though, right?"

She leaned back with a thoughtful expression. "It's an interesting theory, but why are you telling me this now?"

"To be honest, I kind of forgot that I still had the Benuxupane. I only just remembered, but... it has the potential to help the boys, right?"

Desmond licked her lips. "Maybe," she hedged. "It's certainly worth giving this to the scientists and having them run some tests."

A sense of relief washed over me. "Thank you, Desmond," I said. I moved to stand up, but she cleared her throat and I stalled before slowly lowering myself back down.

"I have to admit, I did not expect this conversation from you when I saw you outside. I expected...

anger in light of your brother's decision."

I settled back in the chair, trying to formulate a response. After a moment, I leaned forward again. "It's not your fault regarding Tim," I said. "He probably asked you because he knew I would be opposed to his decision."

"I see. And now?'

I shrugged, uncertain of what to say. "I'm not happy, but as long as you promise he's there of his own volition, I can't argue with you about it."

"Hm," Desmond muttered. "Well, I hope you're onto something with the Benuxupane, Violet. I so desperately want to get those boys out of here. I don't like being in the snake pit longer than I have to be."

I nodded in total understanding. I didn't like living under the uncertainty of a Matrian attack. Even with Thomas assuring us that they thought the base was destroyed—that didn't stop them from sending someone out on foot to confirm.

"I guess what I'm trying to say is… thank you for the polite discourse this time," Desmond said.

I gave a small laugh. "Least I could do, I guess. I am… sorry… for being such a pain."

She nodded seriously, then smirked. "To be honest, you remind me a lot of myself," she said, and I blinked, taken aback. "It's a good thing," she assured me. "I had a similar drive and tenacity… plus a certain attitude about authority figures. It took years to smooth out the rough edges. It's been so long that now, I find I've become the very thing I rebelled against in my youth."

"You're not that bad."

She gave me a scolding look and I sat back from the heat of it. "Okay," I corrected myself, "so maybe you are, but... I can try to meet you halfway, at least."

Curiosity glistened in her eyes. "So, you and your Mr. Croft have decided to stay with us?"

I bit my lower lip and shifted. "I don't know about Viggo, but I'm certainly considering it."

She drummed her fingers on the desk and then nodded. "I think your Mr. Croft is unlikely to want to stay. I got the distinct impression when I met with him today that he doesn't really like me."

"No, Viggo makes everyone feel that way when he first meets them," I said, and she gave me a polite smile.

"I see," she said, doubt thick in her voice. I dropped the subject. I did not want to talk about Viggo. "Well, I'll let you know what they say about this," she said, shaking the little vial of Benuxupane on the desk, and I rose at the dismissal.

"Thanks," I said before turning to go.

I had made it all the way back to my room when I ran into Dr. Tierney, who was sliding a note under my door.

"Is he okay?" I spoke up, and she gave a little yelp,

jumping a foot in the air.

"You scared me," she accused, pressing her hand against her heart and breathing heavily.

"Sorry," I said with a laugh. "So, what was that?" I asked, nodding my head toward the door.

She frowned and shook her head. "Read it yourself," she said, bristling. "I am not your drama coordinator, I'm a doctor for crying out loud!"

I smirked as she stormed off, and then, opening the door, I bent down to scoop the envelope off the floor. Without preamble, I opened the top and slid out the note.

Good for one arrogant, pig-headed, selfish Patrian. Redeemable in Room 3 of hospital floor.

A grin split my face as I folded the letter and slid it into my pocket, heading upstairs.

It seemed my pig-headed Patrian was ready to talk.

CHAPTER 25

Viggo

I was turning the page of a book that Dr. Tierney had given me to help pass the time when the door swung open and Violet stepped in, her face an impassive mask. I smiled at her, but the smile quickly faded under her cool demeanor.

"You, uh… got my message?" I dared to ask.

In response, her hand slid into the pocket of her pants and pulled out a familiar piece of paper. I shifted on the bed, watching her closely as she looked at the letter and then back to me.

"What if I don't want an arrogant, pig-headed, selfish Patrian?" she asked, cocking her head to one side.

I ignored the chill that ran up my spine,

reminding myself that she was still there, still talking to me. "Were you looking for something else?" I asked, picking invisible lint off the blanket.

"How about an… egotistical jerk? Do you have one of those?"

I met her glance with a non-committal shrug. "Maybe," I said idly.

"How about an inconsiderate male?"

"Oh, fresh out, I'm afraid," I replied, and I saw a trace of a smile forming on her lips, striking hope into my heart.

"How about a hot mess? Got one of those for me?"

I grinned, unable to stop myself. "Always, for you," I replied, and she laughed, practically throwing herself on top of me. I spread my arms, catching her, relieved beyond words just to hold her. I smoothed my hand over her hair, keeping her close.

"I'm sorry," I whispered into her ear, and she snuggled closer.

"You'd better be, you jerk," she whispered back, and my smile grew even larger.

"I missed you," I said, nuzzling the top of her head, and she let out a breath against my neck.

"I missed you, too," she sighed. "Oaf," she added.

After a while, she slowly pulled herself away and looked down at me. The sight of her lit-up silver eyes glowing with humor and adoration made it feel as if I was floating. When she looked at me like that, it made everything fade away until only the two of us remained.

I felt myself softening, and finally, that small voice that had been in the back of my mind the past week roared to the forefront, reminding me that Violet had gone through hell to save me. She wouldn't do that unless she cared. And I had chased her off.

I felt guilty all over again, and I started to look away when she grabbed my jaw. "Nuh-uh," she said, shaking her head. "You owe me an explanation. So talk—what was with the dismissal?"

I hesitated. I had been carefully planning what I was going to say during our week apart, but now, looking at her, I wasn't sure I could find the right words, and I was afraid that if I didn't, it would chase her off again.

I felt her hand slide into mine and squeeze gently. "Vi... I just felt like... I couldn't keep up with you. I felt weak and... impotent. It made me worry about the future and my part in yours. I didn't like the idea that I was holding you back. If we were on the run... the only thing I could possibly do to keep you safe is catch a bullet for you."

She frowned, squeezing my hand tighter. "You big dumb idiot," she said, shaking her head. "You're always worried about what you can give to me, or how you can help me... but it doesn't work like that:

We're a team, and sometimes you need help just as much as I do. So keep your Patrian-indoctrinated testosterone out of our relationship, please and thank you."

I laughed in surprise at her words, and then pulled her back in for a hug, one that, I was pleased to note, she returned.

When we broke apart again, Violet managed to look happy and sad at the same time. Reaching out, I touched her face. "What's wrong?" I asked.

I listened as she explained what had gone down with her brother, and how he had opted to return to his cell. I recalled his words earlier today, and frowned.

"Violet, how many boys are there?" I asked.

"Over a thousand. There are fifty-five rows, each row containing twenty-six cells."

I did the math in my head and gaped at her. "*Each one* has a boy?"

Her eyes drifted to the blanket, her mouth twisting downward. "No. Some of the boys... they died in their cells. Most from self-inflicted wounds, but a few starved themselves. I guess... I guess their suffering was too much for them to handle." I grimaced at the news, my heart contracting.

"That's why I took the Benuxupane to Desmond this morning," she added after a minute. "I didn't think about it until today, but maybe it could help them contain these volatile reactions."

I listened intently, but the idea of drugging them seemed wrong to me. These were boys taken at a young age and told there was something wrong with them, and then subjugated to experimentation on their DNA. They didn't need more experimental drugs... they needed discipline and camaraderie. They needed each other, and people to teach them.

"You're thinking of something clever, aren't you?" she said, studying my face intensely, her words more of a statement then a question.

"I... I don't think giving the boys medication is the right solution," I said.

"What do you mean?"

"I mean... medication isn't really what they ultimately need. What they need is discipline, and the opportunity to learn how to socialize again."

Violet's eyes drifted upward, apparently in deep thought as she processed my words. I waited patiently for her response. "What are you proposing?" she asked finally.

"These boys are cooped up. They have been for a long time. In a cell, barely big enough to even exercise in. Children naturally have more energy than adults, and when they are unable to vent it, they start to throw tantrums or get upset. What happens after that, though? They still have energy, with no way to expend it."

Violet nodded slowly, and I pressed on. "We've got to get the boys out of their cells and into mandatory exercise. Break them down—not like they have been before, but in a way that gives them a goal. A collective goal. Have the ones who are more stable help the ones who aren't. Help them rely on each other—after all, only they know what they're going through—we don't. We don't even have the words to help them, but if we can get them to start helping each other..." I trailed off, and Violet picked up the thread, excitement heavy in her voice.

"Then they will start to improve!"

I shrugged. "It's worth a try."

"I think it's a lot more than that. I know that when I was in martial arts classes, I felt closer to my classmates than anyone else, excluding my family. That's really clever, Viggo! Much better than my idea."

I started to reply, before I realized she had bounced off the bed and was halfway across the room. "Where are you going?" I asked, and she cast a beatific smile over her shoulder.

"I'm going to see if Desmond has time to hear your idea," she called as she walked out the door.

I frowned and opened my mouth to protest, but Violet was already gone.

An hour later, Violet was sitting in the chair, watching Desmond's face closely as I explained my idea. Desmond listened attentively to me as I spoke, and I kept a careful eye on her. After I finished, I waited patiently, curious as to how she would react.

Desmond's eyes shifted back and forth between us, consideration on her face. After a moment, she smiled. "There is a lot of merit in your suggestion, Mr. Croft, and I would love it if you took the lead on this. I'd like you to start off with a small group of children—the ones deemed the least dangerous—and send me a daily update. Are you amenable to that, Mr. Croft?"

I eyed her warily, surprised at her rapid agreement. Every inflection of her voice, every change in her face, seemed genuine, and I was beginning to doubt my earlier assessment of her. I had no true reason to doubt her intentions, yet I still found myself feeling guarded and suspicious.

"It is, with two conditions," I said after a pause. I felt Violet's gaze on me, but I kept my attention on Desmond, watching her reactions closely.

She gave a small amused smile, but her eyes were wary. "And what would those be?"

"The first is that Tim is in the first group."

Violet beamed at me, joy lighting up her eyes.

"He can be," Desmond said. "What is your second condition?"

I braced myself before stating, "I want Melissa Dale to help me."

Immediately, dark shadows flooded into Desmond's eyes, and her entire face tightened. "No," she said flatly, her tone low and lethal. "She is not permitted to leave her cell without my permission, and I am not granting it."

I crossed my arms. "I find your reaction to her confusing," I remarked. "After all, she did kill one of your enemies. Regardless of what her status was at the time, if there was anybody who ever needed a second chance, it would be her. Why do you distrust her so much?"

Desmond's mouth twisted in disgust. "Did you forget that she is a spy of Matrus? The instant we give her any freedom, she will use it to try to find a way to escape. If she manages that, she'll bring the entire force of the Matrian wardens here, and the queen will probably assign some of her advanced sisters here. You nearly died the last time a princess came around. Are you so eager to face them again?"

"Did you forget that you were also a spy of Matrus?" I shot back, and she frowned, a crease forming between her eyebrows.

"It's not the same. I changed. My loyalties changed when my son was taken."

"And hers changed when she pulled the trigger and killed a princess," Violet interjected.

Desmond stared at her, then closed her eyes. I could see her warring with indecision, her internal debate playing out in the way she moved and remained quiet. Violet and I exchanged glances while Desmond breathed steadily.

She held that position until she cracked her eyes open. "All right," she conceded through tight teeth. "I will allow Ms. Dale out of her cell, only when there is training. When she is not training, she is back in her cell, and when she is not in her cell, she is in chains. This is non-negotiable, and the only time I will offer this deal. What do you say?"

I shrugged and looked at Violet, who also shrugged. "It sounds good to me," I said, looking back at Desmond and giving her a broad smile.

She narrowed her gaze at me, and then smiled back. "Good," she said cheerily. "Now, I understand you're in recovery, Mr. Croft, but you'll need to get started quickly. Please send me a list of what you need and your overall plan when you get a chance today. I'm giving you a month before we review the results and decide to proceed."

"A month isn't enough time to—" I started to argue, when Violet cut in over me.

"A month will be fine. I'm sure we'll have some positive feedback by then." I glanced at her from the corner of my eye, and she met my gaze with an encouraging expression.

I nodded, following her lead.

"All right, you two," Desmond said, glancing at her watch. "It's time for me to move on... Enjoy the rest of your day."

And, without further preamble, Desmond walked out.

Watching her walk away, I still felt unsettled by her, but only had a vague feeling to support it.

More than once as I was speaking, I had felt like Desmond had been on the verge of denying all of my requests until Violet chimed in. It was odd—could it have been because I was a Patrian? I knew that Desmond had recruited Patrians, but maybe she just didn't know how to interact with them well.

I turned to Violet, feeling baffled. "I don't think she likes me very much," I said after a moment.

Violet smirked.

"What?"

"Nothing," she said with a laugh. "It's just that she said the same thing about you."

I furrowed my brows. "I guess it was the fact that I antagonized her when I first met her."

"What did you say?" she asked.

I shot her a grin. "I called her gutsy for acting so blunt," I responded cockily.

"That does sound like you," Violet replied.

"A devilishly good interrogator?"

She shook her head. "Paranoid is a word that

could be used," she said.

"Hm... I prefer cautious myself."

"Suspicious?" Violet suggested.

"How about vigilant?"

"Disbelieving in a good thing?"

"Could we go with attentive instead? I think disbelieving sends out the wrong message."

"Fair enough," Violet conceded. "Listen... I know you have your reasons for not trusting her, and I get that. Oh, believe me I do. I was hard on her, too... Granted... I kept quiet until after the mission to get your laser, but I've gotten under her skin a few times."

"Really?" I asked. "Over what?"

She gave a little shrug. "Philosophical ideas, mainly. But I have to say... I kind of like her now. She's very... reasonable? I don't know what word to use, but she did keep her promise to help you, and that earned her some trust points in my book."

"Do I have any trust points in your book?" I asked.

Violet narrowed her eyes.

"Barely," she replied dryly and I chuckled, pulling her into my arms yet again.

"Did I tell you I walked today?" I whispered into her ear. She leaned back, her face glowing with pride.

"You did not," she stated.

I nodded. "Three whole steps before my legs gave out."

She pressed her nose to mine. "Guess that means you've got to make it to five steps before you earn a kiss from me," she whispered, a mischievous smile playing on her lips.

"Oh really?" I said, widening my eyes. "Well... challenge accepted."

CHAPTER 26

Violet

I sat with my knees to my chest and my arms wrapped around them, watching intently as Viggo led the group of boys in the drill. The last week and a half had been a blur of activity: Viggo had taken the time to focus solely on getting stronger and preparing his training program for the boys, and I had been with him every step of the way. Today was his first day of training, as well as his first day walking all the way down six flights of stairs. I had been concerned, but Viggo had paced himself, and we took scheduled breaks. We were actually going to be staying in one of the interrogation rooms for an indefinite period of time, until Viggo was good enough to make it up and down the stairs once a day.

I was proud of the progress he had made in the past eleven days. He didn't complain, not once, and he was more reasonable with his expectations. But what made me the proudest was when he actually asked me to stop ahead of our scheduled break. It was a sign that his male-driven ego was taking a backseat, which made me feel closer to him than before.

I watched him as he sat in a circle with the boys, trying to engage them in conversation. He was asking them what their names were and where they were from. Some of the boys were too shy or nervous to answer, their eyes wide as they stared at the much larger male in front of them in fear and awe. Yet Viggo wasn't dissuaded in the face of their timidity—he kept his voice calm and even. I smiled as Tim spoke up, introducing himself to everyone, eliciting an encouraging nod from Viggo. After Tim, more boys started speaking up, earning a praising smile, a proud nod, or a congratulation for their bravery.

Once they were finished, Viggo announced, "That was very good." I was pleased to see some of the boys blushing. "My name is Viggo Croft, and I was born in Patrus. I served as a warden for King Maxen, but if I had been born in Matrus and subjected to the test, I would have failed it like you. Sometimes life isn't fair like that, but I want to help you."

"I'm sure you can't help us," declared one boy, his eyes and posture that of pure hostility. He was around thirteen or fourteen, and stout for his age. As he spoke, I was reminded that the trauma of isolation had affected the boys differently. Tim was exceptionally quiet and slow to articulate, like he had locked away a part of his mind in order to survive. There were several like him, and there were also those who had regressed so far, they were downright catatonic. And then there were boys like this one, who could speak in full, confident sentences.

Viggo looked at the boy and knitted his brows. "Why do you say that?"

The boy scowled and looked around for support, but none of the other boys offered any.

Viggo looked at the others. "Come on," he encouraged. "You have every right to speak up if you feel the same way Cody does."

Cody blinked in surprise as Viggo called him by name. I was impressed as well—I didn't know if I could have remembered his name either, but then again, Viggo had spent a good chunk of his recovery time vetting candidates for the first batch of boys, so I wasn't too surprised that he had memorized their names beforehand.

One of the other boys spoke up, shifting nervously. "The people… the Liberators said they would help us, but we've been waiting for a long time for them to do anything, and all they do is send strangers to try to talk to us."

I frowned—several of the Liberators had taken it upon themselves to try to visit the boys, to remind them they weren't alone, but I hadn't realized that weeks of it had begun to grate on the boys.

"What makes you any different?" Cody asked Viggo loudly, and I saw several boys agree.

Viggo met Cody's gaze steadily. "You have to decide that for yourself, Cody. But I'd like you to give me a chance. I think this might have a lot of potential to help you, if you let it. And, at the very least, you get out of your cell for a day."

Cody looked unconvinced, but backed down. Viggo looked around the circle. "Anyone else have any concerns?"

The boys shook their heads in unison, and he smiled. "Then let's go over the rules, shall we?"

There was a flurry of head movement around the circle, but they all seemed willing to hear him out.

"Now, I know what you're thinking: Rules are awful," Viggo went on. "However, if this is going to work, we have to follow them. All of us, even me. The first rule is simple—Wait."

The boys began whispering to each other, their confusion evident.

Viggo held up a hand and the whispers died down. "See? You didn't wait," he said, and some of the boys chuckled.

"I understand that one of the side-effects of what

happened to you is intense feelings of anger or fear that make you do things you don't necessarily want to do. When that happens, whether it is wanting to hurt someone or run away, I want you to wait before you do it."

The whispers started again, and Viggo let them run on for a moment. One boy stood up and the noise died.

"What do we do after we wait?" he asked in a reed-thin voice.

"I'm glad you asked, Matthew," Viggo said, gesturing for him to sit back down. "Because after you wait, you need to go to the second rule to decide what to do next. That rule is: Look to your brothers."

Again, there was a flurry of whispers and confused looks.

"Look to your brothers, meaning each other," Viggo clarified. "If the other boys aren't reacting the same way as you, then the emotions you are feeling were triggered by your condition. Hopefully, that will help you to calm down, and think about what made you feel that way."

Another boy, who looked far more confident than Matthew, asked, "What good is that going to do?"

"Excellent question, Saul," Viggo said, and the boy nodded and waited for Viggo's answer. "You have to learn to rely on each other. Right now, your emotions aren't in your control, and that scares people. If you ever want to live a normal life again, you have to be able to keep your emotions in check."

"It's not so easy," shouted Cody, his face going red. "You're normal! We're freaks."

"You're not freaks," said Viggo quickly, his voice thundering out loudly, cutting off the boys' conversation before it started. "You're not," he repeated, meeting their collective gaze. "You're still human beings, worthy of respect and admiration. But you have to earn it, and you never will, unless you have the courage to fight back—not just against those who hurt you, but against yourselves."

Several boys nodded, and Cody once again backed off.

I suppressed a smile.

"Now, the last rule just builds on the other two—talk about it. Whatever emotion you are feeling in the moment, you have to try to describe it, and explain what made you feel that way. It will help you identify the things that make you angry or scared, and then help you face them on your own terms."

Silence fell upon the group as the boys considered Viggo's words. One of the boys, Matthew, asked nervously, "Do you really think we can do it?"

I bit my lip, seeing the raw, naked hope in his eyes as he stared at Viggo.

"Shut up, Matthew," Cody hissed, rising to his feet. "Of course we can't—he's just setting us up to fail.

Besides—he's not so tough. Watch!"

I was leaping to my feet when the boy took three running steps and jumped into the air, his fist drawn back to strike. Fear exploded in my chest—Viggo was barely out of the hospital and in no condition to fight an enhanced boy.

Except, as I looked at Viggo, my heart pounding hard, I saw that he was calm and collected. He watched the boy flying through the air toward him, and then moved a few feet to the side. The boy slammed hard into the sand, and Viggo moved swiftly again, reaching out to grab him by the wrist and yank it out from under him. The boy, unbalanced by Viggo's quick move, fell face first into the sand with a small sound, and Viggo moved over to him, placing a knee in the middle of his back, holding him firmly in place.

Viggo turned to the others, his expression calm and even. "Part of your training will include martial arts. I know that you are stronger and faster than most people, but without these classes, you'll never be able to control it, and that will get you or someone you care about hurt."

"What if we… break the rules?" Tim asked.

"Good question," Viggo said, backing off from Cody and helping the boy to his feet. "I want you to understand that I don't expect perfection starting out. That being said, if you break the rules three times, you'll be suspended from the program indefinitely, and have to be part of the last group to go through. The choice is yours." He turned to Cody who was now eyeing him warily. "Thank you for the demonstration, Cody. I appreciate your help."

At this, Cody looked confused, and I grinned, settling myself back down on the floor.

That move with Cody was ingenious. Viggo had undermined the boy's power by acting like it had been planned while simultaneously allowing him to save face among his peers. I watched as Cody trudged back, the other boys congratulating him on helping Viggo, and my smile grew wider.

Whatever Viggo was doing, so far it seemed to be working. I watched as he organized the boys into teams, explaining that their first task was to get the ball in the middle of the room. They weren't allowed to touch anyone else except their own team members, and they had to race to be the first one to touch it. They also weren't allowed to use the same technique twice.

I listened intently as Viggo continued talking to the boys. He had designed several tasks that required teamwork and problem-solving. After this, it was a lesson, followed by another task, followed by another lesson.

I stood up, prepared to go over to congratulate him on a good start, when I spotted Desmond striding toward me, looking like she wanted to talk.

"What a remarkable start your man has had with these boys," she announced as she arrived.

I nodded, feeling immensely proud of Viggo. "How long have you been watching?" I asked.

"Since the beginning, but I was tucked off in one of the side rooms. I didn't want to interfere. Honestly, I didn't know what to expect from this idea, but so far, I am impressed. The potential for it… is really quite remarkable." There was a note of praise in her voice, and something else—something I couldn't quite place.

"Does that mean you're going to hold off on the Benuxupane for now?"

Desmond hesitated. "Actually, that's what I wanted to tell you—I discovered a stockpile of Benuxupane. It's in the same area that you raided for Viggo's cure. I've authorized a team to go after it."

"Oh… Isn't that risky? It's only been a few weeks since the facility was hit… hell, we blew up a warehouse. Wouldn't security be increased?"

Desmond held up a hand. "I've considered this, of course, and I think the team can pull it off."

"But Viggo and his program—"

"Will continue, uninterrupted," Desmond said and I wondered if she could appreciate the irony of her interrupting me with that statement. "And just for your edification, I spoke with Mr. Croft and told him his month started today… I wanted to tell you about the Benuxupane because of what happened after we implemented the other pills. I figured you would want to be informed. But until I am sure that Mr. Croft's program is effective and can be replicated and sustained, I need to have a backup plan in place. I want you to know that I am rooting for your friend's method to work. I don't like the idea of exposing the boys to another experimental drug if I don't have to."

I found it interesting that she shared similar concerns about the Benuxupane as Viggo did.

I turned my gaze back to the boys. "So… uh, how goes the war effort?" I asked, only half-joking.

Desmond gave me a look from the corner of her eye and then leaned back with a contemplative expression. "I know you think we can't do this, Violet," she said.

I saw no point in denying it—it *was* what I thought. "Of course I don't. We're so few, and Matrus is too massive. Not to mention, if you start something in Matrus, it won't be too long before Patrus finds a way to join the fight—probably with the goal of claiming Matrus as its own. I know things are bad now… but could you imagine if Patrus was in charge of everything?"

Desmond laughed. "Violet," she said. "First of all, I appreciate that you are now saying 'we' as opposed to 'you.' That's a very positive step, in my mind, that you consider yourself a part of us. But also… that is such a harsh approach to starting a war, and haphazard. You need to look at the bigger picture."

I stared at her—that was the big picture, as far as I was concerned. "What do you mean?" I asked.

Desmond leaned closer to me, sliding her hands into her pockets. "Imagine you are a mouse. You're walking around, doing mouse things, when you freeze. You realize that in your wanderings, you've stumbled into a clearing, where a massive snake is looking at you like you're lunch. And then you hear a noise behind you, and you realize another massive snake is looking at you like it wants to eat you, too. What do you do?"

I tilted my gaze up to the roof, trying to puzzle through Desmond's scenario. She liked it when people figured things out for themselves, but this time, I didn't have any idea what she was getting at. After a minute, I gave up.

"I don't know—what do you do?"

Desmond stood to her full height. "You get the two snakes to fight each other," she announced. "And once they are embroiled in a war, you find your other mouse friends to watch and wait. It doesn't matter who wins, because once one is gone and the other one is wounded, you and your mice friends can swoop in and kill the last snake."

With that, she smiled and walked away.

I was frozen, watching her back, her words playing havoc on my mind. It didn't take much to understand what she was getting at—she was planning on forcing a conflict between Matrus and Patrus, and then moving in afterward to claim what was left.

I felt conflicted. On the one hand, it was a cruel move, one that would leave innocent people caught in the middle. On the other hand... Desmond had demonstrated to me several times the tough calls a leader had to make for the good of her people. As I stared out at the boys, her words weighed heavily on me—which people were the right people to back? Those that lived blindly in the system, accepting it as divine scripture, or the people who had suffered at the hands of the very same system?

I spent a long time watching Viggo with the boys without paying much attention. My mind was alive with circular logic, trying to decide if I agreed with Desmond or not.

CHAPTER 27

Viggo

I was just coming out of the shower in the locker room to the side of the playground when Violet came in. I was wearing nothing but a towel, but for once, Violet didn't pay any notice, which only indicated her current state of mind. She was upset.

She had stayed with me all day, watching me with the boys. I had also noticed Desmond and her chatting a few minutes after my icebreaker lesson, their heads bent in a private conversation. Afterward, Violet had seemed… preoccupied. I had to repeat orders several times, seeing as I still hadn't gotten the chance to ask Ms. Dale to help me. Desmond wouldn't allow her to come to me—if I wanted Ms. Dale's help, I had to go to her.

Violet would call me paranoid, but I still had my suspicions about Desmond, and her reticence to allow Ms. Dale out was troublesome. I was also worried that Violet was beginning to buy into what Desmond was telling her. Desmond had obviously earned some measure of Violet's respect in the past month, but it was… disconcerting. I still didn't know exactly what she stood for.

Violet sat down on a bench with her back to me, folding her hands and resting her elbows on her knees. Her gaze was fixated on the floor. Although her talk with Desmond had happened hours ago, I could still see the aftermath in her posture. There was an inner turmoil raging within her.

Sensing this was my chance to discover what was going on, I sat down next to her. She turned her head to face me, a small and hopeful smile lighting up her eyes for a few brief seconds before bleeding back into the darkness she was battling.

"Hey," I said.

"Hey," she murmured.

"I, uh, saw you and Desmond earlier," I commented.

Violet released a sigh and nodded. "She was impressed with your first day," she said. "I was too, for the record."

I couldn't miss the pride in her eyes. "It was a good day," I agreed.

"What you did with Cody was genius," she added.

I shrugged. "It seemed like the right thing to do. The kid is strong though."

Her expression morphed to concern. "Are you hurt? I hope you didn't overexert yourself."

I shook my head and laughed. "Relax. I didn't hurt myself. It's just hard not being in fighting form. If that kid had been smarter..." I trailed off, not needing to remind myself that working with these boys came with risk.

Violet leaned into me, resting her head against my shoulder. "Good," she said. "Did you remember to do those exercises this morning?"

I rolled my eyes. "Yes, mother."

Violet gave me a shove with her shoulder, forcing a laugh out of me.

"I mean, yes, dear," I said.

She smiled ruefully, before crossing her eyes and sticking her tongue out at me. I was still amazed by her ability to turn the most unladylike actions into adorable mannerisms.

She gently pushed me back and looked deep into my eyes. "Speaking of parenthood... I have to say, I never saw you as the fatherly type, but..."

I froze, a small tremor of alarm rolling through me that was purely an instinctual reflex, one shared by most men when women started throwing words around like children and father.

Violet, being Violet, didn't miss the flash of panic on my face and broke out giggling. "I wasn't trying to imply *that*," she gasped. "We're not even in a position in our relationship to discuss that."

"Oh, we have a relationship?" I asked with a teasing note in my own voice, and she flushed bright red, her eyes seeking refuge in anything but my gaze.

"I… well…" she mumbled, and I reached over, putting a finger under her chin and forcing her to meet my gaze.

"Relax. I was just teasing. I know we haven't discussed it yet, but that's the great thing with us—we don't have to. We just know."

She blushed prettily and I pushed back a lock of her hair, feeling inordinately pleased that our talk was going so well, if not a little off the rails.

"So, what else did you talk about?" I asked, nudging her with my shoulder.

Violet's smile faded and she stood up, shoving her hands into her pockets and looking around. I watched as she crossed the room and turned, pressing her back against a locker.

"Desmond told me her plans for starting this war," she said finally.

I scooted forward on the bench and rested my elbows on my knees. "And?"

Violet blew out. "She wants to… engineer a war between Patrus and Matrus, and then move in once it's done."

I stood up, alarmed. "What, that's crazy!"

She rocked back and forth on her feet, her gaze on the grey and white tiled floor. "I thought that too… but…"

"What? There's no but, Violet. She's planning on murdering people!"

Violet made a frustrated sound. "I know that, Viggo. But I don't think it's that simple. Not everything is that black and white."

I stared at her, surprised. "How can you say that? All those people who would be caught in the middle of…"

"You don't think I've thought of that?" she snapped. "My cousin is in Patrus. My aunt and uncle—my family. People who still cared about me when everyone else thought I was worthless. Believe me, I'm thinking about it."

I didn't know about Violet's family, other than her brother. My own family was nonexistent—my mother had died when I was young, and my father shortly after I finished the academy. We hadn't been particularly close, and I had been an only child. Still… I had people like Alejandro in my life. He had taken me in, despite my rough edges.

Refocusing on the conversation, I felt a strange sensation, almost like vertigo, that things were spiraling out of control. "I just don't understand what there is to think about," I said. "There's right and then there's wrong."

Violet shot me an incredulous look that slowly became jaded. She gave a slow, bitter laugh and shook her head. "They don't even play by the rules," she said, pulling her right hand out of her pocket to point at a wall. "Look at what they've built. Think about what they've done. They know what they've done here is wrong. That's why they've tried to bury it!"

"So we bring it to light. Let the people decide."

"In Matrus. And when the civil war starts, what do you think happens? Patrus steps in and tries to crush all of Matrus. You cannot tell me that is the right play. There are not enough words in the English language to convince me of that."

I reeled back, quite shocked at her vehemence. "But, Violet… it's drastic. The loss of life alone would be catastrophic."

She swallowed, seeming to back down from her outburst and collect herself. She nodded. "It is. But… I don't really see any other way of bringing down this system. The Liberators number in the hundreds, Viggo. Not thousands. They are a small force who are just actively trying to make things right. To get their government to stop lying and using them and the people they care about. That's what they're fighting for. Not to kill people, but to save them."

I shook my head. My knees were feeling

wobbly—strangely more from this conversation than the exertion of the day. "It's not our fight," I said, after a pause. "We should just go."

Violet tsked, crossing her arms. "How can you say that? You just started with the boys, and now you want to abandon them? And *where* would we go, knowing what we know and having seen what we've seen?"

I opened my mouth, and then shut it, uncertain of how to even formulate a response to her questions. They were valid. I certainly did not want to abandon the boys. I also didn't know where we could go that would be safe. Our options were extremely limited.

But I still didn't want to condone Desmond's plan. "I will never agree that starting a war between the two is the right course of action. I may not have a better plan, but this one... Violet, it crosses the line."

Violet gave a sad toss of her head, her jaw tight. "Maybe it does," she said. "But they crossed the line first."

With that, she pushed herself off the locker and headed for the door. "I'll bring supper to our room," she murmured as she stepped out. Not looking back, she closed the door between us.

I watched her go, and then shook my head and placed my face in my hands, feeling lost and confused.

After a few minutes, I remembered I was on the verge of being late to meet with Ms. Dale. I doubted Desmond would be understanding of my tardiness. It wouldn't surprise me if she just flat out refused to let me see her if I wasn't punctual.

I dressed slowly, not by choice, but by the sheer fact that I was still struggling to do simple actions in any timely manner. It only added to my frustration, however, and I reminded myself that I needed to take it slow. It was hard, though—I couldn't believe what Violet had been saying.

I gingerly pushed myself off the bench, using my arms to help me get into a standing position. I took slow, careful steps to the door and threw it open, moving slowly but deliberately to the stairs.

As I walked, I kept my head down and avoided eye contact with everyone. People must have sensed my mood, because I was aware that there seemed to be a five-foot bubble around me that was keeping people out of my way.

Which was good; solitude suited my current mood. That wasn't entirely accurate, as there was one person I wanted to talk to more than anything. But seeing as she and I were in the middle of an argument, I would have to settle for the next best thing.

Or worse, depending on my point of view.

My footsteps were quiet on the catwalk as I slowly moved down the aisle, leaning heavily on the rail for support. I had to stop more than a few times to catch my breath and rest my legs, but slowly and surely, I kept going. At this time of night, the catwalks were mostly deserted, which I was grateful for.

I made my way down several rows before taking a left turn down one and moving halfway along it. The ramp was already extended, waiting for me, and a guard was standing at the end of it. I nodded to him as I slowly moved forward.

"Sorry I'm late," I said to him. "I'm still injured so I'm a bit slow."

The guard was an older man whom I vaguely recognized from one of Violet's many introductions. He had a cut on his head that was still healing, and it took me a second to remember this was Henrik, the man who had accidentally triggered Violet's brother.

"Henrik, right?"

The older man nodded, giving me a tight smile behind his beard. "Indeed I am."

I nodded to the cell. "She giving you any trouble?"

Henrik chuckled and shook his head. "Nah. She's all right. I just wish…" he faltered, and I tilted my head to one side.

"What?" I asked.

Henrik waved a hand and shook his head. "Never mind. Not my place. You're free to go in, Mr. Croft."

I hesitated, torn between curiosity and going inside. After a moment, I chose to head inside, clapping Henrik on the shoulder as I passed by—I couldn't make a man talk if he didn't want to.

I slowly moved up the ramp, taking my sweet

time, and then ducked into the room, practically col-
lapsing on the floor as I landed. Sighing, I massaged
my thighs and looked at Ms. Dale.

She had raised her head from where her arms
were folded on her knees and gave me a surprised
look.

"Patrian," she said in greeting, and for some reason, I smiled.

"Matrian," I replied, and she smiled in return.

"What brings you to my humble abode?" she
asked.

I reached into my pocket and dug out my handheld, tossing it to her. She caught it, her gaze narrow-
ing on me before turning to the patient files I had
loaded on there.

"What's this?" she asked, scrolling through the
files.

"A job, if you want to get out of this cell," I said.

Ms. Dale scoffed and shook her head, tossing the
handheld back to me. "Desmond would never agree
to that," she announced.

I frowned. "So you know Desmond well, huh?"

She shot me a contemplative look. "You could say
that. Did she really give you permission to let me out
of this cage?"

I shrugged. "Kind of—you'll still be in chains and
have an armed escort at all times, but yeah."

She scoffed again ruefully. "Interesting. How did

you get her to agree to it, and why did you ask for me?"

I rolled my lips between my teeth, rubbing the stubble on my jaw while I contemplated her question. "It wasn't easy, but Violet helped convince her. And I asked for you, because I think I can trust you. I want you to help me train these boys."

Ms. Dale rolled her eyes and shook her head. "I'm not going to do that. If it were girls, maybe, but boys?"

I shot a sharp look at her, suddenly feeling extremely angry. "Really, Melissa? You're going to tow Matrian lines right now? Do I need to remind you of our little conversation in that torture chamber, before I pumped myself with adrenaline?"

Ms. Dale paled and shook her head, but I pressed on, my anger getting the better of me. "Maybe I should go get Violet, and tell her about your role in selecting her brother as a candidate for this place. How you personally rigged his test for certain failure."

I knew I should feel bad about holding this over her, but to be honest, I was still bitter about it, and the need to hide it from Violet. When Ms. Dale had confessed this to me during our private meeting soon after we first arrived in the facility, she had done so out of a sense of guilt, at learning from the twins what this facility was. I saw her guilt, which was why I had to keep it from Violet. She would probably kill Ms. Dale without thinking about it, and while I'd understand her fury, I also had to remind myself that she had killed someone to keep Violet safe. It was the only reason I was still keeping Ms. Dale's secret, but that didn't mean I couldn't use it to extort her.

She darted forward and her hand reached out, striking me hard across the face. "How dare you," she hissed. "I was doing what I had been ordered to do—test Violet's loyalty to Matrus, to see if she was spy material. I didn't know she would react the way that she did, and I certainly didn't understand the full scope of what went on in this facility."

I rubbed my cheek from where she had struck me and met her gaze. "You know, you're in a rare position to actually do something to make up for all of the wrongs you have caused these boys. I suggest you take it."

She settled back on her rear, folding her legs in front of her. I watched her scowl lessen as her anger drained, and she lowered her head until her chin almost touched her collarbone.

I waited.

"How do you do it?" she asked suddenly, looking back up at me.

I frowned, not following her meaning.

"How do you... I don't know... always see things in the right light? Why is your moral compass so much better than mine?"

I widened my eyes. "I, uh, don't know. Honestly...

sometimes I find myself wondering if it is so easy," I replied, my mind drifting back to the argument with Violet. "Even Violet, she..." My voice trailed off, and I immediately regretting mentioning Violet's name. I wasn't in the mood to talk about her with Ms. Dale—not yet. But it was too late.

Ms. Dale's expression had turned curious. "So, this... *wondering* of yours has something to do with Ms. Bates?"

I saw no choice but to nod.

Ms. Dale leaned back. "Well, I'm not a relationship counselor, Mr. Croft... Take it up with her."

I snorted. "First of all, *Melissa*, I would never come to you for dating advice. Secondly, it's more than just Violet... It's about Desmond. And... how... Violet is taking to her ideas."

There was a flash of something across Ms. Dale's face, so fast and imperceptible that I would've missed it, had it not been for our interrogation session after arriving at the facility.

"You know something," I accused.

"I really hate that you can read me so well," she muttered. "But you're right. And if Desmond Bertrand has her hooks in Violet, things are about to get incredibly dangerous for you."

"What do you mean?"

Ms. Dale wet her lower lip. "I know you don't think much of me, but believe me when I say that

Desmond is far more insidious."

"How do you know that?"

She gave me a dark smile. "Because I was once her pupil, Mr. Croft."

I blinked and leaned back, absorbing that tidbit of information. "I see."

Ms. Dale scoffed and rubbed her fingers together. "No, you really don't. Desmond…" She shook her head. "I… I can't explain it."

I shot her a look and she raised her arms in frustration. "It's been decades since I thought she died… Now she's up here, running a rebel faction? She might not even be the same person she used to be," she said.

"What kind of person was she?"

Ms. Dale leaned forward, running the palms of her hand over her pants. "Desmond had this way of making you think, *believe*, that you were special. She could make you forget parts of yourself, and you don't even realize that they're missing until, suddenly, you've crossed a line you would never have crossed otherwise. She was like a virus, one that… gave you what you wanted, made you see what you wanted to see, while slowly manipulating you into a position that gave her the best advantage. She used to prey on vulnerability, using it to get you to do something that fulfilled her agenda, and then discarded you when you become of no further use. But Viggo—Mr. Croft— that was over twenty years ago. I have no idea who she is now, because in all honesty, the Desmond Bertrand I knew would never have betrayed Matrus."

I frowned again. "Are you saying that she's changed?"

Ms. Dale gave a shrug. "I'm saying I don't know who she is now."

I blew out a breath and cracked my neck before we both fell into silence. Eventually I murmured, "Well, let's dwell on that later. For now... can I expect you tomorrow?"

Ms. Dale looked at me and nodded slowly. "Sure," she replied and I smiled.

I stood up and inclined my head to her. "Let me know if there's anything you need, all right? I'll make sure it gets brought down to you."

I moved through the door, pausing as I heard her soft *thank you* follow me out of the room. I turned around, offered her another smile, and then hit the button to close the door, sealing her inside.

CHAPTER 28

Violet

I felt awful. It had been forty-eight hours since my argument with Viggo, and we still hadn't spoken about it. A part of me regretted how adamantly I had come down on him. Actually, all of me regretted it. Yet a part of me still felt upset that he hadn't at least considered the other side of the argument.

Living together had been... difficult. We barely spoke more than two words to each other, and it felt like everything we did was behind a veiled stand-off. It was frustrating. I had opened my mouth at least half a dozen times to bring it up, but each time I did, I reminded myself that Viggo had already made it clear to me that he wouldn't change his mind.

It wasn't as if I hadn't considered the same things

he had. I still had a family in Patrus, like I'd told him. I remembered the girl, Josefine, from Merrymount. I thought of Mrs. Connelly, the kind old woman at the orphanage who had taken Tim and me in after our mother died, and all the other kids she looked after.

Face after face flashed in my mind's eye, reminding me that Matrus and Patrus weren't just ideals founded on misandry and misogyny—they were people. And in war, it was the people who suffered, not the ideals.

I knew Desmond's plan involved a lot of collateral death, and it weighed heavily on me, threatening to further taint my soul with the dark stain of blood. I kept asking myself how could I support her in such a plan. There had to be a better way, one that didn't involve killing the remnants of humanity, and I really believed that the Liberators should be above that. They were supposed to be freeing the people of the lies fed to them by the government, not getting them killed.

But then cold hard reality set in, and I was forced to realize an uncomfortable truth: There was no good way to fix this problem without a regime change, and there weren't many ways of making that happen. Viggo's idea was too optimistic and left Matrus exposed to violence from Patrus. People would die, despite best intentions. Desmond faced the body count head on, acknowledging the toll her method would take, and pushing forward anyway. I couldn't see a third option that would marry the two ideas, and it bothered me.

I rubbed my forehead and stepped through the doorframe that separated me from the training room. Viggo had been up for hours. Desmond had selected the next batch of boys to start training, and the new schedule had sent him into a scramble, trying to come up with how to make it work. He came up with a system where the boys from the first group taught the second group what they had learned, making them responsible for the new group. Today was a trial run, and I was looking forward to seeing how it went.

I leaned against a wall at the back and watched Viggo as he monitored the training and taught his own lessons for the day.

My mind drifted toward the oncoming night and I closed my eyes, dreading it for what it had become. At first, sharing a room with Viggo had been an exciting prospect, to say the least, but now… with this rift between us? I just longed for him to pull me into his arms and reassure me that we were all right. Without that, I felt anxious and barely slept. I hated it.

Viggo wasn't faring much better, given the bags under his eyes. He was sitting with several of the boys, engaging them in conversation. His green eyes flicked over to me, and I bit my lower lip, meeting his gaze. I held my breath, searching for some indication that he was willing to talk to me, or that he recognized I was there to talk, but then his eyes moved away and back to the circle.

I frowned, a moment of insecurity coming over me. Then I set it aside and squared my shoulders, determined to see this conversation happen. I reminded myself that he was with the boys, and they had to take priority. We were adults, and they needed stability, so it was important for them to see that he was there for them. I could wait for him to finish—I had finished all of my scheduled duties for the day, actually exchanging a few of the better jobs for some less-than-pleasing ones so I could have the whole afternoon off to make sure Viggo knew I wanted to talk to him.

With a renewed sense of purpose, I sat down and watched. A collective sound of laughter rose to my right and I turned toward it. I spotted Tim with a group of boys.

They were all participating in an exercise that involved them working together to get a ball that was dangling from the ceiling, probably eight feet over their heads. I watched as two of them locked arms, forming a square with their wrists and hands. They bent their knees and braced themselves, before shouting encouragingly at Tim.

Tim backed up a few paces, and then launched himself at the boys, his face and eyes bright with excitement, his hair whipping wildly around his face as his legs churned, kicking up gobs of sand in his wake.

He leapt, one foot landing perfectly on the other two boys' interlocked wrists, and they heaved. My heart dropped into the pit of my stomach as he flew through the air, his arms reaching out for the ball. He snatched it quickly and then landed in the sand, rolling once and coming back to his feet.

Laughing, he spun the ball on his finger before tossing it at one of the others. With a lazy speed, the other boy casually snatched it out of the air and then dropped it to the ground, kicking it to a third boy. The five boys kicked the ball back and forth, and for a moment, I teared up, seeing my brother in a new and beautiful light.

He was happy and playing, like he deserved to be. I watched as Viggo waded through the boys, a genuine smile on his face as he congratulated them. He held up a hand to Tim, who high-fived him enthusiastically.

In that moment, I felt my problem with Viggo melt away, as I watched my brother's beaming face. He had done something magnificent with the boys, and I was so proud of them all. The sight alone was enough to remind me of something: For all of their differences and flaws, Matrian and Patrian citizens cared about one thing—the future for their children.

That was where Desmond's plan failed and where Viggo's idea succeeded. As optimistic and foolhardy as it was, it allowed people the chance to choose. Hers was artificial, manufacturing finely crafted bullets with no gunpowder. His focused on the positive nature of humanity. Hers presupposed that there was no positive aspect to humanity.

Watching Viggo, I felt infinitely more positive about the conversation that would follow. I kept my eyes on him, waiting for a free moment to pull him aside and make up.

He was walking across the field to where one of the boys was sprawled out in the sand. I watched him approach, his long legs steady and strong as he made his way across the sand.

"What's going on, guys?" he asked, pulling up short in front of the group.

One of the boys looked over to where the boy in the sand was starting to sit up, an angry expression on his face. "He fell," he announced, squaring his shoulders.

Viggo shot him a look, and then looked at the boy in the sand. "Is that true?" he asked.

The boy wiped sand off his face as he glared at the older boy who had spoken. "No! He pushed me."

"I see. Colin—did you push Jacob?"

Colin—the boy who had spoken first—glared at Jacob, his face going scarlet. "Yes, but only because he's a baby!" he shouted.

Viggo cleared his throat, and everyone focused on him. "Colin—Jacob is your brother."

"No, my brother is in Matrus," Colin argued, folding his little arms over his chest. "And he doesn't care about me—no one cares about me."

"Interesting. Why do you feel that way, Colin?" Viggo asked.

"Because they left us up here to have those stupid doctors experiment on us," he practically screamed.

"That's why you think your family doesn't care about you. But what about the other boys in your unit? What makes you think they don't care about you?"

Colin opened his mouth and then hesitated, indecision and confusion marching all over his young face.

Viggo went to one knee in the sand in front of Colin. He was very careful not to touch him, but his face was earnest as he spoke more quietly and directly to Colin. After a few minutes, the little boy scrubbed his eyes, and then went over to where Jacob was standing, holding out his hand.

Jacob accepted it, and the other three boys who had been watching warily closed in on them, whooping and hollering loudly. Colin's face split into a smile, and I smiled too, feeling my heart lighten on seeing that moment of joy on his face.

Just then, I heard a sharp voice. Ms. Dale. She should have looked less imposing with the chains on her wrists and feet and the faded bruises on her arms and face, but she didn't. She strode amongst them with her usual commanding attitude, excess chains dragging slightly behind her. The chains were at least loose to give her more movement during training.

She gave her orders calmly, explained the instructions easily, and commanded the boys' attention for drills. Viggo had asked her to start the boys with basic martial arts training, and she had accepted. I actually had no idea of the entirety of the conversation that took place between them, but Ms. Dale was playing nice, and making a real effort to help the boys.

I hadn't really interacted with her since the night she and I killed the princesses, and I was beginning to regret not being more insistent with Desmond about going to see her before. At the time, I had just been so angry, and a part of me had blamed Ms. Dale for what happened with Viggo, in spite of everything she had done to help.

A heavy hand fell on my shoulder, scattering my thoughts. Looking up, it was Owen.

"Hey, Owen. What do you think so far?"

He grinned and nodded enthusiastically. "This is great. I asked Desmond to sign me up as an instructor, but alas, I have a mission coming up in the next couple of weeks, so I'm on standby. I was here to see if you wanted to train though."

I considered it, but shook my head. "Nah. I'm staying here for Viggo. We need to... talk."

Owen pouted playfully and then nodded. "Yeah... heard some rumors that you guys maybe had a fight."

I rolled my eyes. "No matter where you go, some-body is always in your business."

Chuckling, Owen squatted down next to me. "True story. Do you want to talk about it?"

"No. I'm here to make up anyway, so unless Viggo is super mad at me, which I doubt, then I think it'll be fine."

"What'd you fight about?" he inquired.

"What've you heard?" I countered, and he laughed good-naturedly.

"Fair enough, none of my business. But listen... he's not the jealous type, is he?"

As he asked, his gaze drifted over to Viggo. I fol-lowed his line of sight, and noticed Viggo staring at us intently, his green eyes flashing. I laughed, and then covered my mouth when the boys around us turned to look, waving them off.

"Afraid of Viggo?" I teased Owen.

"Terrified might also be an understatement," he declared, shooting me an over-exaggerated wide-eyed face. I chuckled again.

"Well, don't worry. I'll put in a good word for you when I make up with him tonight."

Owen shook his head, practically vibrating with how much he didn't want me to do that. "Oh no. Don't do that. You start saying nice things about me, and he's gonna find me and kill me."

I snorted. "All right, I'll talk about what a pain in

the ass you are, and how cowardly you are."

"Good," he smirked.

"You'd better get out of here before he gets mad," I said.

"Thanks for having my back," Owen said before he winked and strode away.

I turned back to see Viggo looking at me again and when I met his eyes, he cast a small smile my way. I dared smirk back as I placed my chin on my knees. Our talk couldn't come soon enough.

CHAPTER 29

Viggo

I walked up to where Violet had been sitting, torn between wanting to pull her into my arms and wanting to maintain the distance between us for fear of another fight. She had been patiently waiting for me though, which had to mean something.

We locked eyes as she noticed my approach, slowly picking herself up off the floor with a calm expression. I felt a glimmer of hope slip through my feelings of foreboding.

"Viggo," she blurted, taking a step toward me. "I… was wondering if we could talk."

I gave her a considering look. "I'd like that," I said.

She held out her hand to me and I took it gingerly, allowing her to guide me back to our room. It was slow, painstaking, and way too quiet, but once we were there, I sat down on our nest on the floor and rubbed my legs.

Her eyes took in my action. "How have you been feeling?"

I nodded. "Good. It's taking longer and longer before I feel the need to sit down, so that's something. It's so frustrating, though."

"And… your chest?"

I nodded again, my hand rubbing the area on my ribcage. "Not so sore anymore. Just the legs."

She sat down in front of me, crossing her legs under her. "Listen… about the other day," she said, her eyes on her hands. "I took some time to think about it and… I think you're right. I just… needed time, I guess."

I stared at her. "Are you sure?"

Violet smiled gently. "Of course I am. I forgot to… take in the motivations of the speaker, I guess. Desmond wants to win… you want to be fair. And I think your way is the better way."

I allowed the smile that had been threatening to form on my lips to come to life, and waved her over with my hand. "Come here," I said, and she crawled over to me, until she was inches in front of me. I reached out and gripped her gently by her shoulders. I stared deep into her eyes, and then let out a sigh of relief, crushing her to me and holding her tight. I gave her a long moment to collect herself as her chest heaved. I also gave myself a long moment to just feel her against me.

Then I guided her to a sitting position next to me. I angled my body toward hers until our knees touched. I kept her hands firmly in my own, not wanting to release them just yet.

"So, what do you want to do?" I asked.

"I… I don't know," she answered, with an air of tired frustration.

"I get it. It's hard pissing off the only friends we've got at the moment," I said.

"I've talked to Desmond about these kinds of things before, and it hasn't always ended the way I wanted it to. I doubt this will either."

"So, what are you thinking?"

She pressed her lips together and shook her head, blowing out her breath. After a minute, she turned her gaze to mine and raised an eyebrow. "What are your thoughts?"

I ran through the options in my head. "Well, we can confront her or we can leave."

"We can't leave," she said. "Not with those boys. You're doing fantastic work with them… I don't want to take that away from them, do you?"

"No," I replied immediately. "But then that means we should confront her."

"A part of me wishes I had just… I don't know…

found another way to save your life. Demanded that they made you stable and then delivered you to Patrus so that you could get healed up faster."

I leaned over and cupped her cheeks in my hands. "Violet, no. You're not at fault for this. I mean… how could you have known that she was willing to go to these lengths? You did what you had to do to help the people you care about. It's what I love best about you."

I froze at the words tumbling out of my mouth. I had just admitted that I loved her, which hadn't been my intention. In point of fact, short of a few stolen kisses, we had never discussed what was between us. There was no label that felt applicable in our situation, not that we had even talked about labeling what we had in the first place.

I felt a wave of insecurity rush through me. I had no idea how she would react to this news, and I felt a pang of doubt at her dumbfounded expression.

Until a smile lit up her eyes, causing them to shine in that peculiar way that reminded me of mercury. Her mouth curled up as she reached out with gentle fingers to trace the lines of my face.

"You… love me?" she asked, her heart in her eyes and a teasing quality in her voice.

I felt my expression softening as I nodded. "Of course I do. Think I'd give up my homeland for just anyone?"

She laughed loudly, and I stooped down to lay a

gentle kiss on her forehead. As soon as my lips tasted her skin, something in me shifted slightly, and I felt a sudden need to taste her more deeply.

I pushed her insistently, sliding her down the wall while simultaneously stretching myself halfway onto her. Rolling over on my side with my leg thrown over hers, a growl escaped my throat as my desire for her overpowered me. For anyone else, I was a man of deep control, but with Violet, my hold over myself was tenuous at best. With everything that had happened the last few days... I was fighting off a desperate and primal need to have her. And I was losing.

I stared down at her. Her face was tilted toward mine, angled for the kiss she seemed to sense coming. Her hands were on my shoulders, and I could feel the insistent press of them through my clothes. Bending down, I slid my hands over her hips and jerked her up slightly against me, savoring the feeling of her weight in my hands.

She gave a little sound of surprise as I did this, and then relaxed her legs slightly, allowing my knee to fall between them. I took her invitation, sliding my hips over hers as I settled more deeply into the cradle of her thighs, and she moaned. She lifted both of her legs and wrapped them around my waist, drawing our most intimate parts together until only a barrier of fabric separated us. I groaned, resting my forehead against hers. Our lips still hadn't touched, and I kept

my mouth millimeters from hers, our breaths mingling. Wrapping her legs around me was an entirely
innocent move on her part, but it was like throwing gasoline on a raging fire that was barely being
controlled.

She shifted her hips, unaware of the effect her
squirming was having on me. It took every ounce of
self-control for me to not give her an intimate lesson
on the ways of men and women right then and there. I
knew she wouldn't protest—if anything, she was hungry for it too, given the erratic and enthusiastic movements of her body.

But she also looked vulnerable beneath the haze
of her own desire, and that was enough for me to beat
back the ravenous hunger I had for her. For now. I
was going to have to marry the girl, and soon, before
I would allow myself a taste of what she had to offer.

Because even though Violet would laugh at me
for saying it, I was still respectful enough to want to
do things in the proper fashion. I wanted us married,
and I wanted our wedding night. It was what we both
deserved.

Still, it didn't stop me from pressing myself down
onto her, pinning her hips with my own. I savored the
look on her face at the small press of pleasure, and
took advantage of her parted lips. It was a kiss of wildfire, spreading a slick and insistent heat that threatened to consume both of us. Violet trembled under

my hands as I kissed her, my tongue teasing her own.

She gave an insistent moan, her tongue rising to the challenge, and I growled approvingly in my throat, pulling her tighter against me. I was not gentle, but neither was she, as our two tongues battled each other. Violet tried to roll her hips against mine in an ancient rhythm that was timeless, and I felt sweat forming on my brow at her insistent little cries.

I was pushing her too far too quickly. With the exception of her fiery, passionate kiss in my cabin months ago, I had never felt so close to giving in to my desires for her. My fingers pressed deep into the soft curve of her rear, and she moaned in response, shredding my already fraying self-control.

With another frustrated growl, I pulled my head away from her and rolled off of her, not stopping until my back was against the wall, hoping the distance would help me regain control and focus.

I watched her warily, sucking in deep breaths of air. Her gaze was unfocused as she stared up at the ceiling, as if she didn't trust her own ability to move to a seated position. Her breathing was coming in fast pants, just like mine.

After several long moments, she turned her head toward me and gave a laugh. "We should fight more often," she suggested wryly.

I pushed a hand through my hair, still struggling with my own control. "Later," I announced, giving her a small smile. "After we decide what to do about this situation."

She nodded, her mouth returning to a flat line. She smoothed her hands over her clothes and then sat up, turning to face me. "Right," she murmured.

"So…" I drew a deep breath and swallowed. "Talk with Desmond about her plan?"

"Right. Probably better to do it in the morning," she said.

I nodded. "Right," I drawled, and she narrowed her eyes at me.

"Sorry. A little distracted. I think… I'm going to take a walk," she announced, rising to her feet.

I gave her a cocky smile. "Afraid to be alone with me?"

"No. Just, uh, cautious," she retorted, her hand on the door.

I smiled, inordinately happy that we had made up. "Oh yeah? Prove it," I said, knowing I was potentially starting up the flame again. She froze, her back to me and then twisted round.

"Arrogant Patrian," she spat.

"Impetuous Matrian," I replied.

She came back in and folded over at the waist to press a swift and—thankfully—chaste kiss to my lips. "I'll be back in a little while," she said.

"And I'll be waiting," I replied huskily, watching her disappear into the hall.

CHAPTER 30

Violet

Two weeks later

I was becoming more and more frustrated with Desmond, and was beginning to think that she was purposefully pushing us aside. I had requested to have a meeting with her twelve days ago, and since then, it had been scheduled, rescheduled, and then pushed back six times.

I had taken the first two cancellations at face value—one time there was an op that ran into a problem during a mission, and Desmond needed to be there to problem solve. The second time, there was a food shortage due to a waylaid shipment that required her undivided attention.

But when they had started to stack up, I sat down with Viggo and suggested that we were being pushed back intentionally. Viggo had urged patience, and I had agreed, but now, with this latest cancellation, I was angry.

I threw open the door to our room and slammed it shut behind me. Viggo, who was lying on the floor looking at some files glanced up at me, his brows rising.

"Desmond?" he asked archly and I let out a breath of air, nodding tightly.

Viggo leaned forward. "What do you want to do?" he asked.

"Tie her up and force her to listen to us?" I deadpanned.

"Aggressive problem solving," he said. "I like it."

I groaned and tossed myself into our nest behind him. "I just don't get it! She can't know what we want to talk about, so why is she putting us off?"

I turned my gaze over to Viggo, who was frowning thoughtfully. "Are we sure she doesn't know what we want to talk about?"

"Hm," I murmured. Was it possible that Desmond somehow knew that we were opposed to her plan? If so... why was she just leaving us alone? Why would she just leave us hung out to dry, forgotten about, but still within her group? It seemed... impractical.

"I have no idea," I said, "but I guess it's possible. I'm still not sure why she wouldn't act on the knowledge, if she has it."

Viggo was silent for a long moment. "Maybe... she can't. We've kind of insinuated ourselves in here. You've got a rep for being a solid field agent, and I've sort of made myself indispensable with the work I'm doing with the boys."

I nodded before climbing back to my feet. "I gotta go," I told him, shoving my hands in my pockets. "I promised Tim I'd go spend some time with him."

"Want me to come?"

I smiled and shook my head. "Nope. Strictly sibling time. Besides, you get him for much longer than I do."

Viggo's face fell and I immediately regretted my choice of words. I meant it as a joke, but clearly Viggo thought I was serious.

"Whoa," I said, holding up my hands. "It was a joke. Seriously... I love all the time you spend with him. Besides, I don't want you to be accused of favoritism," I added, leaning over to kiss him on the cheek. "Even though I know he is your favorite."

"He really is my favorite," he said, before cracking a smile at me.

"Smart man," I said as I exited the room.

The sound of his chuckle filled the hallway behind me, and I smirked. Despite the frustration I was feeling with Desmond, Viggo had a way of making it all better. It put a little spring in my step as I headed downstairs.

As I approached Tim's cell, I was struck with another moment of happiness to see that the ramp was extended and locked in place, the door wide open. The boys in Viggo's training program were given limited freedoms, but this one was a big one that Viggo had pressed for. It demonstrated his and the Liberators' trust in them.

I felt another surge of pride toward Viggo as I walked up the catwalk. He was so good at coming up with plans and executing them. Not to mention, he knew when to be strict and when to grant freedom. I was constantly amazed by his thoughtful nature, and his ability to build something from nothing.

I swung through the door, knocking gently on the interior concrete. Tim was already inside, kneeling down and rubbing Samuel's belly. The brown dog writhed in ecstasy, his tail making a whump whump sound against the floor. Tim was so focused on giving attention to the dog, that he failed to notice me for several seconds.

When he did, however, I felt my heart constrict at the smile that broke out across his face. The transformation couldn't have been more significant in my eyes. Gone were the wary shadows that turned his light gray irises dark. Even his posture had changed—he no longer slouched when he stood—now his back was straight, his shoulders squared. There was a quiet sense of confidence in him that hadn't existed until several days ago.

"Violet... Late," he said, after taking a moment to scrutinize his watch.

"Sorry, kiddo—I had to chat with Viggo for a few minutes."

He nodded politely. "Viggo... He's a... good person."

I smiled and nodded, seeing that Viggo's conversation class still needed a little work. "I think so, too, but I'm really glad you like him."

Tim nodded again, and I opened my arms to him. Hugging... was hard for my brother, so I was never offended when he declined. However, I must have caught him on a good day, because he smiled broadly, making me ache in all the best ways.

He stepped into the circle of my arms and wrapped his arms around me, giving me a hug so hard that it forced me to laugh as he picked me up and spun me around in a circle. Just as quickly as it started, he dropped me, and took a step back. There was a slight strain in his face, but the smile remained.

"I am so proud of you," I stated, and he blushed. I knew that touching things was painful for him, but the fact that he was willing to set aside the pain for something as simple as a hug... So different he was from the boy I had rescued from the cell.

I sat cross-legged on the floor, and he followed suit. "I can really see the difference," I said, reaching over to unravel a curl on his forehead.

He pulled away with a small laugh. "I'm not ... a child, Vi," he reminded me, humor laced in his voice.

I grinned, unable to contain it. "No, but you'll always be my baby brother," I said, managing to slip my hand through his defenses and ruffle his hair gently.

The look he gave me was mutinous, but his eyes sparkled. For just a second, everything that had happened to him slipped away, and I could imagine that this was how my brother would have been, if he'd never been taken in the first place.

"Happy for you... and Viggo," Tim said excitedly. "Training is good. Skin hurts, but I'm... controlled. Friends. It's good."

"I think so, too." I rested my head back against the wall, feeling content for a moment, when the problem with Desmond began worming its way back into my mind. What would I do if she decided to never meet with us? I couldn't force her to sit down, despite my earlier statement to Viggo. And Tim was starting to take root here. It wouldn't be fair to drag him away from his brothers.

I sighed, irritated.

"What's wrong?" Tim demanded.

"I'm sorry, Tim. I'm just… I'm having a hard time dealing with some stuff right now."

"Like what?"

"It's… I don't really wanna talk about it."

"Violet… not following the rules," Tim said, his eyes drifting toward the floor as he shifted nervously.

I looked at him, confused. "What rules are you talking about?"

"Viggo's rules! Whenever you feel something…"

"Stop," I repeated thoughtfully.

"Then look," he replied.

"Then talk about it," I finished.

He nodded.

"When did you get so grown up?" I asked.

"Dunno… But you should follow the rules."

I groaned in a comical fashion and he chuckled. "Fine, smart guy. You win! I'm a bit stressed out because I've been trying to have a meeting with Desmond, and she's been putting me off."

Tim gave me a side-long glance, not directly making eye contact.

"Don't like Desmond," he said after a moment.

I paused, frowning. "What? Why not?"

He hesitated, screwing his face up as he thought. "Comes here… Talks to us."

"About what?"

His shoulders went up and down. "Matrus. Patrus. Says… they're bad. They'll hurt us."

"Does ... she say why?"

Tim met my eyes and gave another shrug, but he looked... sad. "Says we're different. People hate us."

My frown intensified. "She shouldn't be saying that. It's the governments who have done bad things... not the people."

Tim nodded, his brown locks bobbing. "More. Jay hates her."

I racked my brain to remember who Jay was. "You're going to have to help me out, buddy. Jay?"

"Ber...trand?" he drawled, sounding it out.

Realization dawned on me.

"Desmond's other son?"

He nodded emphatically. "He's... scared."

"Uh-huh," I replied, rolling that bit of information over in my mind. I knew of Desmond's second son but had never been directly introduced to him... But why would her kidnapped son be afraid of her? That... didn't make any sense. Wasn't she doing this to help him?

I rose to my feet. "I'm going to find Viggo. See what he thinks about all this."

Tim nodded, holding up his hand with his index finger and thumb connected in a circle. He had just started picking that up from Viggo.

"Okay. If you see Desmond again... maybe come find me?" I said.

He repeated the gesture and I chuckled, waving

at him. As I walked away from the room, however, I felt a prickling unease settling in under my skin, as if warning me that something dangerous was coming.

I had no idea what yet, but it was both disconcerting and vaguely familiar.

CHAPTER 31

Viggo

I pushed through the door leading to the boys' area. Shortly after Violet had left to visit her brother, I had gotten a note passed to me by Henrik, who told me it was from Ms. Dale. It only had four words scratched on it: *We need to meet.* Curious, but not overly alarmed, I had gotten up and dressed, then made my way downstairs.

Everything was becoming much easier as the days went on. I was walking again, and was even able to jog for a small period of time. I was careful not to push myself too hard too fast, but even as I made my way downstairs, I had noticed the change. It was like I was settling back into my own body again, and needed less breaks and rest stops than before. I had even managed to work up to doing some pushups and sit-ups in the morning—with Dr. Tierney's permission, of course.

I made my way along the ramp to Ms. Dale's cell with a nod to her guard—not Henrik; he was off shift now.

Ms. Dale watched me as I entered, her eyes wary and her face tight.

Dusting my hands, I placed my back against the wall and slid down it until I was sitting across from her. She gave me a wry look.

"You know, I think you might be sending love letters wrong," I commented. "You were supposed to give it to me to give to Henrik." I rubbed my hands over my pants with a congenial smile.

She rolled her eyes at me. "Please, as if I'd be interested in that old coot."

"He's certainly interested in you, considering he went out of his way to play delivery boy on your behalf. Practicing a play from your Patrian seduction book?"

If looks could murder, I would have been vaporized in an instant, given the way she was eyeballing me. She took a deep breath, relaxing the hard edges of her face, and nodded at me. "How are you recovering?" she asked.

"Is that why you brought me down here?"

She gave me a stern glare.

"Better," I replied. "I've started doing some jogging

and I feel stronger."

"Good... We need to start moving with alacrity," she said, her voice grim.

I arched a brow. "Alacrity? Sure you don't want to try moving with obfuscation first?"

Ms. Dale shot me a disdainful smirk and leaned forward, draping her arms over her knees. "Mr. Croft, big fancy words aside, we have a problem."

"What's up?"

Her eyes glittered dangerously. "Surely you've noticed the change in the boys by now, right?"

I frowned, my mind racing through recent events. My work with the boys had kept me busy—so busy in fact, that more and more Liberators were coming to me to see if I needed help. They seemed like good people, so I had agreed and shown them the ropes.

As for the boys—they seemed... determined. A lot of the initial excitement was gone, but there was a fire in their eyes when they did the exercises. A hungry desire that manifested itself during class. They were attentive—far more than any child should be—but I had just attributed it to their genetic modifications.

"The boys have seemed... eager lately."

"No, Viggo. They're thirsty. For blood."

I paused, and then broke out in a laugh. Ms. Dale stared at me with a mixture of irritation, impatience and incredulity. "I'm sorry," I said, once the laughter had subsided, "but that is really melodramatic."

Ms. Dale huffed in annoyance. "Did you know Desmond has been meeting with the boys in the training program?"

The smile dropped from my face as if someone had turned off a switch.

"What?"

"I guess they didn't mention it to you," she said, a smug smile playing on her lips.

I had to hand it to her, she was quite good at gloating. Well, that was fair—I had spent the majority of my time with her gloating. However, if she was keeping information from me out of spite, then that was a whole other story.

"No. They did not. Care to fill me in?"

"Desmond has been spending time with the boys in the evenings and before breakfast. She knows all their names and has even given some of them gifts. She goes on walks with them, and encourages them to tell her all about what they are learning."

"How do you know this?" I asked.

"I got tipped off the other night... By Henrik of all people."

I suppressed a smile at that bit of information. "Interesting. And you're sure nothing's going on between you?"

"Be serious, Viggo," she hissed. I watched her reach into her pocket and pull out a folded piece of paper. "She's giving them this to read," she said, thrusting out the paper.

I grabbed the piece of paper from her hand and gingerly unfolded it. It was a pamphlet, written in noticeably basic language. I read the first line, blinked, and re-read it.

"*The Patrus/Matrus Threat?*" I said, meeting her gaze.

"It's propaganda. Bad propaganda. It paints both nations as bigots."

I winced. "Well… it's not exactly a lie," I said slowly.

Ms. Dale's face darkened. "Viggo, it's fear-mongering. I thought you were trying to actively avoid that."

I nodded, considering the implications of what she was saying. I tried to follow Desmond's logic, searching for some rational explanation as to why she was doing this. It seemed strange that she wouldn't run it by me first. After all, she had seemed very positive at the onset, even offering to send more help in her electronic messages.

I considered that maybe she was wanting to do it to spend time with them and do her part to help out the program. But that didn't explain why she would keep it secret, or why she would feel the need to make something like the pamphlet to back up her assertions.

The only thing I could think of was that she was trying to somehow influence their loyalty, but even that was a bit of a stretch. The boys spent almost all of their waking hours with me and Ms. Dale—I doubted their loyalty could be bought for something as simple as candy and a few pamphlets supporting anti-nationalist propaganda.

Could it?

No, there was no way it would work. I knew my boys; they couldn't be influenced so easily. There was something else going on, something we just weren't seeing.

"I want to say she's buying their loyalty," I announced finally. "But I can't see how she could be. The boys can't be bought with treats. We must be missing something."

"You're right—I know we're missing something; I just wish I knew what. She always was a clever one... always came at a problem sideways."

"What do you mean?" I asked.

"Well, I touched on it before, but Desmond used to *inspire* fanaticism. She's good at it. Do you remember... oh... thirty-some odd years ago? It was a bit before your time, but the bombing of the Patrian grain silo?"

"Yes." My father had told me about that day when I was younger. Nearly seventy-five men and women had died from the resulting fires—it had burned down nearly a third of the reserve supplies as well as over a dozen homes and warehouses in the district. Putting it out had taken three days. No one ever claimed credit for it, but at the heart of every rumor, the insinuation was that the Porteque gang was responsible.

"Desmond arranged the whole affair, and she manipulated those men from the Porteque gang from *inside their operation.* She inserted herself as one of their 'obedient' women and married one of the men. Then she whispered to him—who knows what—about how women needed to find their place just like she had. She had those men worshipping her—in their own way—and convinced them that destroying the grain silo was the only way to get the government's attention. Three men killed themselves bombing that place, and Desmond disappeared into the night, damage done."

"So... you think she's after the boys, trying to win them over to later use them in her war efforts."

She shot me a glance of confirmation. "I trust those boys, but Desmond is insidious—always thinking, planning, scheming. She's been worming her way in since she saw the success of your program... I'm worried about the boys. They're vulnerable, and Desmond is reminding them of who got them to where they are and who will continue to help them. And... I'm guessing our names are not being mentioned."

I rose abruptly to my feet and moved to the door.

"Where are you going?" Ms. Dale asked.

"I'm going to go track Desmond down and talk to her," I announced.

"Viggo, you can't! If you tip your hand too soon, then she'll use whatever she has to bring you down. And Violet."

"Then what do you propose I do?" I asked, pausing.

"Find a way to watch one of her meetings. Maybe get into her office and snoop around. See if you can't find out what she's doing with the boys."

"And if I find out her intentions aren't good?"

A cold hard light glimmered in Ms. Dale's eyes. "Mr. Croft—Viggo—have you ever assassinated someone before?"

I shook my head. It was hard for me to think about—killing someone in cold blood. I knew I could kill someone in self-defense. I could also kill someone while protecting another person. But cold blood? It felt... wrong. Cowardly and unfair.

"I thought as much. It's not in your nature, Mr. Croft." She shifted, straightening her legs. "Which is why, if you do find something out, you'll need to let me out of here. So I can take... precautions."

I stared down through the corrugated holes in the floor into the bleak darkness below. "It's not in my nature to hurt people," I replied, meeting her gaze head on.

She shrugged. "I could argue that killing her would be protecting people."

"This feels... wrong, Melissa."

Her mouth tightened and she gave me a sad look. "You might think so, Mr. Croft," she whispered. "But go to one of her secret meetings. Find out what she's telling the boys, and then come back and tell me if you still think it's wrong."

I frowned, but nodded. "I'll... check it out. But beyond that... I am not committing to anything."

CHAPTER 32

Violet

The next night, Viggo and I were creeping quietly along the catwalks. I had an electronic winch on a wheeled cart next to me, and Viggo was carrying several lengths of rope. It was late, and there weren't many people around.

When we had met up late last night, I had explained what Tim had told me and Viggo had told me about his conversation with Ms. Dale. We'd spent hours going over what we should do, and finally had decided that this was the best course of action.

Earlier in the day, I had met with Tim and asked him to show me where Desmond usually met with the boys. He had led me to the electrical substation and explained, as best he could, that Desmond brought the boys down there to hold discussions and debates in secret.

This had concerned both Viggo and me enough that we had come up with a drastic plan to try to hear what she was telling the boys. That plan included me getting lowered down dozens of feet to listen in through an audio transmitter that Tim would be carrying in his pocket. I didn't like the idea of putting Tim at risk, but Viggo had insisted that it was the best way.

We had already considered just trying to sneak down the stairs, but it was risky—if the boys were indeed becoming loyal to Desmond, they would alert her to our presence.

I bit my lip as I pulled up the facility blueprints. Desmond had sent them to me to help with the bomb disposal project, and now I couldn't be more grateful that she had. If I'd needed to ask for them, it would have drawn suspicion over what we were doing.

As it was, I wasn't so certain that Lynne, a Liberator who worked in the equipment room, had accepted my flimsy excuse when I checked out the winch and rope—I'd explained that Viggo needed it for training—but there wasn't much to do about that now. The bug I had stolen outright, convinced it was safer to steal, as checking it out officially would raise red flags. Luckily, I had spent more than a few hours in the supply closet, so I'd known exactly what I was looking for.

I studied the map, then moved about ten feet to the left of the door. According to Tim, no one would start showing up for the meeting for another ten minutes, which meant that Viggo would lower me down by the winch, secure the rope to the handrails, and then detach the winch, wheeling it over to Tim's cell.

I would have twenty minutes from the start of the meeting to listen in. Unfortunately, the transmitter on the bug wasn't strong enough for both of us to listen from up on the catwalk, hence the need for me to once again lower myself down into the dark pit that waited eagerly beneath our feet.

I checked my watch nervously. "You ready?" I asked as Viggo carefully applied the brakes to the wheels.

Normally, the winch would be flat on the ground and bolted in. We didn't have time for that, so we were doing this differently. Viggo was going to brace it himself as he lowered me down, and then carefully disconnect the line and tie it off. There would be several seconds where my weight and life would be completely in his hands.

We had discussed leaving the winch there to hold me up, but I was worried it would be noticed. Viggo had expressed his uncertainty about holding my weight—which had led to a really amusing few minutes of me teasing him for calling me fat. He had already regained so much of his strength that I was confident that he had recovered enough, and I had somehow managed to convince him of that.

He was in the process of threading the rope through the machine. "Yeah, ready," he whispered as he ran the line through the carabiners on my harness. "Are you sure you want to do this?" he asked, his green eyes finding mine.

I swallowed. "Yes. It has to be me. You're the only one who can support my weight. I can't support yours."

He nodded, but I saw a flash of doubt. I gripped his jaw. "I trust you," I whispered. "And I love you… You can do this."

Viggo leaned down and kissed me hard. Then I turned slowly and looked down at the pit.

We both can do this.

Viggo took a deep breath and straightened. "When I transfer the line, it's going to be jerky. You have to remain calm and not struggle, okay. If you start swinging too much, I won't be able to tie off the line."

I nodded rapidly several times. "I will, I promise."

Viggo guided me to the handrail and helped me over it. I felt shaky, just like when I had done this over a week ago, when I had disarmed the explosives, and I questioned the wisdom of what we were doing once again. But then I thought of those boys and what was at stake, and slowly lowered myself down, surrendering my weight to the rope as Viggo pressed a knee into the winch.

I heard the soft whir of the machine as it lowered me, and focused my gaze on my hands gripping the rope, trying not to think of the darkness below. As I descended, I slowly let go of the rope with one hand, reaching into my pocket to pull out a small shielded light that I had also pilfered from the supply closet.

Clicking the button, I carefully angled my body around until I was facing the wall that was between me and the service station, keeping my gaze steadily fixed on it. I counted the bolt holes that had been punched in the concrete, using them as a distraction to keep my mind from the gaping abyss ready to swallow me up.

The seconds crept by, turning into a minute, and then two, when my descent finally came to a stop. I shivered, trying to think of anything but what Viggo was about to do.

I felt the rope shudder under my hands and resisted the urge to cry out. The rope creaked ominously, and I felt myself swing. I leaned my body weight forward slightly, steadying myself and the rope.

After a few seconds, I gasped as the rope gave a little, and then sucked a deep breath in, realizing that it was just Viggo letting off the slack he needed when he'd tied the rope.

I gazed up and saw the dark blurry shape of his head as he looked down. He held out his hand and I raised my own, shining my light behind it so he could see.

I heard the faint sounds of his footsteps followed by the creaking of wheels as he made his way to Tim's cell, and I exhaled. I let go of the rope with one hand, reaching into my other pocket and pulling out the earbud, realizing I should have put it on sooner.

Then there was nothing to do but wait. Viggo was in the process of giving Tim the transmitter, showing him how to turn it on and off. I doubted Desmond would think to sweep the boys for transmitters, but just in case she did, Viggo would explain to Tim what to do and how to handle it.

I tried to keep calm, but without something to focus on, it was difficult. The dark was terrifying, even my little flashlight wasn't enough to keep it at bay. As I stared through it, I got the distinct impression of a predatory beast, circling tightly, waiting for any opportunity to strike.

I closed my eyes. *Okay, Violet. You're dangling from a rope with no secondary line above a bottomless pit, about to spy on a woman who may or may not be trying to manipulate some children for nefarious reasons. You've got this, right?*

Just then I heard the pitter-patter of feet, light and soft, barely detectable on the catwalk, and breathed a sigh of relief. It would only be a few more minutes before Tim turned on the transmission. I could hold on for that long, and once the transmission was happening, I could use that as a distraction.

Although it was less than five minutes, it felt like I had been hanging there for an eternity. I was almost convinced that the transmitter wasn't able to penetrate this amount of concrete when I heard a sharp burst of feedback in my ear, causing me to jerk in surprise.

The rope creaked again, and goosebumps erupted on my skin as Desmond's voice started coming through the microphone, loud and clear.

"All right my darlings, sit down, sit down. Do you have all of your candy?" she crooned in a way that I had never heard before.

There was a round of affirmative words before she continued. "Now, does anyone have any questions as to the reading I gave you last night?"

A jumble of voices followed her question, presumably from the boys all clamoring at once. "Calm down, one at a time. Antoine?"

"What's a threat?" came a tiny, slightly nervous sounding voice.

"That's an excellent question—a threat is someone or something that can hurt you. Who's next? Cody?"

The earbud fell silent for a second.

"The pamphlet said that if Matrus or Patrus ever found us, they would want to experiment on us again.

Is that... true?"

"Unfortunately, it is very true, Cody. I know this because I used to be a spy for Matrus. And in my time, I learned that there was no stopping people in power from using other people to keep their power. Make no mistake boys, for all the harm that Matrus has caused you, Patrus would do the same."

"I don't understand why we don't just join up with Patrus," came a small shout. "They don't like Matrus, and neither do we. Maybe we can become... friends."

"That's a good suggestion, Peter, except... Patrus would never accept you. You're born of a Matrian. They rarely let males from one side move to another."

"But we could fight Matrus! And then take it!"

I could practically feel Desmond's smile through the earbud. "I admire your spirit, Stephan, but it's not that easy. Patrus would want control of Matrus... they wouldn't want to give it to you."

"Well, what should we do?" asked a new voice.

"What do you want to do?" replied Desmond.

There was some murmuring, and then another boy spoke up. "What do you think we should do, Des?"

I frowned at the intimate use of her nickname, something she only let a handful of people use. The entire conversation thus far was making me uncomfortable. I mean... she wasn't lying to the boys, but she was painting a pretty grim picture of their reality.

I wasn't sure they needed so much harsh truth this soon.

"Well, I can't tell you what to do," she replied. There was a slight pause before her next sentence stopped me cold. "But I can tell you what I plan to do. If you'd like to know."

A chorus of shouts encouraged her to tell them, and her warm chuckle filled the air. "All right, calm down. Imagine you're a mouse," she started and I squeezed my eyes closed and grimaced.

I listened to her give the exact same scenario she had pitched to me to the boys. But instead of being appalled and thoughtful like I had been, the boys reacted to it very differently.

"Wow, Des," chimed in Cody's voice. "You're really smart!"

There were loud sounds of agreements and I exhaled, resting my forehead against the rope. Of course the boys liked her scenario, they had no concept of what war meant in terms of human life.

I felt the rope jerk under my hands and panicked for a moment, thinking that the line was about to snap. I pulled back my sleeve and checked my watch. Had twenty minutes flown by so fast? I was shocked to see that it had.

The rope vibrated with tension and I clamped my teeth shut to keep from making a noise. Not that I thought Desmond could hear me through all this concrete. I just didn't want to take the risk of alerting someone else.

The line jerked again and then I felt myself begin to rise in the air. I kept myself focused on Desmond's voice answering questions and reminding the boys that if they wanted to help her, all they had to do was ask, and felt a roil of nausea that wasn't exclusively related to my fear of heights. As I neared the top, I risked a peek and saw Viggo already leaning over the edge, his right hand outstretched.

I knew better than to reach for it—it could make me start to swing—and just held on tight. He grabbed me by the collar of my shirt as I reached the top, hauling me up a few inches so I could grab the top bar of the handrail. I slowly climbed up and over, his hand on my arm to prevent me from falling.

Once my feet were firmly planted on the other side, I looked up at him and shook my head while his hands were fast at work, unclipping the rope from the carabiners.

"It's bad, Viggo," I breathed. "She's carefully eliminating all hope of them having somewhere to go, then graciously allowing them to join the Liberators, if they 'choose' to. Except that it's no choice at all, given the way she's talking about Matrus and Patrus."

"It doesn't make sense," Viggo said as he carefully coiled up the rope. "Why would they fall for that so easily?"

I opened my mouth to respond that they were children who didn't know better, and then stopped, reminded of the fact that they weren't all children. Most of them were traumatized young adults, betrayed by the system. So why were they being so agreeable with Desmond?

"I don't know," I finally said. "But all she did was ask if they all got some candy and then got right down to discussion."

Viggo threw the rope over his shoulder. "All right… I'm going to get this back to supply and see if I can't check out one of those suits," he whispered. "You get to your brother and wait for me there."

I stared at the door a few feet away. "What are you going to do?" I asked.

"I'm going to go into Desmond's office and see if I can find proof."

"Proof of what? She's just talking to them."

He nodded. "And giving them candy. All of them. Has your brother been eating it?"

My jaw slackened. "I-I don't know. I don't think so—he doesn't like her."

"Good. I think she might be drugging them."

"With what?"

Viggo shook his head. "I don't know. Something that makes them more compliant. Willing to listen and accept."

"Viggo…" I said, feeling extremely doubtful.

He set his hands on my shoulders and gazed deep into my eyes, his own glowing intensely. "Violet, I know these boys. They question everything. Aggressively."

"Okay," I said. "But then what's your play?"

Viggo picked up the handle to the wagon and started walking, and I followed. "If I can find tangible proof, I'll bring it to the rest of the Liberators," he said. "If we can get them on our side, they'll oust her as the leader."

I gulped, but felt a faint glimmer of hope. "Then I hope you find it," I whispered. I moved up next to him and pressed my lips against his rough cheek. "Good luck," I said as I moved down one the aisles, heading for my brother's cell.

CHAPTER 33

Viggo

I carefully made my way to the supply room, a small area off to the side of the training room, originally designed to be an observation post. Knocking on the door, I gave Lynne a friendly smile as she looked up at me.

"Hey, just returning the equipment we borrowed," I lied casually.

Lynne nodded and stood up from her chair, picking up a clipboard on the side of the wall. "That didn't take long," she commented, as she held out the clipboard.

I accepted the pen she handed me. "Yeah, Violet isn't big on heights. She just thought it would be good if I was familiar with it, in case the need ever came up."

Lynne's head bobbed up and down in agreement. "Yeah. It's smart. We get a lot of cross-training over here."

"It's a really good idea," I said as I signed my name with a flourish. "Speaking of which, I was wondering if I could check out one of the camouflage suits. I really need more practice now that Dr. Tierney has given me the go-ahead."

Her eyes drifted down to my chest and then flicked back up. "I wasn't aware that she had," she said, smiling.

"Just the other day, actually. I think you were off duty."

"Tuesday? Oh… I traded shifts so I could try to spend more time with my brother," she said.

I watched as she went over to the rack of suits hanging on the back wall, checking the sizes. After a moment, she walked over and set it on the table in the middle of the room.

I walked closer, dropping the two lines of rope I was carrying into the bin. I then moved over to the opposite side of the table and waited patiently. I watched her write down the inventory number, as well as my name and the date and time in very neat handwriting on the piece of paper on the clipboard. When she was done, she turned the clipboard around. "Just sign," she said brightly.

I signed my name a second time, and then gathered the suit in my hands. "Thanks" I said, holding it up as a farewell.

She smiled again, a dimple forming in her cheeks. "Don't mention it," she said, her voice suddenly lower and huskier, catching me off guard.

I gave her a surprised look, and she threw me a long slow wink before moving deeper into the office. I shook my head and suppressed a smirk, hoping that Violet never found out that Lynne had a thing for me. I couldn't imagine a jealous Violet, and I certainly didn't want to.

Heading for the locker room, I checked my watch. I had just enough time to get changed and make it to Desmond's office before she finished her pow-wow, according to Tim's timeline.

I quickly changed and then headed to the stairs, moving upward. I didn't regret lying to Lynne about Dr. Tierney giving me the go-ahead on the suit, I just wished I had more than Violet's description of how to make it work. It felt... too easy in some way.

Then again, for a man recovering from heart damage, I really hoped that whatever electrical surge she had described wouldn't aggravate my condition. I maybe should've let Violet do this part, but it was too late to go back now.

Pulling the door closed behind me, I checked the stairwell and decided to give the suit a little test run. Carefully tensing my muscles, immediately I felt the pins and needles that Violet had described. I quickly relaxed my muscles, shaking out my arms and legs.

That was… intense.

I placed two fingers on my pulse and looked at my watch. It was elevated… but not too high. I gave a few more experimental tenses, smiling as I saw the stairs through my hands, and then relaxed again. Violet had also said that maintaining the suit for a long period of time was extremely difficult, so I needed to save my energy for that.

I headed up the stairs. Once I reached the top, I spun the hand wheel gently, grateful that it was well-oiled, and then pushed it open an inch at a time, checking the gap to make sure it was clear.

Luckily, it was so late that all of the scientists were gone—in bed or otherwise indisposed. I stepped through and quietly pulled the door closed behind me. I knew it would close itself, but I wanted to control it.

I made my way across the lab and into Desmond's office, sifting through the papers on her desk, skimming the documents for something—anything—that would help me convince the others that Desmond was not acting in the best interests of the boys.

There was nothing there. Blowing out, I put the files down and looked around the room. She wouldn't be using the computer—it was still tied into the Matrian system, and she had ordered them all to be shut down after the bomb incident.

Maybe her handheld? I looked around her desk,

shifting some of the files around. Nothing. Gritting my teeth, I opened the drawers on her desk and nearly gave a jump for joy when I found it. Activating it, I quickly pulled out my own handheld and started to jack them together when I heard the distinct sound of footsteps, heading toward me from the stairwell.

I hurriedly set her handheld back in the drawer and closed it while tucking mine back into the pocket in my forearm. Then I moved off to the corner and clenched my muscles, watching the lab through the window-walls of the office.

Desmond appeared, walking at a slow, steady pace. I watched as she entered the room, crossed to the desk to grab some files, and then walked out, retreating the way she had come. I kept my muscles tense and moved cautiously toward the drawer where her handheld still was. If I could just reach it…

Then came the slow, deliberate sound of a gun cocking.

I stalled, turning back to the door.

Desmond was standing there, staring back at me. Her lips were twisted in a disturbing smile, the rest of her face hidden behind goggles that were a famil-iar hue of red, indicating thermal scanning. A stab of frustration coursed through me as I slowly raised my hands and faced her and her pistol.

CHAPTER 34

Violet

Tim's eyes were wide as I quickly explained our plan to him. I expected him to balk or show at least some doubt, but after I'd finished, he nodded, his eyes alive.

"It's... a good plan," he whispered, stroking Samuel's fur.

I stood up, feeling nervous, but also confident. Once we had evidence on Desmond, things would be better. And who knew, maybe whoever succeeded her would let us continue to work with them. I had really come to like the people here and would hate to have to leave like this.

I started to check my watch for the umpteenth time, when I heard crackles that sounded like a microphone coming in over speakers.

Then I heard the distinctive sound of Desmond's voice, rich with disdain, like sugared venom. "Violet Bates," she announced. "I would like to invite you to meet me in the training room. That is… if you'd ever like to see your precious boyfriend again."

The icy hand of fear crept down my spine, before I felt a bolt of pure annoyance. I let out a bitter laugh, startling Tim. He gave me a look of concern, but I waved it off, pinching the bridge of my nose between my fingers. "Sorry, Tim," I said after the moment of laughter had passed. "It's just… we're never going to be those people who get to sit in the spectators' stands, y'know?"

Tim thought about it a second, and then smirked back at me. "Nope," he agreed. "But… not boring."

"Not boring," I muttered as I weighed my options. Given Desmond's message, she wasn't likely to give me a lot of time to do much. I looked at Tim, who was watching me closely, his face shark-like in anticipation. I rubbed my temples. The options weren't good. I needed to get to the training room.

But Tim didn't. Neither did Ms. Dale. If I could just get them out, maybe even using the dreaded ventilation system to help get them past Desmond and the Liberators, then they stood a chance. Viggo and I would have to find some other clever means of escape.

"Tim—you need to get Ms. Dale and run. Use the ventilation shafts to move if worst comes to very worst and keep heading up. You have to go down to that room again, and then follow the other hall. There's a ladder that will take you up."

He shook his head, denial stamped on his features. "No," he said stubbornly.

"Tim, I can go help Viggo, or I can stay and make sure you get out alive. If I go and help Viggo, then I have a chance of saving him."

"How?"

In response, I pulled out a pistol—another object I had pilfered from the supply room. I had tucked it into one of the many dangling bags on the harness, and then slid it out when Viggo wasn't looking. I hadn't been sure he would approve at the time. The ammunition was live—meaning that it would kill.

Tim's eyes went wide as he stared at the gun. "Oh," he replied.

I tucked the gun back against the small of my back. "Go," I said, urging him to the door. "And don't forget Samuel," I reminded him. It was an unnecessary reminder—the dog followed him everywhere.

Suddenly the same crackle filled the air. I turned, half-expecting to see Desmond right behind me on the ramp, but she wasn't. Still, a bead of sweat dripped from my forehead.

"Ms. Bates, you only have a few precious minutes left to save him," she said, practically singing the words in her triumph.

I took a step onto the ramp. "Do it, Tim," I ordered, my voice coming out harshly.

I didn't look back as I marched down the row. He wouldn't argue with my back to him, and I didn't have time to entertain his argument, even if he planned to. Viggo's life was on the line—again—and if Desmond thought she was going to take him from me when I had just gotten him back, she had another thing coming.

Namely, a bullet.

I threw open the door to the stairwell and marched up the stairs. I could already hear hushed whispers filtering down the stairwells. Someone was standing with the door wide open, waiting for me.

I wasn't sure that she had any idea where I had been, but if she had, I prayed that Tim hurried before someone caught him and Ms. Dale. I took a deep breath and forced my face to relax. I straightened my spine and squared my shoulders, then continued up the stairs.

Stepping through the doorframe, I nodded at the Liberator who was holding it open. I vaguely remembered her—I thought her name was Phyllis, or maybe Phoebe—and I was a little surprised when she nodded back. So was she, given the flush of pink across her high cheekbones, and the speed at which she pulled the door closed behind me, avoiding eye contact.

Her reaction reminded me that not everyone in

the room was bad. They were just being misled by a very disturbed individual.

The same disturbed individual who was standing in the middle of the largest patch of sand with a man kneeling in front of her.

I marched through the crowd, who regarded me with curiosity, disdain, and some outright hatred. The last came from Meera, who shouted something incoherent at me before shoving me hard. I was surprised by her vehemence, until I remembered Solomon. Things had been strained, but she had tried. I guessed that was over now.

Her shove caused me to lose balance and I fell to the ground on my hands and knees. A few people cheered, but the rest remained silent, waiting for the scene to unfold before them. Given how Desmond had gotten everyone down here—likely by sending them messages through their handhelds—it would prove to be theatrical.

I drew in a lungful of air and glanced over to where Meera was standing when a flash of movement caught my eye. I lifted my gaze and saw Nissa standing practically on top of me, her face marred by a frown, which intensified as our eyes met. She took a step back, and I felt hope crumble in my chest.

Convincing these people that I wasn't their enemy was going to be impossible. Desmond had spent years with them—she knew them better than they knew themselves, it seemed. She had molded them all into believing in her, creating a sense of devotion that would be impossible to overcome in these circumstances.

Her plan wasn't a secret: They had come to terms with it already. And who could blame them? They were the outcasts of societies that had wronged them, and Desmond represented a very real way of dealing a blow to the institutions. They didn't care about the people they hurt in the process: All they cared about was revenge.

I also highly doubted that they would believe me about Desmond drugging the boys. If I mentioned it, it would seem like a desperate claim, trying to taint the reputation of someone they loved.

I stood up and continued walking, doing my best to ignore the snide comments and yells. The sand crunched under my feet as I marched through it and stopped about thirty feet from Desmond.

"Let him go," I said, my voice ringing out loudly, and, thankfully, calmly.

Turning her back to me, Desmond held the microphone to her lips. "You see," she cried. "Why else would she come, if she weren't a spy?"

The crowd murmured in agreement, and I felt my brows draw up in confusion. "*What* are you talking about?" I asked, taking a step forward and looking at the audience. "I came up here because you were threatening my boyfriend!"

I felt Viggo's eyes on me, but I kept my focus on Desmond and the crowd. Desmond was trying to convince them that I was working against them, but I wasn't about to make it that easy.

Desmond turned back to me, shaking her head sadly. "We trusted this girl—we trusted her with our deepest secrets, never knowing that she was really working for Matrus. And her boyfriend here for Patrus."

She planted a foot on Viggo's shoulders and gave him a little shove, sending him tumbling to the ground. He sat up quickly, shaking the sand off his face. I held my ground, staring at her. "Seriously? This is the best you can come up with? That I work for Matrus and him Patrus? There are so many problems with that I don't even know where to start!"

"Enough, Ms. Bates. We are tired of your... deceptions. I have suspected you for some time, ever since that... special meeting you wanted to schedule with me out of the blue... mere days before seeing our plan finally come to fruition. You see... when I started this operation, I knew that both countries would eventually figure out that something was up and send agents to investigate. I don't know how, but you must have been tipped off that Lee was working with someone else. You probably didn't know who then, but you and your partner here—as unprecedented as it seems—started working together once you realized how effective we could… would… become.

"But then you got impatient. You bided your time, put on the good soldier act, all the while waiting to be clued in to the details of our plan. And when that didn't work, you got more impatient and had your boyfriend sneak in to my office to steal the plans that we have spent years putting into motion and escape like rats in the night. Do you deny it?"

The crowd hushed, waiting for my answer. I didn't address Desmond—instead, I turned to the crowd. "You don't actually believe this, right?" I said incredulously. "Most of you saw the aftermath of the twins—the princesses—we killed defending ourselves. How could I do that if I was a Matrian spy? Why would I?"

The crowd murmured, and I took that as a good sign; I hesitated, and then decided to go for it. "She's right—Viggo was in her office, snooping around—but not to report her location to her enemies. He was there because… we suspect Desmond is giving the boys a drug to make them more complicit to her ideas! She's trying to use them, the same way Matrus used them!"

The crowd hushed and then someone shouted, "Where's your proof?"

I looked at Viggo, who shook his head grimly. "Desmond caught Viggo before he could find it. But that doesn't mean it's not true. Ask for her handheld! Check it out for yourself."

Desmond gave me a bored look and glanced at the crowd. "Go ahead. I have nothing to hide—you all knew about the Benuxupane. I've been giving it to them in small doses to see if they showed improvement, and they have. Why do you think they've been getting better faster?"

I felt stunned by her declaration. "You promised you wouldn't start administering it until you had determined whether or not Viggo's plan would work!" I shouted.

"I had determined that his program was helping, but not fast enough. Certainly not fast enough for the family members who want nothing more than to have their children returned to them, healthy and whole."

I paused, realizing I was on a slippery slope. "Okay, but what about this grand idea? Have any of you stopped to think about it? What it means? She doesn't want to target the nobility or the people in power—she wants to manufacture a war between two countries. One that will kill innocents. Now, I don't know about you, but I still have family living out there. People I care about, getting killed in the name of a war that they don't even understand! I can't live with that. Can you honestly tell me you can?"

The crowd fell silent, and I could see the thoughtful expressions on many of their faces. For a second, I felt certain that my words had swayed them, until someone in the back shouted, "Traitor!" The entire room crumbled into shouts and jeers.

Desmond sauntered over to me and I held steady, keeping my hands at my sides. She twisted her wrist, letting the microphone drop from her mouth and point toward the ground, before giving me a pitying smile.

"You know, Violet," she said, her voice soft and low, "I never imagined that it would come to this. But now that it has, I hope you can appreciate the irony as much as I do."

"You're a snake, Desmond. No wonder your son wanted to be free of you."

Her smile flickered and faded into a scowl, and she turned back to the crowd. As she did, I took a step back and pulled out my gun, pointing it at her head. Someone in the crowd screamed in warning, and Desmond whipped around, coming face to face with my gun.

My finger tensed on the trigger, and my heart hammered in my chest as I prepared to carry the weight of what I was about to do. Spill more blood. Claim another life.

A roar at the back of the crowd reverberated off the walls with such intensity that the clamor of the crowd was drowned out, causing voices to fall silent in unison. A pale white and dark blur leapt over the crowd, landing to a skidding stop in front of me.

As the dust settled, I found myself staring at one

of the boys, who had put himself directly in front of my gun, standing between me and Desmond, his face contorted with anger and determination. People shifted as more boys began to pour through the door that I had passed through minutes ago. Several more came to stand between Desmond and me. The rest pressed in, forming a circle around us.

My hands shook as I took in the development. I heard a familiar cry of pain, and turned back in time to see my brother and Ms. Dale hauled unceremoniously into the circle around us. One of the boys tossed a squirming black bag in between them, and I heard a yip from Samuel.

Grimacing, I turned back to Desmond, who grinned at me, daring me to pull the trigger with the boys in the way.

Reluctantly, I lowered the gun and the second I did, the boys rushed at me, grabbing me and forcing me to the ground.

"My boys, please—be calm!" Desmond shrilled. "Let's put that training to good use! Drag them all to the airlock, and let's make a sport of it."

Desmond's announcement was met with a chorus of cheers, and I squeezed my eyes shut, unable to accept another failure on my part.

CHAPTER 35

Viggo

The five of us—including Samuel—were hauled upstairs through the levels and marched out by several of the boys, with Desmond bringing up the rear, a self-satisfied bounce in her step. I did my best to ignore it, but it was hard to ignore the boys giving me sidelong glances with pain in their eyes.

They looked at me like they wanted to ask why I had betrayed them. As if I could give them an answer to something that wasn't true.

It hurt that the boys hadn't trusted me enough to question Desmond's lies, even if they were being fed a drug. It hurt that they felt I had betrayed them. And at the center of all that hurt was Desmond—whatever she was planning, however she planned to achieve it, looking at those boys made me feel a rage that I had never known before.

I was supposed to be protecting them from people like her, yet I had missed what was going on. If I had been more attentive about what was happening under my nose, I probably could have done something to stop her.

As it was, I kept my mouth shut. I knew that no amount of reasoning with the boys would work now. From their point of view, Violet had pulled out her weapon first. That made her, as well as the rest of us, the aggressors. We were a threat, and we needed to be eliminated.

We reached the final set of stairs, and I felt a coldness in my gut, wondering what exactly Desmond had planned. Would she throw us out of the airlock without a mask, leave us to choke for breath and then suffocate from the toxic fumes of The Green?

No. She had mentioned something about the boys making a "sport" of this. That meant a fighting chance, if only a slim one. I needed to bide my time and see what she had planned. Depending on what it was, it might mean I died a few minutes sooner, fighting for all our lives.

Ahead of me, Violet marched forward, resolute. I felt a pang of sympathy for her—she probably wished she had pulled the trigger before the boys had arrived. As I thought about it, however, I realized that this might be better. Even with the training, the boys still had the potential for volatility, and shooting Desmond would have caused a strong reaction in them.

I realized now that my own rules for the boys would have backfired in a way, had Violet pulled the trigger. Most of them would've reacted, seen the others react, and then acted upon their instincts. In a single moment, I could've lost her, lost everything. I was grateful that she had decided to back down.

We were shoved unceremoniously into the antechamber. Most of the boys remained in the halls and stairwells—this floor wasn't open enough to hold all of them. A few of the team leaders stood inside the room, glaring at us. Desmond pushed through the group of boys, placing gentle hands on their shoulders and whispering words of encouragement.

She stepped into the room and raked us with a gaze. "Change," she ordered.

She must have sent for someone to bring regular clothes, because within seconds of her order, articles of clothing were passed up from the back. Desmond snatched them one by one, tossing them casually on the floor.

I ignored her as I bent over and grabbed the clothing. Tim, Ms. Dale and Violet weren't wearing invisibility suits, so they had no need to change. I turned my back on them and began changing.

"So, Ms. Dale," I said conversationally, as I stepped

out of the suit. "How do you think Desmond's going to kick this war off?"

There was a long pause behind me, and then Ms. Dale responded. "It's… tough to say, Mr. Croft… Starting a war is not an easy business. It requires resources, timing, and careful consideration… Whatever it is, it has to be big."

I nodded, sliding the pants over my hips and buttoning them quickly. "Like a bombing, maybe?" I asked, casting a quick glance at Desmond to read her expression.

"That might work," Ms. Dale replied. "But it'd have to be at a target vulnerable enough to cause a public outrage."

Desmond's face tightened as her smile began to fade. I hid my face, subsequently hiding my grin, and quickly slipped the shirt over my head. "I see. Like an orphanage?"

Ms. Dale scoffed. "A bit cliché, but it could work. However, I think if it were to be truly believed as an act of war, an orphanage isn't political enough. It's all emotion, no real target. No, if it were to be believable, it would be a political target, as well as an emotional one."

I nodded and sat down on one of the benches, forcing one foot into a shoe. Violet sat down next to me, flashing me a questioning look. I knew she was curious about what Ms. Dale and I were doing, but I couldn't stop to explain right then, so I gave her a tiny nod of my head.

"I guess maybe… if you really wanted to make the people angry, you would have to assassinate a public official," I drawled on.

"I suppose so," Ms. Dale said. "It would have to be someone in the public eye, someone who was beloved enough to stir them toward war."

I nodded, stepping hard into one shoe and stealing another covert glance of Desmond. She had planted a bored expression on her face with a faint air of impatience, but I could tell she was listening intently.

"Well, what about the queen?" I suggested.

I caught a flash of Ms. Dale's smile as it quickly formed and faded. "Actually, she would be a great target, Mr. Croft. Especially considering the tragic death of her mother before her."

Desmond's eyes narrowed, and I felt a pulse of triumph as I looked up and met her gaze. "That's your target, isn't it?" I said softly. "You plan to make it appear as if Patrus killed the new queen."

Desmond smirked at me and gave a little shrug. "Even if it were my target, you'd never get there in time. I've already sent my best agent to handle it—whatever it might be."

I frowned, thinking. Violet stood up beside me and faced Desmond. "Who did you send?" she demanded, her voice constricted.

Desmond gave an exaggerated roll of her eyes and stepped over to the suit display, studying it idly. A tense silence reigned before she finally sighed and turned around.

"I supposed it doesn't hurt to tell you, seeing as you'll be dead within a few hours... I sent Owen."

Violet's face flushed with horror, and I felt a pang of jealousy again. Until I remembered the fire and passion that we had shared recently. I knew Violet loved me. Her concern was for someone she had become close to during our time here. She was worried about her friend, and I could understand that.

I stood up and dropped my arm over Violet's shoulder. "I'm sure he'll be all right," I whispered.

Desmond's chuckle tore a hole through my reassurance, and I turned, allowing my anger toward her to surface. "What's so funny?" I spat.

She shook her head and waved it off, but I took a step forward aggressively. Immediately, the boys moved forward, thunderous expressions on their own faces. I clenched my fists, torn between wanting to punch the smug look off Desmond's face and not proving the boys wrong.

Desmond held a hand up toward them and made a little backward motion. The boys stepped back reluctantly, and she moved closer to me, until we were almost touching. When she spoke, her voice was pitched so low that it was almost difficult for me to hear her. "My dear boy, what makes you think Owen is going to be all right?"

I glared at her as she stepped back, and Violet stifled a cry behind me, making my anger burn more intensely. After all, it was a cruel logic—sending a man to plant a bomb and live would only endanger the entire group. No, better to kill that person, so that she was the only one who knew the secret.

"You're a monster," I hissed.

Desmond laughed. "Oh, Viggo, Viggo, Viggo," she chided, her smile growing even wider. "Surely you've heard that one man's monster is another man's hero. I do what others can't or won't, and I do it with pride. I can and will make changes to this world, our world, and I will make it a better place. Just you wait."

I shook my head. "Thousands of innocents will die for this. Please, you have to see reason! I understand you have hatred for Matrus, and even Patrus... but the toll it will take... It's not worth it!"

Desmond shrugged. "Casualties of a corrupt system cannot concern the just and the oppressed. Not if we ever want to take back power."

A few of the boys nodded in agreement. It was clear that Desmond was beyond unreasonable, she was insane—but her words were reaching into the darkest parts of the boys and speaking to them exclusively.

Desmond held out her hand. Immediately, several masks were held up by the boys, and she began grabbing them and tossing them to us one by one. I glowered at her, but placed the mask over my face, making sure it was tight and secure.

"So here's how it's going to go," Desmond said. "You are going to be given a... hmm... three-hour head start to escape. Then I'm going to send the boys after you, to implement some of the skills you've been teaching them. They will be ordered to kill you on sight. I would say good luck, but honestly... I am saving my good luck for the boys you betrayed." She reached out and patted the shoulder of one of the boys—it was Cody, the boy who had challenged me on the first day of training. He smiled viciously at me and I swallowed, trying to maintain my calm.

The boys started to push in on us, forcing us to fight or go into the airlock that stood open behind us. I was the last to be pushed in, making sure to keep steady eye contact with Desmond as I backed into the smaller room. Once I was inside the doorframe, one of the boys closed the doors, sealing us in.

I turned to the others. "All right," I breathed. "It looks like we're going to have to get to the river as fast as possible."

The room began to fill with gas, and I felt my eardrums tighten and pop as the air pressure changed slightly. Violet gazed at me from behind her mask, her eyes reflecting her concern and apprehension.

"Viggo, many of the boys are faster than us—we

won't get that much of a head start on them."

I nodded. "It's true, but if we can make it to the river in time, we'll escape," I promised.

I looked into each set of eyes and nodded confidently at them. They seemed to accept my words, which was a relief in its own right. I certainly wasn't confident, but I had hope that we would make it. At the very least, I knew I could buy them some time, if necessary.

Just then, the gas stopped filtering in, and the light on the door leading to the toxic forest beyond turned green.

I nodded to the others. "Go," I ordered firmly, as I pushed the door open.

CHAPTER 36

Violet

As soon as my boots hit the soft mossy earth, I started running, heading in the direction of the river. Desmond had given us nothing save the clothes on our backs and the masks on our faces, so I had to use the small amount of early morning sunlight filtering through the trees to best determine our direction.

We were lucky that the sun had begun to rise because we had a lot of ground to cover, and no light to illuminate our way when it got dark. We needed to put as much distance between ourselves and the boys as possible. I heard the others' feet hitting the ground as we ran, and I slowed down, allowing Tim, who was guiding Samuel, and Ms. Dale to pass me so that I could run with Viggo at the rear. Once we were jogging side by side, I shot Viggo a look.

"Why the river?" I asked.

Viggo glanced at me. "I managed to call for back-up," he said with a subtle smile, and I felt a smile forming on my own lips. He was doing his whole ambiguous shtick, and to be honest, I enjoyed it. It was difficult to explain, but it nurtured a hope that we would live to see his next move. It was almost like an incentive on his behalf—living so I could see what he had in store.

"So… she's already sent Owen into Matrus," I remarked, curious about what Viggo was able to glean from the earlier conversation.

Viggo nodded once, keeping his eyes on the path in front of us. "Yes. Which means Owen is several hours ahead of us. He might even be taking an alternate route from the river to get there—it's a straight shot down. Or he might have potentially jumped the border between The Green and Matrus and hiked in."

I frowned—it was plausible, I supposed, but it would take time. We had a chance of bypassing him on the river. If Desmond had thought there was any likelihood that we would catch up, she would've kept that information private, which meant she had provided another way for him to get in.

"I think he might already be there," I said, dodging to one side to avoid an overhanging branch. "She wouldn't have told us if she thought there was a chance to stop him."

He absorbed this information as we ran, the sound of our feet hitting the dirt intermingling with the sound of our breathing. "Possibly. You worked with them on an op before. What was the general set-up?"

I filled him in on everything that had happened after the boat—being smuggled in, meeting Thomas, getting information and gear, and then execution.

"I think we can safely assume that most of that is not going to happen," Viggo said.

"Why?" I asked curiously.

"Because it's a solo mission—that means... Look out!"

Shouting an expletive, Viggo reached out and grabbed my arm at the same moment I started to turn. Then I was tumbling to the forest ground, the world shifting on its axis until up was down and down was up. Viggo uttered another curse behind me, and I lifted myself off the ground to my hands and knees, whirling around so I could see what was happening.

A massive silver python was wrapped around his torso and legs, the heavy muscular coils already starting to constrict. He had thrown an arm around the snake's neck and was squeezing hard, but with little effect. The snake thrashed back and forth, trying to dislodge Viggo from its neck, while he struggled to hold on.

I shot to my feet, looking around for something—anything—that I could use as a weapon. Viggo was shouting something, but I couldn't make it out—his voice was strained from the compression of his lungs. His face was turning a hue of scarlet that made my heart leap into my throat and his name escape my lips.

Racing over to the closest tree, I leapt up and grabbed a branch with both hands. It sagged under my weight, but didn't break. Grunting with effort, I shifted my weight, pulling myself up and then dropping hard. There was a sharp cracking sound, and then I fell to the ground, my legs not prepared to hold my weight. I clutched the bit of broken branch in my hands and scrambled toward where Viggo was still struggling with the snake.

I could see his strength fading. Adrenaline coursing through my veins, I hefted the branch over my shoulder like a spear and raced toward the pair. The snake's head was thrashing back and forth, but I was certain if I could first shove the broken end into one of its gleaming black eyes, I would be able to kill it.

Suddenly, the spear was yanked from my hands and the next thing I knew, I was staring into the determined eyes of my brother. He lifted the branch over his shoulder, took a measured step forward and then threw it, grunting as he did.

The branch was not aerodynamic, but Tim's reflexes and hand-eye coordination had been enhanced, and I winced as the branch hit with a wet thud, a good foot of it embedding itself into the snake's skull. The snake shuddered, and then its head hit the ground with a heavy thud, its coils becoming slack.

I raced over to where Viggo was still half entangled in the coils. Grabbing them, I quickly pulled him out. He was gasping, but the blood-red color of his face was beginning to dissipate.

I wrapped my arms around him and held him tightly, shooting a grateful glance at my brother. He offered me a little smile in return. Pulling back a few inches, I looked deep into Viggo's eyes. His labored breathing was still fogging up the clear plastic face of the mask, but I could see his eyes clearly.

"Idiot," I said softly, so only he would hear.

He coughed, hard, and then grinned up at me, his green eyes twinkling. "Saved your life," he breathed, his words punctuated by tiny coughs here and there.

I shook my head at him, and then helped him up. Ms. Dale and Tim came to stand next to us.

"Viggo… okay?" Tim asked.

Viggo smiled at him and then began coughing again. I took a step closer, concerned, but he held up a hand, and I stopped, even though I didn't want to. After a moment, he took a deep breath and nodded, straightening up. He then reached over and grabbed Tim by the shoulder, pulling him into a massive hug. My heart soared at the image of Viggo and my brother bonding. Viggo was gentle in his hug—he was conscious of Tim's sensitivity.

Even that was enough to bring tears of happiness to my eyes. It was strange, but even though we were on the run, with the threat of death looming over us, I felt optimistic about the future. We were going to evade the boys and escape. I clung to this hope with the same certainty that I needed oxygen to live.

Viggo released a blushing Tim and turned to the rest of us. "We throwing a party?" Viggo said hoarsely.

Ms. Dale eyed him wryly. "Not yet, but if you can get us out of here alive, Patrian, I'll buy the first round."

"Well then… if I didn't have a reason for living before, having the pleasure of seeing you buy me a drink is a damned good one," he replied with a laugh. He took a few more experimental breaths in, and then nodded. "All right, people, that's a good enough break—let's run."

Tim beckoned to Samuel, and we wordlessly fell into line and began running again. Viggo set the pace—so at first it was a light jog, but after a while, it became faster. I wasn't sure how long Viggo could keep it up, though—I had already begun to see the strain in his face, although he stoically tried to hide it.

I brought up the rear of the run, with Tim behind Viggo and Ms. Dale in front of me. We ran in a straight line, but a few times Tim scampered off, ducking under some branches or diving through the brush. The first few times, I'd watched in confusion, but after the fourth time, I put on a burst of speed and raced up to him when he rejoined our little formation.

"What are you doing?" I asked.

Tim glanced at me and then looked ahead. He was definitely exerting himself more than the rest of us— sweat was dripping from him at a phenomenal pace. However, his breathing was less labored than mine, and he still showed signs of going strong.

"Messing with… the trail. Trying to leave… fake ones. Distract the boys," he responded.

"That's really smart. How'd you learn to do that?"

He nodded his head toward Viggo's back, and I smiled—of course Viggo had taught them survival. They lived in The Green, after all.

I accelerated and moved up to Viggo. "Where do you think the attack is going to happen?" I asked.

Viggo had recovered from the struggle with the snake, but I could tell we would need to take another break soon. Still, his discomfort didn't keep him from answering my question.

"Matrus. I doubt that Desmond has informants in the queen's inner circle, but with royalty, it's all about location, location, location."

I let out a small chuckle—hard to do when running—and then asked him, "So he knows where the queen is going to be?"

"So do you—don't you remember what celebration is coming up soon?"

I frowned, and then started doing the math in my head. The Patrian calendar was different than the Matrian one, and I hadn't really paid much attention to the dates when I was serving my time in the re-education program. It took me a minute to remember.

"The Solstice Celebration!" I exclaimed.

Viggo nodded. "Yup—the queen does her little ceremonial blessing of the waters at the Moon Temple, right?"

I nodded. The tradition began when Matrus was founded. It was in celebration of the lunar New Year—a symbolic act of embracing femininity and the power that it bestowed in wisdom, endurance, and patience. The ceremony was held in a small temple just outside the palace that had been built in a cave which had housed the first settlers who'd fled Patrus and its laws.

Suddenly, an image of the silver case with the egg sitting in Desmond's office flashed in my mind's eye and I gasped. Viggo shot me a curious glance and then slowed to a stop, taking the opportunity for a break.

I turned back, my heartbeat doubling.

"Vi… what is it?" he asked.

I looked at Viggo and then back at the way we had come. "The egg. It's still in the facility."

Viggo glanced back at the miles of forest between

us and the building, and sighed. "It's gone, Vi. We can't go back for it."

I nodded, having come to that conclusion myself. "I know," I said. "Sorry… it just feels weird not having it."

He nodded, his expression pensive. "Okay… We need to keep going. Time's running out."

Letting the egg go in my mind, I turned and we continued moving.

It was hard to gauge how long we had been traveling so far, but I knew we were running short on time—we must have passed the three-hour mark.

I could feel the seconds ticking by, each one more tense than the last. I kept a wary eye out, looking for anything unusual in the underbrush.

Which was how I noticed some rustling in the trees to the left of us that seemed to be keeping pace and then some. At first I thought we might have attracted the attention of some other predator, but through a break in the trees, I saw what clearly looked like legs and shoes. I felt a moment of alarm and had opened my mouth to warn everyone of it when it suddenly burst through the foliage just in front of Viggo and rushed right toward us.

CHAPTER 37

Viggo

The cramp in my side had been intensifying over the last few miles, and it felt like my chest was about to come apart, but I sucked it up and pressed on. I had no choice but to keep running—if it killed me, it killed me. I would be dead soon if I stopped anyway.

I had been keeping a wary eye on our surroundings, when a boy crashed through the brush, rushing toward us.

I slid to a stop and turned to face him fully, my mind instantly working to figure out how to disable him without harming him. I didn't recognize him—he was moving too fast for me to pick out any key features or characteristics—but it didn't matter, so long as I could get him under control.

I curled my hands up into fists and assumed a fighting stance, watching the boy as he barreled head-long toward us. I braced for impact, intent on using his momentum against him by rolling him over my back, when Tim darted between us, turning to face me.

"Don't!" he pleaded, his eyes wide with fear.

I froze and watched as the boy behind Tim slid to a stop as well, panting hard. He leaned over and coughed, sucking in air. It was obvious he had been running for a long time in an attempt to catch up. As he straightened, I recognized him.

"Oh. Hello, Jay," I said and he offered a wave, still wheezing. I looked at Tim. "What's going on?"

Tim shifted nervously and looked at Violet. "Didn't go to Ms. Dale first," he said, addressing his sister. "Went to Jay. Asked for help."

"So… Jay's here to help us?" Violet asked, looking relieved.

"I didn't want to stay with her," Jay said from behind Tim, looking both uncomfortable and disturbed. "When they brought you upstairs, I stayed below and grabbed some things that I thought you might need." He shrugged off the large backpack he was wearing and held it out. The bag was over-packed, and I could see the seams straining.

I accepted the bulging bag with a grateful smile. "I'm glad to see you here with us, Jay." Jay flushed, a dark red spreading across his cheeks. I patted his back and handed the bag to Violet. "Any chance any of the other boys being with us?" I asked hopefully.

Jay's embarrassment turned into deep sadness, and my heart ached for him. It was clear from his reaction that they had all chosen Desmond, not me, and my heart constricted again in pain thinking about the boys and how they saw me now. It made me beyond angry that they were yet again being used for someone else's aim.

Jay had taken a step back from me, his eyes wide in alarm, and I realized that my feelings regarding the situation were currently on my face. Sighing, I squatted down, bringing myself lower than him to make him feel more secure. "I'm sorry, Jay—I'm not angry at you. I'm angry at Desmond for using the boys like this."

Jay nodded slowly, his eyes downcast. "My mom isn't a good person," he whispered, and I felt my chest tighten further. No child should have to feel that way about his mother.

"Come here," I said softly, holding an arm out to him. He stepped closer and I pulled him in for a hug. I rubbed his back as I felt him shake a little bit, tears falling from his eyes. "It's going to be okay, Jay. I promise." It was the only solace I could offer to the boy, but it was one I meant. I didn't know how yet, but I was going to make it right for him. I was going to do more than that—I was going to protect him.

Violet let out a gasp and I reluctantly let go of Jay and turned toward her. Violet had been busy during my chat with Jay. All the items from the bag were laid out in an orderly fashion. Jay had done well— he had grabbed three pistols with several magazines of ammunition and two boxes of ammo. He had also grabbed five of the aerosol canisters that helped keep the vicious creatures of The Green at bay, as well as several tins of food, a few pieces of fresh fruit, two lightweight blankets, a knife, three flashlights, a compass, and three canteens.

Yet Violet's attention was completely on the two identical silver cases sitting in front of her, gleaming in the muted light. "How did you know to grab these?" she whispered, her eyes coming up to stare at Jay.

Jay looked up at Tim, who flushed and ran a hand over his hair. "I told him—they're important."

She stood up, her brows drawn together. "But how did you know to grab the one in the cabinet?" she asked, taking a step closer.

Tim shrugged. "You're sneaky. Also… don't like Desmond. No egg for her."

Violet grinned and kissed her brother on the cheek. "You did really good, baby brother," she announced with a smile. "And you, Jay." She rested a gentle hand on his shoulder. "I just want you to know how brave I think you are. And I want to thank you for believing in us."

Jay blushed again, but beamed at her, his eyes glowing from her praise. Licking his lips, he tentatively wrapped his arms around her neck in a hug and she returned it warmly. The entire exchange was touching, but I could feel time marching merrily forward without us.

We needed to get going.

"We should keep moving," Jay said, echoing my thoughts, as he took a step back. He looked over his shoulder, back the way he had come. "I spent some time laying a few false trails, but it won't buy us a lot of time… Maybe an hour or two at the most."

"I agree," I said. "Everyone drink some water, but not too much—you don't want it sloshing around in your belly while you run. Once we're finished, we'll begin moving again. Violet, help me repack the bag. The three of us will take turns carrying it." I looked at Ms. Dale, who nodded at me, her face reflecting her tension and eagerness to continue our journey.

"The five of us," contradicted Tim, his voice and stance carrying a stubbornness that I was beginning to recognize as a trait in the Bates family.

I smiled and nodded. "All right—the five of us," I agreed. I handed the water bottles out to Ms. Dale, Tim, and Jay, allowing them an opportunity to drink first as Violet and I repacked the bag. Within minutes, we were running again.

We had packed the bag well—the contents weren't shifting around or bouncing against my back as I moved, which was a bonus. While I ran, I turned my mind toward Desmond's plan and the implications it might have on our world if she succeeded.

Who knew what Desmond's political aims really were? She had only been clear on what she didn't like—how could someone so tyrannical and cold-blooded be different than the regime before? I didn't think it was possible or likely that much would change—instead I feared things would get worse in her grab for power. After all, if she was willing to use her own sons to carry out her dirty work, who knew what she would be willing to do to maintain power.

Power—there it was again. It baffled me how much people were willing to do and sacrifice in order to gain and keep it. There was a depraved lunacy in the pursuit of it that spoke to the darker side of humanity. I was content without power, so it was hard for me to imagine why anyone would go to such great lengths to acquire it.

That didn't stop me from appreciating the irony of the whole situation. Here we were, so-called enemies of Matrus, tearing through The Green in a mad dash to save the very institution that had labeled us as such. Well, I wasn't sure of my status, but I was pretty sure they didn't expect a Patrian male to attempt to save Matrian lives. However, I was likely an enemy of Patrus at this point—I had failed in my mission to return Violet to Patrus to face justice for her crimes. And that meant that I was also working to save Patrus from a senseless war that it had no idea was coming.

It was enough to make me chuckle, and help me keep going in spite of the exhaustion that was sending warning signals rolling through my body that I needed to stop and sit down.

The sun had long since faded, and we had paused shortly before to pull out the flashlights that Jay had provided. Now we ran in pairs, with one person holding a flashlight to illuminate our path. Occasionally, Jay and Tim would break off to help disguise the trail to buy us more time. We paused more than once to drink water, catch our breaths, or pass the bag. Even with all that activity, the hours slipped by in a tense silence with no sounds save for our footsteps and labored breathing.

The steady sound was lulling us into a false sense of security. After hours of not seeing anyone other than Jay, we were beginning to nurture the hope that we had somehow lost any pursuers. I had thought it through, and I was fairly confident that the boys would have likely stopped when night fell. The forest was a scary place during the day, and for all of their enhancements, they were still young enough to fear the dark and the creatures that inhabited it.

It turned out that we were all wrong on that

account.

Just as I began to hear something new over our falling footsteps, a shout came up from the forest behind us. I skidded to a stop, my muscles protesting the sudden change in status. Whipping around, I cast my flashlight toward the forest behind us; I was breathing heavily behind my mask, sweat dripping down my face and chest.

Ms. Dale had already pulled her gun, much to my annoyance, and Violet's hand was twitching, like she wanted to hold hers. I held my breath, straining to hear.

The seconds turned into a minute as I listened intently, my muscles twitching from overuse. A faint rustling drew my attention, and I took a step forward, staring intently at the intermingled vines, branches, leaves, logs, and bushes, trying to make out anything through the wild chaos of the forest.

I heard the rustling again, drawing closer. Something was behind us, approaching at an alarming speed. I turned back to the others and nodded.

"Run. As fast as you can. Get to the river."

Violet and the others nodded and turned, beginning to run in spite of the clear exhaustion that was stamped into them. Fear was a powerful motivator, however, and they ran, ignoring their aches and pains with one singular goal in mind.

I followed closely behind, keeping an eye out

behind us. The new sound I had begun to hear was exactly what I had hoped—the river. Hopefully the bridge was still there, but who knew how long we would have to search the banks before we found it. I wasn't even sure if it was further to the north or south, and I only had Alejandro's word that it was there.

Still, I clung to the hope that we would see it and be able to cross it before the boys behind us caught up.

Violet was the first to spot the river, and let out an excited, albeit ragged, cry. "Over here," she shouted, her boots kicking up clumps of earth. I pelted after her, coming to a stop a few feet away from the water that seemed to glow. The trees parted here, allowing the light of the moon to illuminate the banks of the river.

I quickly scanned up and down the river and gave an audible sigh of relief when I saw a gigantic overturned tree connecting the two banks a few hundred feet north of us. "There," I said, pointing to the natural bridge.

The others began racing toward it. The tree was ancient—probably the oldest thing in the forest, given its size. Even sideways, the trunk was wider than I was tall by three to four feet, and it stretched all the way across the water.

Violet was in the process of scaling the trunk to get on top when a sharp crack of a breaking tree branch came from the dense tree line directly behind us. I didn't stop to look, just began shoving our group up the trunk as quickly as I could. I climbed up behind them, about to urge them to run, when I realized I didn't have to. They weren't wasting any time.

Normally, a crossing like this would be slow going. Even though the trunk wasn't submerged in the water, the tree trunk was slick—one wrong move would send us into the water. However, we didn't have the luxury of being cautious. We ran toward the other side. About halfway across, I heard an excited shout, and turned back to see two boys break through the tree line and leap up onto the tree trunk, not even breaking their stride.

Adrenaline surged through me, and I raced across to the other side. As I approached, I looked at Tim and Jay. "Push the trunk in the water," I bellowed as I brought myself to a full stop, whirled around, and dropped to a knee. I pulled my gun and aimed at the boys who were still crossing. Immediately Jay and Tim began pushing, and I could feel Jay's impossible strength as the tree that likely hadn't moved in a long time shifted slightly.

The boys opposite me felt it too, and froze, their eyes bulging. I exhaled, trying to find the air to shout again. "Go back, boys, or we will defend ourselves."

The tree moved again, rolling slightly under my knee, and I used one hand to steady myself, staring down the barrel at them. The boys took in me, the gun, Jay and Tim, and finally took a slow step back, much to my relief.

The log shifted again, and I met their gaze solidly. "Run," I said.

They ran.

I held my position for a moment longer, and then staggered to my feet and moved toward the group, dropping down heavily on the ground. I moved next to Tim and Jay and pressed a shoulder to the tree, struggling against the weight of it. Violet and Ms. Dale shoved in next to us, and together we strained. The log resisted at first, but under our combined efforts, it shifted slightly. We continued to push for several more moments, our strength fading, when suddenly it began rolling so fast that I almost fell face first into the mud.

The massive tree rolled into the river with a splash, and we hurried backward to avoid the toxic water.

I looked at everyone and smiled. "Well… that was easy, right?"

Everyone groaned except Violet, who rolled her eyes at me—and then groaned.

CHAPTER 38

Violet

Hours had passed since we helped Jay shove the giant tree trunk into the river. Viggo had led us several hundred feet down the riverbank before announcing that this was where we'd stay for the night. All of us had laid out the blankets and eaten some food, and I took first watch. I woke up Tim for the next shift, and then promptly passed out.

We probably would've remained sleeping had it not been for a loud voice calling Viggo's name. I jerked awake with a start, managing to wake Viggo in the process.

"What?" he said as he bolted upright. I stood up slowly and moved over to the riverbank, looking down it. Ms. Dale was already there with her gun drawn, indicating that I had only gotten about two hours of sleep. A bright light was shining from the bow of a boat, blinding me with its intensity. I raised my arm, shielding my eyes from the light.

"Who's there?" I called, holding the gun against my thigh and slightly behind me.

There was a metallic scraping sound as the light panned right and away. Blinking my eyes to rid them of the black spots dancing across them, I slowly focused on the image of a boat drifting closer. As I squinted, I saw a familiar head of white hair, topped by an equally familiar cap.

I started to smile when I saw Alejandro's face, and then hesitated when I began to wonder what he was doing there.

Until his smile broadened when he saw Viggo, his eyes glittering with merriment.

"My boy!" he crowed, and Viggo laughed. I stared at the two and a massive click fell into place as I recalled Alejandro's missing friend. I shook my head, chuckling at my own idiocy.

"Hey, Alejandro. I see you got my message," Viggo called, stepping up next to me and dropping a casual arm over my shoulder.

Alejandro's smile grew even bigger—which I didn't think was possible—as he took in Viggo's action. I felt my cheeks grow hot under his scrutiny, and gave him a little wave.

"Hello, Alejandro," I said.

"Hello, girl. It's good to see you again! Who's that with you? Two boys... a dog... and a lady. Hello, ma'am. Gentlemen. Canine." He whipped his hat off his head and bowed deeply. "By the way... does anyone know who tried to sink me by throwing a massive log into the river?"

Viggo chuckled and shrugged. "It's a good tale, but one better told on the move, wouldn't you say?"

Alejandro guffawed and nodded. "Well then, stop lollygagging on the shore and let's get a move on! You know how I love a good story..."

An hour later, we were all lounging on the boat, save Jay and Tim, who were sleeping below in Alejandro's room. Alejandro had listened intently as Viggo filled him in on everything—and I did mean everything, from me coming to Patrus to steal the egg to the events leading up to now.

Alejandro nodded, and shot a few of us some considering looks, but remained quiet until the end of Viggo's story. Once Viggo had finished, Alejandro took a moment for himself, silently considering the implications of everything.

"So, let me get this straight—Violet stole a stolen egg with a partner who tried to kill both of you.

Violet flew that partner's flying machine into The Green and crashed. Meanwhile, Viggo gets assigned to hunt her down, but in the midst of this, Viggo shoots Ms. Dale, then y'all find a building built mostly underground. An abandoned building, save for some one thousand boys who were experimented on and given advanced abilities. You were discovered by a rebel faction, led by Violet's now dead partner's mother, and she wants to manufacture a war between Matrus and Patrus so that she can destroy both and assume control over both nations, uniting them under her command?"

"Yes," I said, nodding emphatically. "That about sums it up."

Alejandro blew a breath of air out of his mouth, fogging up the plastic visor for a few seconds. Cursing, he whipped it off his face, used the sleeve of his shirt to wipe it clean, and pushed it back on. He then leaned forward and gave us all a look.

"This is serious. Patrus is already buzzing like an angry wasp's nest."

"What do you mean?" Ms. Dale asked.

Alejandro studied her for a moment and then sighed. "After the bombing of a storage facility, rumors started up, speculating who was responsible. With no one coming forward to take credit, the rumors shifted toward agents of Matrus, trying to undermine the Patrian regime. A few days later, there was another explosion—this time at a hotel hosting a meeting between government officials. Only two were killed, but several more were injured. Later, a bomb was discovered on a boat that was supposed to carry King Maxen that day. The next day, another bomb detonated in one of the hospitals. In one of the children's wards. A male children's ward."

I felt suddenly nauseated. It had to be Thomas, working under Desmond's orders. Possibly even with other Liberators—ones I hadn't met or who were working for Desmond from the inside. All those people... all those children. It was beyond cruel.

Alejandro reached out with one hand and took my other hand into his own, his eyes glistening from unshed tears. "So, what I mean to say is... how can I help?"

Viggo shook his head, his face pale. "This is the first step of Desmond's propaganda war," he said. "Her plan is to make it look like retaliation for the attacks on Patrus. It's a tinder keg about to explode." I could feel the tension radiating from him, and reached out with my other hand to take his, squeezing it gently.

"We couldn't have known," I whispered, and Viggo met my gaze. I could see his eyes were also glistening. I stared back at him. "We have to make this better. We're going to, right?"

Viggo stood up and walked to the starboard rail,

looking out on The Green as we slid past it. "How long would it take us to get to Matrus?" he asked, turning to face Alejandro.

Alejandro stood up and pulled his handheld out of his pocket. "I can get you there in… twenty-six hours," he said.

I grimaced. It was cutting things close, but it was the best we could do. I looked to Viggo, and he nodded. "That'll be great, Alejandro," he said, reaching out for the older man's hand.

Alejandro clasped hands with him, and they shook on it.

I looked over at Ms. Dale, who was wearing an expression I didn't recognize. "Ms. Dale? What's wrong?"

Startled, Ms. Dale turned to me, pushing a few locks of her hair away from her mask. "Something… feels off. This feels too simple for Desmond… I fear that we're missing something."

I frowned, considering her words. "You think there's something deeper going on? Some deeper game she's playing that we're not seeing?"

Ms. Dale shook her head, her expression one of frustration. "I don't know… it just feels off. I don't have anything to offer as proof, Violet. Just a gut feeling."

I fell silent, unsure of how to respond. However, I had a sneaking suspicion that Ms. Dale was right as well. This plan was grand, and impressive, but I also felt like something was off.

But experience had taught me that wild speculation would get one nowhere. Until we knew differently, we had to act on the information we had, and pray that it would help prevent a war.

CHAPTER 39

Violet

I stood holding Viggo's hand as crowds of people pushed past us, making their way to the temple. We had arrived a little earlier than expected. Docking had been… interesting. Ms. Dale had used her credentials to get us past the inspection officials, claiming that it was under Queen Elena's direct order that we be allowed in, quietly and without any whisper of our appearance. I had kept my head down as she aggressively, but expertly, handled the situation.

With a final look of longing, Viggo dropped my hand and disappeared into the throngs of people, mostly women, who were making their way into the Temple of the Moon. I watched him leave, heading for the line of men filed up on one side, and turned to Ms.

Dale, who offered me a tight, nervous smile.

"Be careful, Violet," she said and I nodded, pulling the hood of my stolen jacket up over my head.

"You too," I murmured.

I watched as she too disappeared into the crowd, leaving me alone by the temple steps. Our plan was crude, but we had no other options. Viggo would patrol the area where the men were, and I would be down in the main part of the temple, keeping an eye out for Owen as well. Our plan was to confront Owen and try to draw him outside. I had been adamant about not hurting him if we could avoid it, and everyone had agreed.

It went unspoken that if we couldn't get him to see reason, we would have to kill him. It was a harsh reality, but as I stared at the undulating crowd of women and children, I realized it was the only way. I couldn't let Owen kill all these people.

I went in with the crowd, keeping my pace moderate and my eyes moving. Most of the women were wearing ceremonial robes—pristine white gowns that were modestly pinned together at one shoulder. At the steps of the temple, there was a growing pile of trinkets that women were placing into a small natural pool of water that flowed from the cracks of the cliff face, collecting at the base.

The tradition had been started during the first ceremony of the moon, when Queen Natasha had pulled a beautiful blue stone out and called it her hopes for the future of Matrus. She had placed it in the waters, and asked that the waters that had sustained them thus far to also help sustain her dreams for the future.

Now, many women participated in the ritual, dropping items that they had carried with them throughout the year. According to tradition and belief, if their hearts were pure and intentions good, the waters would find their greatest hope and grant it to them.

I watched as a little barefoot girl stepped up to the fountain and kissed a small porcelain doll she was holding. She placed it in the waters, bowed at the pool, and then skipped back over to where her mother was waiting. The woman took the little girl's hand and disappeared into the temple.

Steel slid into my spine as I continued through the crowd.

The mouth of the cave had been widened during the years, painstakingly chiseled out by hand. It was now wide enough to fit ten people standing side by side. I made my way up the steps, moving around women who were chatting or waiting for someone.

The cave mouth stretched inward for ten feet, the sunlight from outside illuminating the brown and black stones that glistened. I could see the line of men standing behind a cordon of rope, waiting to be led down to the balcony at the back of the chamber. I couldn't see Viggo, but I knew he'd be able to make it down all right.

I followed a group of women down the natural spiraling staircase. The light from outside quickly disappeared as we made our way down, but torches had been lit and placed in sconces, which helped illuminate our way.

I gave a brief glance to each woman who was wearing a more modern outfit, just in case Owen had somehow managed to slip in on the women's side, but he wasn't among them. Still, I didn't let go of my hope that we would find him. We had to. I couldn't bring myself to consider the alternative.

The stairs went down forty feet before ending in a circular chamber. As I moved off the last step onto the landing, I stared. I had forgotten how beautiful this room was. A massive chandelier hung almost twenty feet overhead, with thousands of candles illuminating the ceiling above. The ceiling was photo-luminescent, so the light being generated by the candles caused the ceiling to glow in soft blues and purples. Alternating red and purple tiles cut in a hexagonal pattern circled the floor. Inside of it, smaller, multi-colored tiles had been cut in creams, whites, grays, and blues, forming a mosaic of the Mother.

The Mother was a symbolic image of femininity, one that encapsulated the ideals of what made women great. I remembered when my mom had taken me up to the highest gallery and had me look at it from above.

In one arm, the Mother cradled her infant, while in her opposite hand, she wielded a stone. She stood resolute, determined, ready to destroy anyone who harmed her baby. She was strong, feminine, brave, and wise.

I made my way to the center of the room, standing over the Mother's heart, and looked around. Suddenly, three large thumps sounded, and a bell chimed. Immediately, everyone dropped to their knees. I knelt down a second later, keeping my eyes low as the queen descended the steps. Each step she took was sounded by a chime and I could hear the whisper of the fabric of her long train as she moved.

We all kept our eyes down. No woman was to lay eyes on her from when she entered the temple until she waded into the pool just under the waterfall, stripping her dress off and allowing the waters that sustained her to bless her, which, symbolically, meant Matrus.

Elena's arrival was a bad sign since it meant that Ms. Dale had failed to get her warning to her in time. I kept my eyes down, but didn't close them in prayer. Instead, I looked around, studying each of the women who knelt around me, their eyes closed and their lips moving.

About halfway down the stairs, a high, undulating

cry went up, and the women started to sing, their voices rising in the cave in a harmonious beseeching of the moon to grant all women blessings of good fortune. The song grew steadily as Elena made her way down the stairs.

Once she reached the bottom, the singing stopped, and a hush fell on everyone. There was another whisper of fabric as she slowly disrobed.

"Mothers, daughters," she said, her voice ringing out like a bell. "As I step into the pool of water that sustained us during our exodus, I make my body into a vessel, ready to absorb the wisdom of the Mother."

"The Mother," everyone echoed reverently.

"The Mother who guides us, grants us strength, gives us patience, and teaches us to be brave. It is in her name that we beseech—guide us through the next year. Make us prosperous, dear Mother, and help guide us from the darkness of oppression to the light of freedom."

"In her image," the celebrants concluded.

There was a sound of water splashing. I could hear the water shifting as she moved to the waterfall. Then came several sounds of her grunting as she sought out handholds in the rock face, climbing up to a boulder that stood directly under the waterfall. She didn't make a sound as the frigid water pelted her skin.

"Mother!" Elena cried, and I pictured her standing on the boulder, her arms uplifted and head tilted back as she beseeched the Mother on behalf of her people. "I am not a perfect woman. I have been in turmoil over those I have lost in the last year—my own mother and sisters have fallen in pursuit of your image. Please, grant me the strength to lead these great women in their stead. Please, grant me the wisdom to keep our enemies at bay. And if all else fails, grant me the bravery to stand up to those who would do us harm, so that I may serve my sisters in my duties to them."

"Bless her, Mother!" the assembly cried.

Just then, an angry shout sounded in the hall and I opened my eyes and looked up toward the balcony containing the men. I could see a few bewildered faces as two men pushed through, grappling with each other.

I rose from my knees and gazed up, seeing Viggo and Owen struggling with each other over a bag Owen was clinging to tightly. Viggo said something to Owen that I couldn't make out, and Owen shook his head, pulling harder. Other women were starting to stand, pointing at the fight between the two men. I, however, was fixated on the bag. That was where the bomb was.

"Bomb!" I exploded, pointing up at the balcony. "Bomb! Run!"

It took a moment for my words to register, but when they did, the room erupted in panic, everyone screaming as they fled for the stairs. I caught a glimpse of Elena as she was grabbed by several wardens and whisked up the stairs.

Viggo grunted and I switched my attention back to the gallery, watching the scene unfold. Viggo had managed to wrest the bag away from Owen, but Owen wasn't giving up. Raising his hands in desperation, he shoved Viggo hard. Viggo stumbled toward the rail, his hip hitting it hard. Owen raced closer and shoved again.

"NO!" I screamed as Viggo teetered on the edge, clutching the bag to his chest. I watched in horror as his weight shifted impossibly out over the balcony, his feet coming off the ground as he started to fall. I felt another scream building in my throat as I took a step toward him, when Viggo's hand snaked out, grabbing a stone jutting out just below the banister.

He dangled by his fingertips while Owen cursed and turned to flee. I kept my gaze on Viggo and looked around for some way to help him get down. I ignored the cries and shoves of the women who were still fighting to get to the stairs and looked up, my eyes resting on the chandelier.

"Viggo," I rasped. "Can you make it to the chandelier?"

Viggo grunted, his arm flexing as he painstakingly swung his body around to look at it. "Needs to be lower," he called back, and I could hear the strain in his voice, which spurred me into action. Starting at the chandelier, I looked at the thick length of rope suspending it in the air and followed the line down. I raced over to the wall, grabbing several women and dragging them along with me.

"Help me," I yelled at them, grabbing the rope. I held it taut while the women tentatively unwrapped it from the peg suspending it in place. Luckily, the chandelier was lifted and lowered using a pulley system, but I was glad that I had grabbed them—it was still heavy.

Together, we slowly let out the rope, dropping it down further and further. I shot a glance at Viggo over my shoulder, keeping an eye on him as he watched the chandelier. "That's good," he shouted. "Hold it there, and get ready for some more weight."

The other women looked at me and I met their inquisitive gaze with a no-nonsense one of my own. "Just do it," I ordered, and they nodded. Several other women noticed what we were doing and came over, grabbing lengths of rope and bracing themselves.

I heard Viggo grunt and the sound of shoes scraping on stones. The rope shivered from the impact of his body. "Go, Violet," he shouted, and I gritted my teeth, nodding to the others.

"Slowly," I commanded, using one foot to brace myself on the wall as we let the rope out a few inches at a time. My forearms were straining and my shoulders ached, but I felt relieved when I heard the sounds of boots hitting the ground. We lowered the chandelier the rest of the way to the ground before I whirled around and launched myself at Viggo, binding my arms around him. He held the bag away from his body, but wrapped one strong arm around my shoulders.

"We're okay," he wheezed. "And... we got the bomb."

I snatched the bag out of his hands and opened it. The same material Owen and I had scraped off of the columns in the facility had been packed tightly into the bag, a silver detonator leading to a digital clock that was counting down. There were five minutes on the clock, much to my relief. I pressed the edges of the clay around the timer down and peeked under it, checking for any additional detonators or wires underneath.

"I'm going to pull the detonator," I said, before looking up at him. "Just in case I'm wrong... I love you."

His lips twitched in a smile. "Yes I know. Just pull it."

I rolled my eyes at his arrogance and then slowly, carefully, slid the silver pin out. I exhaled in relief when nothing happened, and then looked at Viggo. "Okay, now carefully pull the timer out. Slowly."

Viggo grabbed the timer and did as I asked. I pressed my cheek against the clay so I could triple check that there wasn't a secondary detonator, and breathed a second sigh of relief when it came up easily. Viggo pulled it one way while I pulled the bag another, and we both carefully took a step back and lowered our respective items to the ground, several feet apart.

Once the bomb was out of my hands, I threw myself at him, wrapping my arms around his waist.

"We did it," he said, nuzzling the top of my head.

I snuggled against his chest. "I knew we would."

Viggo reached for my chin. Panning my face upward, he'd lowered his head for a kiss when something hard slammed into both of us, knocking us to the ground.

It took me a moment to realize that a pair of wardens had hit us, one of whom was now on top of me with a knee planted in the small of my back.

"What are you doing?" I exclaimed, trying to twist around to look her in the eye. "We stopped the bomb! We saved everyone!"

"Quiet!" the woman on top of me ordered, her hand going to the back of my head and gripping my hair to still me.

I looked over at Viggo, who was also struggling. But he didn't get an order for silence when he started to break free. The warden on him made a tsking sound, stood up quickly, and kicked him in the face so hard his head snapped back and he fell to the ground unconscious.

I started screaming and struggling, trying to claw

my way over to him. The woman who'd kicked Viggo looked at me, then back to him, and shook her head, pulling a pistol out.

"Sister," she said, and my screams died in my throat as she aimed her gun purposefully at Viggo. "Come quietly or I will execute this man here and now, temple property be damned."

I had no choice but to stop struggling and let the wardens take me.

CHAPTER 40

Violet

Every part of my body was shaking as I paced the length of the cell I had been shoved into. I felt agitated, both mentally and physically, and pacing was the only way to keep in the screams that were building in my throat.

I had been in the cell for hours. Viggo had been taken somewhere else after we had arrived at the palace. He had been unconscious when I last saw him, blood streaming from a cut in his forehead. I had done my best to explain everything on the ride over, but the wardens were stone-faced, content to let me talk until my voice gave out.

I couldn't be more grateful that we had convinced Tim and Jay to stay on the boat with Alejandro and the eggs. We'd known that there was a good chance we would get caught, which made it important to keep the eggs out of the situation. We'd kept them in reserve, as a backup plan if this didn't go well.

The door swung open and a warden stepped into the prison chamber, making her way to my cell.

"What's going on?" I asked as she slipped the key into the door. She looked at me, her blue eyes stoic and flat. I took a step back from the bars, turning around and dropping my arms behind my back.

The cell door swung open. Grabbing me just above my elbow, she marched me out and through the open door on the other side of the room.

We were in the royal palace, and as I stepped into the hall, I felt a tug of déjà vu. It hadn't been that long since I had last been here, and nothing had changed. The warden guided me up several flights of stairs, to the very topmost level of the palace. I passed by the portraits of Queen Rina and her daughters, taking a moment to gaze at Elena's profile, before I was shoved into a familiar office.

My stomach clenched at the memory of Queen Rina and Mr. Jenks' lifeless bodies sitting in the now-empty chairs in front of the table. Instinctively, my eyes went to the table to see if Lee's words were still there. Of course they weren't—the surface had been sanded down and re-stained.

A solitary figure stood by a window, staring out at

the city below. Queen Elena. She was clothed now, her blonde hair coifed in curling waves artfully pinned into place. I heard the wisp of skirts as she turned, her hands folded over her abdomen.

As I met the new queen's gaze, I felt a rush of excitement. This was my chance to explain what had happened and try to get a way out for me and Viggo. Stepping forward, I offered her a bow, noting the look of surprised pleasure on her face.

"Hello, Ms. Bates," Queen Elena said, her voice soft. "Please, have a seat." She held out an arm toward one of the chairs on my side of the table, and after a moment's hesitation, I sat down.

She moved over to her own chair, opposite me, and seated herself, smoothing the front of her dress with both hands before resting her arms on the table.

"You know, Violet, I have been thinking a lot the last few hours, and I have to say, you are a rather fascinating subject to think about."

"Your majesty, please… where is Viggo Croft? Is he… is he all right?"

Elena smiled and leaned back in her chair, watching me. "Such devotion to a Patrian… how I admire that."

I frowned, unsure of what she was talking about. Leaning forward, I tried a different route. "Your majesty, you have to understand—he's innocent. We both are. We saved the ceremony."

"No, actually, what you did is what you have been doing all along—annoying me with setbacks," she announced, standing up. "You see, I had a plan, but then you came along, and kept forcing me to adapt it."

I gaped at her as she moved over to a rope hanging from the ceiling and pulled it once. The doors behind me swung open, and I stared as a woman with a familiar face marched in with an unconscious person slung over her shoulder. I watched as Ms. Dale was deposited on one of the couches with a grunt.

Straightening, the familiar woman rotated her neck and then looked at the queen. I recognized her as Tabitha, second in line for succession. She was muscular, her limbs and neck bulging, while Elena was slender, like a willow reed.

"Thank you, Tabitha," Elena said. "And now… Desmond?"

My jaw dropped to the floor as Desmond appeared, seemingly from nowhere, in front of the queen. "As always, my dear girl, it is an honor to serve," she said, bowing deeply.

Elena smiled and embraced the older woman, placing her forehead against Desmond's in a sign of complete trust. Then Elena broke from her, coming around the table to sit back down.

I stared at Desmond as she moved behind Elena and leaned against a shelf.

"I… I don't understand," I breathed, shifting my

gaze between the two women.

Desmond shot me a piteous look while Elena gave me a feline grin. "Violet, you've seen the facility," the queen said. "You know what Mother and Mr. Jenks did to me and my sisters." I nodded and she continued. "Do you know what gift I was given?"

I shook my head. I probably should have looked it up, but it hadn't seemed as important to me when Viggo was in his coma and Tim was struggling to fit in.

Leaning forward, she rested her chin on her hand and sighed. "I really expected more from her, Desi," she said, and Desmond shrugged.

"I never said she was bright—that distinction belongs to her better half."

"What is going on?" I demanded, coming to my feet.

Elena sighed and waved her hand, and Tabitha's hand came down on my shoulder, forcing me down with a strong squeeze. Drumming her fingers on the table, Elena eyed me. I glowered back.

She laughed then, a chiming sound that was almost child-like, and leaned forward. "You have been the fly in my ointment, Violet, so I think it's only right that I share with you a few things… Before I have you executed as an agent of Patrus, who attempted to kill me and several women in an unprovoked attack."

"What? Why?"

"Honestly, I rarely get the opportunity to be honest with anyone. When Mr. Jenks made me, he made me to be smart. Very smart. By five, I could read as if I were ten or eleven. I was solving algebraic formulas at six. Everyone was so proud. Until they realized the downside of the treatment. Each one of us got our own slew of problems. Tabitha has a short temper and a thirst for violence that I don't think will ever be sated. Lena can't be touched. Ever. And I? I'm what you would call a sociopath. Do you know what that is?"

I shook my head and she leaned closer, as if she were telling me some deep dark secret. "It means that I don't feel things the way you do. Love, happiness, guilt?" She laughed then, that same delighted laugh as before, only it sent shivers down my spine, warning me of impending danger. "I feel none of those. I am… unburdened by them. It gives me clarity of focus.

"When I was twelve, I realized that I was going to be queen. And it made me curious about the queens of the past. So, I studied and read every bit of history and news that I could find about them. And do you know what I found?" She nodded encouragingly at me, her smile bright. I met her gaze and shook my head again. "Nothing worth reading about," she said, her voice dropping lower.

She stood up and moved back over to the window. "Our ancestors didn't come here to survive, Violet. They came here to thrive. Every queen, including my mother, was a stopgap. A way of maintaining the status quo. The only interesting thing my mother ever did was make me and those like me. And that was enough for me to formulate the beginnings of a plan."

Turning back toward me, she leaned against the window sill. "Desmond has always been working for me," she announced.

Although the truth had begun to dawn on me the moment Desmond had appeared here, as Elena spoke, it felt like all the oxygen had been drained from the room and I was in free fall, about to impact with the ground. My mind rattled with all the implications, sweeping through my memories to find any clue that I had somehow missed in my time around Desmond. I kept returning to one memory – the delayed timer hooked to enough explosive to bury the entire facility. Thomas had mentioned a code... did that mean Desmond had it? Would she have entered it if we'd failed? Then there was the propaganda that Desmond had been feeding the boys. That had been against Matrus as well as Patrus. Why?

The queen chuckled, kicking her feet against her skirts in a childish way. "Worth all the headaches you caused me, to see that expression on your face."

As I stared back at her in horror, she blew out. "My mother had done a great, yet terrible thing. I knew she would feel guilty eventually, so I started... putting things into motion. First, I had the egg stolen—by

Desmond. She handed it over to a Patrian operative, and threw my mother's operation in jeopardy. My mother tapped you to go get it, but then things went sideways… Clearly, Lee was not as loyal as his mother. Desmond hadn't believed my doubts about him, but who could blame her—he was her precious son. Still, it was easy enough for me to see, which was why I predicted he would go against orders and kill the queen while leaving King Maxen alive… Of course, he believed that Mother was the queen that Desmond was always talking about. The fool."

Desmond's face was stony as Elena moved away from the window and over to the bookcase, where she ran her hand over the books' spines. "No plan ever survives first contact," the queen continued, "so a lot of what happened afterward was a bit of a race to get what you possessed, and bring you in for a nice grand public execution. Desmond let me know that you had popped up, and I ordered her to do just that. However, she saw something more in you, a tool that could be used to help us. And you helped us, Violet… You got us the Benuxupane.

"To be honest, I didn't realize what Maxen intended it for… He is clearly smarter than I've given him credit for. But after learning about what it could do for the boys, I knew we needed it. You see… your involvement in the whole affair has forced us to adapt and change our plans. I was hoping to have more time to force the relationship with Patrus to deteriorate, while giving Desmond and her merry band of fools a chance to tame the boys—my thanks to your Mr. Croft for assisting us there." She shrugged. "Doesn't matter though—even though you stopped the bombing today, it still counts as a threat to the queen at one of the most sacred rituals of our people. With the Benuxupane, we have control over the boys and most importantly... we have you and Mr. Croft. The two malicious agents who confessed to being Patrian agents all along, trying to undermine the Matrian way of life."

Elena stepped close to me and reached out to stroke a lock of my hair. I flinched back, my skin crawling, and she smiled.

"So, thank you, Violet," she whispered. "Without you, none of this would have been possible."

I looked away from the queen and stared at Desmond for several moments. My brain now felt paralyzed, my mind stunned by all the revelations that had just been dropped on me.

But then, surprising myself and the women before me, my lips slowly curved upward in a smile.

I wasn't sure why I was smiling. I just felt such a cold rage begin to consume me—over everything Elena had said, every lie I had believed—that I suddenly felt unpredictable. Dangerous. Manic, even.

Concern flickered in Desmond's eyes, which only

caused my smile to grow.

From the corner of my eye, I noticed Elena's head start to turn away, and before I could think twice, I jolted to my feet in one powerful, fluid motion. Elena jerked her focus back to me, and I felt a rush of pleasure at the alarm on her face as I lunged for her, my fist making contact with her nose.

She flailed back with a shriek, and her foot caught on the train of her dress. There was a sound of fabric ripping as she tumbled to the floor. I whipped around and saw Tabitha coming toward me, her eyes flat and hard. I leapt onto the table and before she could defend herself, I smashed my boot into her face. Her howl came like music to my ears. My kick wasn't enough to bring Tabitha down, but she staggered back, blinded with pain and gripping her nose as trails of blood flowed between her fingers.

I jumped to the floor and raced over to Desmond, who had been distracted with helping Elena.

"I hope you're listening up, bitch," I hissed, glaring down at the older woman. "I'm going to get out of here, and when I do, I am going to tear down *everything* you have built piece by piece. I'm going to stop your war, free those boys from you, and then I'm going to grant your greatest wish."

Desmond sneered and I heard the doors fly open behind me.

"And what would that be?" she asked.

I moved closer, feeling immense satisfaction as she faltered slightly, and I bared my teeth at her. "I'm going to reunite you with your oldest son," I said, as I snapped a hand around the back of her neck and slammed her face into a table leg.

Desmond groaned while I raised my hands and took a step back. Turning, I found myself face to face with six wardens—each pointing a gun at me.

But I wasn't finished here just yet.

I glanced over to where Elena was picking herself up from the floor. "And *you*. You, Elena, I'll hand over to your younger brothers."

I watched the queen give me a confused, yet vicious look, and then smiled when I saw the blood drain from her face as my meaning dawned on her.

I returned my attention to the six wardens eyeing me and gestured to the door behind them. "That way back to my cell?" I asked.

The wardens glanced at Elena, who was looking daggers at me, her face cold and hard. "Take her away," she said as they slapped a pair of cuffs around my wrists.

"I'll see you later," I promised the queen, but in my heart I meant soon.

As the wardens led me out of the room and into the hallway, I knew that my surge of rage-ignited confidence wouldn't last, and I didn't know how I was going to escape this place or our planned execution.

All I knew was that I had to.

For the sake of Viggo, my brother, my family in Patrus, and every single citizen of our God-forsaken nations, I had to stop the war.

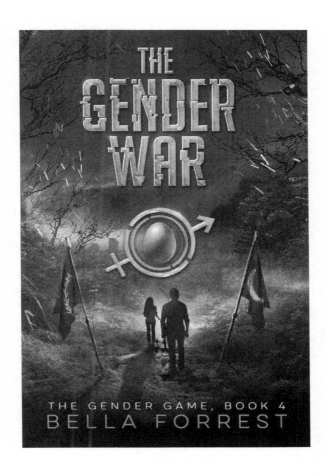

Dear Reader,

Thank you for reading! I hope you enjoyed *The Gender Lie*.

The next book in Violet and Viggo's journey, Book 4, *The Gender War*, releases February 9th, 2017.

If you visit www.morebellaforrest.com and join my email list, I will send you an email reminder as soon as The Gender War is live.

You can also visit my website for the most updated information about my books: www.bellaforrest.net

Until we meet again between the pages,
—Bella Forrest x

ALSO BY BELLA FORREST

THE GENDER GAME

The Gender Game (Book 1)
The Gender Secret (Book 2)
The Gender Lie (Book 3)
The Gender War (Book 4)

A SHADE OF
VAMPIRE SERIES

SERIES 1:
Derek & Sofia's story

A Shade of Vampire (Book 1)
A Shade of Blood (Book 2)
A Castle of Sand (Book 3)
A Shadow of Light (Book 4)
A Blaze of Sun (Book 5)
A Gate of Night (Book 6)
A Break of Day (Book 7)

SERIES 4:
A Clan of Novaks

A Clan of Novaks (Book 25)
A World of New (Book 26)
A Web of Lies (Book 27)
A Touch of Truth (Book 28)
An Hour of Need (Book 29)
A Game of Risk (Book 30)
A Twist of Fates (Book 31)
A Day of Glory (Book 32)

SERIES 5:
A Dawn of Guardians

A Dawn of Guardians (Book 33)
A Sword of Chance (Book 34)
A Race of Trials (Book 35)
A King of Shadow (Book 36)
An Empire of Stones (Book 37)
A Power of Old (Book 38)

A SHADE OF DRAGON TRILOGY

A Shade of Dragon 1
A Shade of Dragon 2
A Shade of Dragon 3

A SHADE OF KIEV TRILOGY

A Shade of Kiev 1
A Shade of Kiev 2
A Shade of Kiev 3

BEAUTIFUL MONSTER DUOLOGY

Beautiful Monster 1
Beautiful Monster 2

DETECTIVE ERIN BOND
(Adult mystery/thriller)

Lights, Camera, GONE
Write, Edit, KILL

FOR AN UPDATED LIST OF BELLA'S BOOKS,

please visit her website: www.bellaforrest.net

Join Bella's VIP email list and she'll personally send you an email reminder as soon as her next book is out!

Visit to sign up: www.MoreBellaForrest.com

Made in the USA
San Bernardino, CA
31 December 2016